Jocelyn
SELF INTO SILVER

WANDA E. PALMER

TATE PUBLISHING
AND ENTERPRISES, LLC

Published by Tate Publishing & Enterprises, LLC
127 E. Trade Center Terrace | Mustang, Oklahoma 73064 USA
1.888.361.9473 | www.tatepublishing.com

Tate Publishing is committed to excellence in the publishing industry. The company reflects the philosophy established by the founders, based on Psalm 68:11,
"The Lord gave the word and great was the company of those who published it."

Published in the United States of America

ISBN: 978-1-63063-896-2
1. Fiction / General
2. Fiction / Christian / General
14.03.03

~ Dedication ~

To my friend Priscilla Moore. This book would have never been written without you.

To the author of Amazing Grace, My Lord and Savior, Jesus Christ.

~ Acknowledgment ~

I would like to thank my editor, Judy Hurst, for all of her hard work.

To learn more about Navajo culture, go to www.discovernavajo.com.

"Hey, Jocelyn!"

"Hey, Marcie, what's up?"

"Penny's having a party at her club. Do you want to go?"

"Oh, I don't know. Her parties are pretty wild, and there are usually a lot of navy guys there."

"What do you have against the navy? If it weren't for them, there wouldn't be a Groton."

"Mom says that the navy is not good for the families. The men are gone too much and for too long a time."

"You're just going to flirt with 'em, not *marry* one!"

"I know," Jocelyn laughed, "But what if you fall in love with one of them. Then what?"

"Lighten up. You're way too serious." Marcie slammed her locker shut and started off to her next class. "Let me know if you change your mind," she threw over her shoulder as the warning bell rang.

Jocelyn hurried to her next class, trying to dismiss the party from her mind.

After school, Jocelyn expected Marcie to bring up the party again as they walked home from the bus stop. When she didn't by the time they reached Marcie's house, Jocelyn didn't know what to think. It was as if she wanted Marcie to talk her into it. She was still trying to figure it out as she entered her own backdoor.

"Hi, honey. How was your day?" Winnie, the Meyers' housekeeper, greeted her. She was always interested; it wasn't a rhetorical question.

"Fine, Winnie. Is Mom home?"

"She was in her study, the last I knew. Want a snack?"

"No, thanks."

Jocelyn went up the back stairs to her room and put her things down on the desk in her study. She then went down the hall to her mother's study.

"Mom?" she called as she tapped on the open door.

"Hello, sweetheart. How was your day?" Mary Meyers looked elegant as usual in a light blue suit. As one of the leading real estate agents in town, she rarely dressed casually. She felt she was on call all of the time, even when working at home. She got up from her desk, and they sat on the couch.

"It was fine. I made an A on that English paper."

"That's great! I thought you expressed yourself well on that one. Are you about ready for the chemistry final?"

"I think so. Mr. Peters went over it all again today."

"Do you still want to study chemistry in college, dear?"

"Yes, Mother, I do."

"Then I hope you ace the test," she said.

"Thanks. I need to talk with you about a graduation party at Penny's club. Her parties are usually pretty wild, with a lot of navy guys there."

"Do you have any reason to go? Those sound like two strong points against going."

"Well, Marcie wants to go, and it is a graduation party."

"Let's talk with your father over dinner, but it doesn't sound like you really want to go."

"Okay. Thanks, Mom. I'll go study."

Over dinner, the Meyers family discussed the party.

"Jocelyn, what do you want to do?"

"I want to go because Marcie wants to, and it is a graduation party. But Penny's parties have a reputation for being wild with a lot of navy guys there."

Jocelyn's oldest brother, Matthew, suggested she go because it was the last high school senior party before graduation.

"You don't want to miss it and regret it. If it's a bust, you can always leave early," her brother James suggested.

"You'll have your phone. Some Ensign gets fresh with you, the Three Musketeers will rescue you." Robert laughed, but Jocelyn knew they would. It was the good part of having three protective older brothers.

"So, Jocelyn, what do you think? You don't have to go."

"I guess the guys are right. I'll go with Marcie, and we can leave early if we don't like it."

"By the way, Jocelyn, have you decided where you want to go on your graduation trip?" Father changed the subject.

"I can't decide between Vermont, Maine, and Prince Edward Island."

"Prince Edward Island," Brianna stated. Since she started reading L. M. Montgomery's books about the island, it had been her only destination.

"Thank you, Brianna, for your vote, but it's Jocelyn's choice," Father reminded her. The talk revolved around the merits of each until Mrs. Meyers reminded everyone that she had to leave for a client appointment, and that homework and chores needed to be completed before TV.

The family told her good-bye and then went about their evening tasks.

Before starting her studies, Jocelyn called Penny to accept the party invitation and Marcie to tell her about it. They decided to go together, and Jocelyn would drive.

The chemistry test the next day was not as hard as Jocelyn feared, so she felt she did well on it. The history and math finals were on the following day, so she focused on those that night.

The next night was the Coast Guard Academy Ball. It was a good end to the week. A neighbor, Stephen, attended and hence had asked her. They had always been friends, her only male friend, and since he was shy, he asked her to go with him.

They were having a good time until one of the other guys asked her to dance then tried to pick her up; she quickly returned to Stephen. She refused to dance with anyone else the rest of the evening. They laughed and talked together, and after the last dance, he kissed her on the cheek and promised her they would be friends forever. Neither one was willing for more commitment than that. They felt they had their whole lives before them, and she hated men.

The following week seemed to fly by. She had finished her term papers and had only one final exam. Friday afternoon arrived almost as a surprise.

"Hey, Marcie."

"Hey! Senior week with nothing to do but graduation practice, and then graduation. I can hardly wait."

"Me too. Do you have your speech finished?"

"Just about. I wish you were giving it." Marcie had beaten Jocelyn for the valedictorian place and speech by one hundredths of a point.

"When do you want to leave for the party?"

"How about seven thirty and take the beach highway? At least the whole evening won't be a bust. It's always so beautiful along there. We should get a sunset as well as the water." They both laughed as they walked out of the building.

At 6:55 p.m., Jocelyn's sisters were camped on her bed critiquing her dress, shoes, purse, and hair. One minute she wanted to walk out, the next she was making the suggested adjustment.

Mother came in. "You look lovely, dear. Do you need any help?"

"I think I already have more help than I can use." Jocelyn waved at her sisters.

"Okay. Everyone out." Her sisters wished her a great time as they filed out of the room.

"Better?"

"Yes. How do I look?" she asked as she spun around.

"You look fine. Have a great time." Mother hugged and kissed her.

Jocelyn looked at herself once more in the mirror. "Thanks, Mom," she said and left.

Father met her on the stairs and hugged, kissed, and wished her a great time.

"Here she comes!" The boys ran to the foot of the stairs and cheered, all talking at once, and then followed her to her car, each with his own admonition. She waved as she left the avenue. She was still laughing at some of the crazy things her brothers had said as she walked up to Marcie's door.

Marcie was notoriously late, so Jocelyn figured she would have to sit with her parents until she was ready. Jocelyn rang the bell and hoped Mrs. Rogers would answer it as she never knew what to say to Mr. Rogers.

"Oh, hi. Come in and sit down," Mr. Rogers said. He then yelled up the stairs, "Marcie, Jocelyn's here. Get a move on." They went into the den.

Jocelyn sat on a chair, which was miraculously free. She wondered where all the cats were. Helping Marcie get ready, she guessed. Marcie thought there were fifteen after the last batch of kittens. Mr. Rogers was hidden behind the paper. There was a show on TV she had never seen before. The more she saw of it, the more she wished she could turn it off or change the station. She looked around the room and realized she was actually twiddling her thumbs as she had read in novels. This struck her as funny, but she suppressed her laughter.

Finally, Marcie rushed into the room, with her mother talking to her. "Let's go," Marcie said breathlessly.

"Let's go? Here, give me a hug. Ralph, doesn't she look good?"

"Umph."

"Have a good time, dear. Do you have the directions?"

"Yes, Mom," Marcie said as she walked out.

"Okay. Do you have your phone? Call me when you get there."

"Oh, Mom." Marcie closed the car door.

"Bye-bye."

"Bye." Quietly, she turned and asked, "Jocelyn, do I really look okay?"

"As far as I can tell. I'll check you over when we get there."

"Oh, it's all right. The beach road, remember."

"I remember. Remember when…" They were off in a cloud of remembrances and excitement. The sunset was gorgeous, which made the drive even more interesting than the usual sights along the road. Soon, they turned into the club grounds.

"Wow. This must be a big party."

"Surely all these people are not here for Penny's party. There must be other functions going on as well."

When they got to the door, a doorman in a tuxedo asked who they were there to see and then asked for their invitations.

Open-mouthed, the girls looked at each other and then back at the doorman.

"I didn't know we would need them to get in."

"Neither did I."

"Marcie, Jocelyn, it's sooo good to have you," Penny greeted them in her oily voice. Then to the doorman, she said, "I'll take care of them."

"Yes, miss."

"Come along. We're over here." The girls quietly followed, having thought their evening was over before it even started. "You're a little early. Mostly everyone won't be here for an hour or so."

"But you said eight."

"Oh." Penny waved off the objection. "Let me introduce you to who is here." As they moved from group to group, Jocelyn felt more and more out of her element. The ball last week had been fun. This seemed a chore.

"Now that you're acquainted, get yourself something to drink and mingle. Someone else just arrived."

The girls looked at each other and picked up cups of punch. Jocelyn tasted hers, looked at it, and wondered where to set it down.

"Don't you like it?" A young naval officer, whom she hadn't noticed, was next to her. "Here." He took the cups and led them to the canned sodas.

"Thanks."

"Yes. Thank you."

"I'm Mark Denton."

"I'm Marcie Rogers."

"I'm Jocelyn Meyers."

"It's nice to meet you, ladies. Are you from here?"

The girls nodded.

"Where are you from?"

"New Mexico."

"How did you get into the US Navy?" Marcie asked.

"Marcie, New Mexico is a state!" clipped Jocelyn.

"Yes. Have you heard of Texas?"

"Yeah."

"Have you heard of Arizona?" Mark asked.

"Yeah."

"We are between the two."

"Oh. Out west. Do you still have trouble with the Indians?"

"Marcie!" Jocelyn admonished.

"It's okay. I'm half-Indian, so you'd better watch out!"

Marcie blushed—"Oh, there's Winnie"—and rushed off.

"Please forgive her. Marcie knows better, she's just flustered."

"That's okay. She's not the first and probably won't be the last."

"Are you stationed at the submarine base?"

"You might say so. I'm in Submarine School."

"I hope you don't get claustrophobia."

"No."

"How did you choose the navy? After all, you're a long way from the ocean in New Mexico."

"Many reasons. My grandfather was a marine in World War II. Several of my uncles were in the service. I didn't want the marines or the army because of their nature, but the family wanted me to carry on the military tradition. You don't get shot at on a submarine, I thought. Also *Hunt for Red October* was a favorite movie of theirs."

"I don't think I've ever seen that movie."

"I could probably quote it to you." He laughed. "How do you know Penny?"

"She's in my class at school."

"You are a senior in high school?"

"Yes. We graduate next week. How do you know her?"

"Actually, I don't. Her father is one of my instructors. When he gave me the invitation, it sounded like an honor for a select few. When I got here, I realized that was an exaggeration."

"I hope you enjoy it anyway. Have you graduated from college?"

"Yes. Last year. Do you plan to go to college?"

"Yes. This fall."

"What do you plan to major in?"

"Chemistry. I would like to research cures for common ailments."

"Like the cold?"

"Exactly. When I was little, I had a friend who died from a bad cold that turned into the flu. It was awful. Also, we have Baker here."

"What is Baker?" He asked hesitantly.

"Oh, they make penicillin and other medications. They have a whole department that just researches cures."

"Really. So, I guess you'll live the rest of your life here in Groton, Connecticut."

"Oh, I'd like to travel too. What is New Mexico like?"

"I could talk all night about it. Let's get some more to drink and sit down. Oh, would you like something to eat too?"

"That sounds good."

They filled their plates, got more sodas, and found a relatively quiet corner to talk.

After a good conversation, Mark looked at his watch and said he had to leave. "It was good getting acquainted. I would like to keep in touch, if you don't mind."

"So, I'll have a submarine pen pal."

"That's submariner."

"Sorry."

"That's okay."

They exchanged phone numbers and addresses.

"I really need to be going. Curfew, you know."

"Sure. It's been nice talking with you. I wonder what happened to Marcie?" As Mark moved off, Jocelyn started hunting for Marcie. She finally found her in the bathroom, looking disheveled and crying her eyes out.

"Marcie?"

"Let's get out of here."

"Sure. You got your purse?"

Marcie piloted them out to the car almost faster than Jocelyn could walk. After they were out of the parking lot, Jocelyn asked, "What happened?"

Marcie told her of her evening in between fits of sobs. It sounded to Jocelyn as if she had been raped! They got to Marcie's neighborhood long before she had calmed down enough that Jocelyn felt she could go inside, so she parked down the street.

They talked for over an hour before they felt Marcie could face her parents.

"Remember, just say you're tired and want to go to bed. Make no promises."

"Dad would go after him with a gun!"

"I'll call Mark tomorrow and see what he thinks."

"Oh, Joss…" The girls hugged again.

Jocelyn restarted the car and stopped at the curb in front of Marcie's house. Marcie wiped her face again. Jocelyn checked her mascara. Marcie put on a false smile and walked into her house. The next morning, Jocelyn had no idea how early was too early but felt that eight was safe. When someone answered the phone, Jocelyn couldn't remember Mark's rank. She forgot that it was on his address he had given her. She asked for Mark Denton.

"Jocelyn?"

"Mark?"

"Yes. I didn't expect you to call so soon." He laughed.

"Mark, something happened last night to Marcie. We need your advice about it."

Mark noted the stress in her voice and seriously questioned, "What happened?"

Jocelyn told him, and he asked a few pertinent questions. Then he gave her some sound advice.

"I'll check on this end. You talk to your folks. I'll call you later. She needs to be checked out at a hospital as soon as possible."

"Okay. There's always someone here, so you can leave a message if I'm not back."

"Talk to you soon. Bye."

Jocelyn went downstairs to find her parents and told them what had happened to Marcie. Then she took Marcie to the emergency room. The doctor felt he had some good evidence and called the police.

Mark talked with the men he had seen at the party. Most of them were in groups joking about what they had seen and done.

A large group had congregated in the lounge of the barracks. It sounded like a game of one-upmanship to Mark, each one bragging more about his exploits than the last. He noted their comments, especially what one man said. In private, he jotted down names and comments in a notebook he carried. Then he called the house to speak to Jocelyn.

"Meyers residence, Winnie speaking."

"Hello, this is Mark Denton. I met Jocelyn Meyers at a party last night. May I speak with her?"

"Miss Meyers is not taking calls. May I give her a message?"

"Did she take her friend, Marcie, to the hospital?"

"Uh. May I give her a message?"

"No, thank you. Oh, yes. Tell her Mark Denton called."

"Mark... Denton... and your phone number?"

He gave it, concluded the call, and went to the hospital, certain Jocelyn was there because of Winnie's hesitation. He parked and walked into the emergency room. He spied Jocelyn quickly and joined her.

"Hello."

"Hey, Mark. Thanks for coming. The doctor's in with Marcie. We didn't think of coming to the emergency room. Thanks for telling us."

They talked quietly until Jocelyn saw a policewoman enter and go to the desk.

"Mark, look. Let's go."

He put his hand on her arm as she rose. "They'll call us when they want us. We'll keep an eye on that room."

Jocelyn sat on the edge of her seat, eyes glued to that door. Their talk became disjointed and confused. The doctor came out and headed toward them. Jocelyn met him with Mark close behind.

"Are you Jocelyn Meyers?"

"Yes. How's Marcie?"

"And who are you?" He looked at Mark.

"Mark Denton. I met these ladies at the party least night. I think I have some information the policewoman can use."

"Okay. Come on." The doctor led them into the cubicle. "These are her friends," he introduced them to the policewoman.

The policewoman suggested going to the station house to free up the emergency room space and asked if Mark knew who Marcie had been with.

"No, but I know some who went to the party, and I'd like to help."

"Okay, follow me to the station."

They settled in the interrogation room. Mark got out his list of men that he knew had been at the party.

"Marcie, describe the attacker," the policewoman requested.

As she described the man, Mark marked off names and wrote down the description. The policewoman asked what he was doing.

"Well, I wrote down the names of everyone I knew was there. As she describes the man, I'm marking off the ones who don't come close to her description. I'm also writing down her description to see if it triggers a recognition."

"Good. Please continue, Marcie."

Marcie started repeating herself. The policewoman directed her thoughts. When the officer went out to get the sketch artist, Mark went with her.

"Officer, I have a couple of names. This one with the star beside it was bragging about a conquest this morning, and he fits the description. The other one also fits the description, but it could be someone else."

"Good work. You would make a good police officer. Ever thought about it?"

"Well, I'd like to be Captain of a submarine, but thank you for the offer."

The officer contacted the Submarine Base Police Office and gave them the information on the two men and then called Penny's house to request a copy of the guest list. She wasn't up yet, so her father took the call. He objected but relented when she said it was for an investigation.

Afterward, Jocelyn asked Mark to follow them to her house. They went into the music room and talked. Even Marcie found Mark engaging as he promised to help all he could with the investigation. He asked Jocelyn if he could see her again and then left.

His hopes for a girlfriend budded. He was only half Navajo, so the nice Navajo girls weren't interested in him and the rest of the girls he met thought he was subhuman. He enjoyed talking with Jocelyn. He decided to pursue a friendship with her, hoping for more—a lot more—marriage.

Jocelyn took Marcie back home and helped her talk with her parents. Mr. Rogers exploded as they knew he would, calling a lawyer friend at home. That lawyer didn't handle this type of law, but gave Mr. Rogers names and numbers of some who did. Mr. Rogers asked for the most aggressive one, left a message with that office answering service, and called three times Monday morning prior to the lawyer arriving in the office. The lawyer talked briefly with Marcie on the phone, made an appointment to see her, and requested her friends be there, too. Mark couldn't get off at that time, but got the lawyer's information and made an appointment for when he was free.

At the police lineup, Marcie easily identified the man, who was the one that had been bragging. Mark was asked to testify.

Marcie spent most of the summer with Jocelyn. At first it was just for moral support, but when Marcie learned of her pregnancy, she needed a lot more. Mrs. Rogers took her for the abortion, but never went with her to the lawyer's office or the trial. Mark and Jocelyn supported her there. Mark got off for the trial since he was testifying and often drove Jocelyn and Marcie to the courthouse.

When the verdict announced the man guilty, the girls embraced. Marcie actually hugged Mark, who was quite startled by it. They celebrated with a special meal and drive.

The girls were accepted at the same college, so planned to be roommates. Then Jocelyn noticed Marcie's outgoing personality became withdrawn. Her parents noticed. Her mother took her to a psychologist friend. They had to put her in a mental hospital to recover from the rape and the abortion. By August, Jocelyn was preparing to attend college, whereas Marcie was recovering. They drifted apart. Jocelyn focused on school and Marcie stared off in the distance. Jocelyn later learned Marcie had become reclusive, working from home.

Mark called Jocelyn often. They enjoyed talking. She had never talked with a guy like she talked with him. He invited her to a movie. They went walking on the beach. She invited him to luncheon. He took her to dinner.

The first time she invited him to dinner at her house, she told him it would be formal. "What?"

"A tuxedo," Jocelyn said.

"I don't have one."

"Everyone has a tux!"

"I don't."

"What do you wear to a formal navy function?"

"My dress uniform."

"Then wear that." She sounded exasperated.

"Why? It's just a meal."

"Not at my house. My brothers will be in tuxedos and my sisters and I will be in formals, like my parents."

"What's the special occasion?"

"Dinner!?!" She stressed.

"Okay, I'll wear my dress whites."

When he arrived with his bouquet, he was ushered into the back parlor by Winnie, who announced, "Mark Denton has arrived."

He presented his flowers to Jocelyn who handed them off to Winnie. He shook hands with her family as Jocelyn introduced him. He had never been in such a formal situation for a normal dinner. He was sure it had to be a special occasion. He was used to awkward greetings when people met him, but her family welcomed him.

James asked, "What's your pleasure?"

Mark noticed everyone had a glass in their hand.

"Water would be fine."

Robert said, "You gotta have something in it: scotch, rye, gin, bourbon..."

"A bottle of water is fine."

"Maybe he wants a beer," James suggested.

"No. Just water."

Winnie entered and announced dinner. Mark was relieved. In the dining room, he noticed each brother formally seated a sister as their father seated their mother. He sat where indicated between Jocelyn and her mother. He found the glasses full and a plethora of silverware. His Navajo stoicism stepped up and he followed Mrs. Meyers in the utensils to use with each course. He found her charming. She found him a curiosity. She had rarely had someone at her normal dinner table who was not in her social circle.

Mark tasted the clear liquid and found it was just water. Winnie kept his water glass full as she kept everyone's wine glasses full. When the wine changed to accompany the new course, she replaced his untouched glass.

Jocelyn emptied her wine glass at each course. Mark didn't count, but realized that night how much wine she consumed and wondered how much she had prior to his arrival. After dinner, they adjourned to the back parlor for more drinks. On the way back to the base, Mark argued with himself about pursuing Jocelyn. He hated alcohol. The whole family obviously drank a lot. He was not sure she had realized he was saying good-bye, she was so inebriated. On the other hand, she and her family accepted him.

Jocelyn felt very comfortable with Mark. He didn't flirt. He didn't try to kiss her. He didn't even try to hold her hand. They just talked. She started calling him.

Mark often came to visit Jocelyn. She enjoyed spending time with Mark, even though she treated him like another brother. In many ways, they were opposites. He was shy. She was gregarious. He needed time to himself, which was a challenge in the midst of the crowded conditions of a submarine. She found people interesting and exhilarating, but did not mind being alone with her own thoughts. He liked to grow things and usually had a plant in his quarters. She had a brown thumb and felt she could kill cactus (he gave her one, and she killed it). His taste in music was limited to his tribal music. She liked classical and always had season tickets to the symphony, the ballet, and the opera. He preferred the outdoors. She was content to stay inside. But they could discuss anything.

Jocelyn attended a nearby girls' college and enjoyed it very much. Of course, some courses were harder than others, but she learned early on to ignore most of the comments made about the professors. Just because someone else thought a certain professor was easy or hard did not mean that she would think so too.

When Mark was transferred, she corresponded with him. His first boat (as he called his submarine) was based in Hawaii. Between her sophomore and junior year, he got her a room for a week at a Navy Lodge hotel on the beach there and sent her a plane ticket.

She was looking forward to her trip. She would fly by herself and meet him at the airport in Honolulu. While her father had been a United States Senator, she had gone with her family to Washington, D.C., every fall, home for Christmas, back for the spring session, and home for the summer. But this time, she would be by herself all across the country and then over to Hawaii.

It would be two years since she had seen Mark. He had been another brother before. She wondered what it would be like to be with him now. They always had fun together.

Then Hawaii! She had researched it on the internet. He said they had a full schedule of tours and luaus, whale and volcano watches. It sounded exciting.

He had asked that she wear her full suit instead of her bikini, and she had found two that were still in good condition. She had shorts and tops with some wraparound skirts to go over the shorts when she needed a dress.

Her mother gave her a talk about men and not kissing and petting. She didn't like guys that way, so it wasn't a problem to her. Each of her brothers had a private talk with her, saying that guys only wanted one thing from a girl. She insisted Mark wasn't like that, but when she was by herself sometimes she wondered. She pushed those thoughts away. Mark wasn't like that, and she wasn't interested.

The family took her to Trumbull Airport, hugged and kissed her, and wished her a good time. In New York's Kennedy Airport, she easily found her gate. While she was waiting, a guy tried to talk with her. She told him she was going to meet her fiancé and turned him off. She was good at turning guys away. She had had plenty of practice from all the coast guard and navy guys in Groton.

When the stewardess came, she bought two bottles of rum and got two glasses of coke. After those, she settled for a nap. When she awoke, she ate her lunch that Winnie had sent her and opened the bottle of wine she had brought. She needed help when she got to Los Angeles, and the stewardess got her transport to her next flight. She slept most of that flight.

Mark got worried when she didn't come out. And then someone came pushing a wheelchair, calling for him. He stepped forward.

"I'm Mark Denton."

"She's plastered. Here are her tickets. I can get you a sky cap to help you."

"Please."

The sky cap got her bag. Mark took her purse, picked her up, and carried her to the baggage claim. The sky cap got her luggage and helped them to a cab. Mark gave him a good tip.

At the Navy Lodge, he loaded the bags onto a cart and pushed it before them as he carried Jocelyn. He was glad he was strong. A bellhop took her things and helped him into the room. He laid her on the bed and paid the man, with her mumbling the whole time about coming to see him. He found the almost empty wine bottle in her large purse. There was a connecting door between their rooms, which he had opened. He went to his room and found a jar with a special powder in it.

He knew she drank a lot. Her family had wine with every meal. After supper, they would adjourn to the back parlor for drinks and often had pre-dinner drinks. He had decided when he was at Sub School that she was an alcoholic. If he were to marry her, he'd have to fix that. He mixed the powder with the wine in a glass. He sat it down and waited.

She got up to go to the bathroom. On her return, he met her with the glass and water for himself.

"Jocelyn, what about a little nightcap?"

"Mark, where did you come from?"

"Let's sit on the balcony and have a drink."

"Sure. What are *we* doing tomorrow?"

WANDA E. PALMER

"We're taking a tour of the island. Here."

He sat next to her, not sure how soon she would react to the powder. He held up his glass. She tapped it with hers and then drank hers down. He had expected her to sip hers. He had heard a person sips wine. He rushed her to the bathroom and sat on the side of the tub, holding her head over the toilet. She threw up for such a long time that she was spent when she stopped. He helped her brush her teeth and wash her face then put her to bed. He went to his own bed but had to help her again, so he slept on the floor in her room.

His mother had said it might take several times before the person stopped drinking. He was willing to wait. When Jocelyn started stirring the next morning, he went to his room and closed the connecting door. He showered and dressed and then went to her hall door and knocked. He had ordered a champagne breakfast, which was brought to her room at nine.

She was dressed, but she looked awful.

"Hi. How about breakfast on your terrace? I've ordered it for us."

"Okay. Say, Mark, I don't feel so good."

"We can hang out here today. It's probably jet lag. Come out to your balcony." He took her hand and led her out. "It's a beautiful day. How was your flight?"

"Oh, it was great."

"Excuse me. I think that's our breakfast." He tipped the man, put the powder in one glass, and added the last of the wine. He filled his glass with water. "Here." He looked at her and felt a twinge of guilt, but then he remembered why he had to do it. He refused to live with an alcoholic. If he could cure her, he would marry her.

He gave her the glass. This time, she drank it like a soda. He put some of the food on a plate and watched her closely. A few moments later, he was again holding her head over the toilet, helping her brush her teeth, and then laying her down on the chaise on the balcony.

He ate. She moaned. He gave her the glass again, helped her throw up, cleaned her up, and lay her on the chaise.

"Mark, I think something's wrong with that wine."

"Oh. Sorry. Here. I'll get you some champagne." He added the powder and poured the champagne in. The results were the same. She requested rum and coke from the room fridge, but still it was the same. Everything she tried made her throw up.

She felt awful. "Maybe I have the flu."

"Oh, that would be a shame. I'll take care of you. Why don't you take a nap, and I'll stay on your balcony. Call if you need me. Here's something to drink." Then he rushed her to the toilet again.

"Maybe you're allergic to alcohol."

"I've never been before, and I've drunk a lot."

I know, he thought to himself. "Well, try some water. You'll get dehydrated."

She had no problem with the water. She took a nap while he ate the breakfast, hoping his plan was working.

When she woke up, he offered her more champagne and then the other drinks. She turned them all down. She did drink more water. She was hungry. He gave her some toast from breakfast, and that did okay. He suggested an apple, and that did okay too. He gave her the champagne, and she gave it all back.

"Mark, maybe you're right."

"About what?"

"That I can't drink any more."

He wanted to jump up and down for joy. He said, "Oh. Are you still hungry? I'm getting hungry. What if we try the restaurant downstairs?"

"Okay. Let's find the bathroom first, just in case."

"I won't be able to hold you there."

"I know."

"You need to get cleaned up. I'll clean up the room while you take a shower. You'll feel better."

"Mark, you won't try anything will you?"

"What?"

"You won't try to have sex or anything, will you?"

"*No*! If I were like that, I could have taken you last night. I spent the night on your floor and helped you throw up. Do you really think I'd do that to you?"

"No. I told my brothers that you're not like that. Say, you're not gay, are you?"

"No. But Jocelyn, I will marry…"

He turned away and went to clean the balcony. He had wanted to say that he would marry her. She watched him a while then got her clean clothes and took a shower. He cleaned up the room and made the bed. He put the trash on the cart and put it into the hallway.

The water was turned off on the shower.

"Jocelyn?" he called at the bathroom door.

"Mark!"

"I need to clean up too. I'll come back to get you when I'm ready."

"Okay."

She was relieved. Mark wasn't like that! She got dressed, fixed her hair, and sat on the balcony, awaiting his return. She was feeling better. It was a nice day, and the view was beautiful. She hoped she would be okay for the rest of her stay.

There was a knock on her door. She opened it to Mark. She laughed. He joined her.

"You look like you feel better."

"You don't look so bad yourself, Ensign."

"I made Lieutenant, remember?"

"Sorry, my dashing young Lieutenant." She took his arm.

He was glad he had her room key. She never even thought about it. They had lunch and joined the afternoon tour. They enjoyed the tour, which ended in a luau. He ordered virgin drinks for them. He had his powder, but hoped he wouldn't need it.

When he returned her to her room, he wanted to kiss her and follow her in, but she reached out her hand to shake his and told him she had a good time.

"When in the morning?"

"I'll call you. How long does it take you to get ready?"

"About a half hour."

He opened her door and held it for her.

She looked in his eyes and said, "Good night, Mark," and then closed the door.

He stood there looking at the door until someone else came down the hallway. He went to his room, took a shower, and went to his balcony. He sat down on a chair and daydreamed about Jocelyn.

He took his powder with him, just in case, as they went on whale watches and tours of the islands. They walked on volcanoes and around the Pearl Harbor Museum. They watched the surfers and the ocean through a glass-bottom boat. They saw green sea turtles and amazing flowers at the botanical garden. They enjoyed waterfalls, deep bays, and towering mountain peaks. They watched dances and listened to music native to the people. They ate delicious food and drank interesting liquids. They learned the history of the islands. He even took her on his submarine for a dinner. He only had to use his powder once more. He couldn't hold her that time, but she returned to the table saying that she couldn't drink alcohol anymore.

They talked about the flowers in the rain forest and decided they both liked flowers. They watched the animals in the zoo. He tried to put his arm around her, but she kept removing it. He held her hand, but she kept taking it away, so he stopped trying.

WANDA E. PALMER

He watched her a lot. Sometimes he enjoyed her reaction as much as the sights they were being shown.

"Oh, Mark, it's hard to believe the week is almost over. I've had a great time."

"Jocelyn, I wish I were escorting you back home."

"That's okay. You need to see your family."

"Thank you. Maybe sometime you can visit my family with me."

"I'd love to."

"I'd like to see you again. If I get stationed in Groton, may I visit you?"

"Of course, Mark. You're a part of the family."

"Jocelyn, I'd like to be more than just another brother to you." He reached toward her.

"That would be nice Mark." She looked in his eyes.

"May I kiss you?"

"No, Mark." She stepped back. A chair was behind her. She sat, surprise all over her face. They laughed.

He promised himself he would never tell her what he had done. She never drank again as far as he knew. They had a great time. They could laugh and talk and discuss and agree to disagree. There was a good friendship between them, but he wanted to marry her. They continued to correspond.

~ *2* ~

During her junior year, Mark was stationed back in Groton. When he was free, he would often visit the Meyers family, and Phillip Meyers soon told him he was part of the family and that he could join them anytime.

One evening at dinner, Mark requested to talk with Phillip. "Of course, son. Let's go into my study."

They were gone for a long time when Mr. Meyers requested someone to ask Jocelyn to join them. She was in her study, reading.

"Hi, Dad. You want to see me?"

"Come in, sweetheart. Mark and I have been talking about a lot of things. He would like you to visit with him at his home when he returns from his upcoming submarine patrol."

"There are some things you need to know before you decide. I am Navajo. My father died when I was young, so my mother went back to live with her family. We live in the traditional Navajo Way. There are many traditions in a traditional Navajo family. I would like to stay a month as I will have that much leave coming, but I understand that their way will be a great culture shock to you."

Jocelyn looked askance at him.

"My elders are revered. My grandfather only speaks Navajo. We wear Navajo clothing and live in a hogan, which is one large eight-sided room. My mother has a sheep flock, the wool of which she uses to make blankets, which she sells. The women grow a garden. The men hunt to supplement the mutton diet. We eat mutton stew most meals. There will be a cleansing ceremony for me when I first arrive to be sure I am back in harmony with nature."

She was sure he was exaggerating. Her disbelief evident on her face.

"We live forty miles from the nearest city. We get most of our purchased supplies and mail from the trading post ten miles away over very rough track. We don't go there very often, at most once a week. When we arrive in Albuquerque, most of my extended family will be there to meet me. The men will squeeze into the cab of a pickup truck. The women will pile in the back with the children."

Jocelyn looked at him with less acceptance of everything she was hearing.

"We get thirteen inches of rain a year and are very grateful for that. Plants and grass and trees only grow where there is water. So the landscape is mostly rock—weathered to unusual shapes. I will show you and teach you, but there will still be a major shock when you get there. I have seen how you live. As your friend, I want you to see how I live. We can talk openly together. Before I show you about my world, I want you to promise me that you will continue to be open and honest with me. If it doesn't work out for you to stay the whole month, I will bring you back."

"Jocelyn, Mark and I have discussed this, and I think it's something you should do. But, and this is an important *but*, it is all up to you. You're free to say no. You're free to return at any time. You're under no obligation."

Jocelyn was unsure of what she thought. It sounded hard but exciting. It was an adventure but a scary one. It sounded too extreme to be true.

"Do you have any questions now?" Mark asked.

"I don't know. I think I'll need to know more," she answered tentatively. "Are you sure you're not exaggerating?"

"I'm sure. Thank you for listening to me."

"Jocelyn, I think, for many reasons, it would be best to not talk of this to anyone just yet. You need to decide without being pulled by other opinions."

"What about Mother?"

"We will talk to her tomorrow."

"Dad?"

"Yes, dear?"

"My mind is a blank whirl. I can't seem to latch onto anything."

"That's okay. You have time."

"May we start now with some of the pictures I brought?" Mark asked.

"I guess so."

As she looked at the pictures with Mark and Father, Jocelyn's mind quit spinning, and she enjoyed learning about Mark's world. She agreed that it was a long way from Groton, Connecticut. At one point, she asked, "Are you sure this is a part of the United States?"

Over the following weeks, Mark taught Jocelyn about his world. It was very complicated. She was enjoying learning how to say hello confidently until he casually remarked that she had to be careful how she pronounced the word, or she could call Grandfather a louse. They covered a few other important words like grandfather, mother, uncle, aunt, good-bye, and thanks. He covered how to approach a house, how to enter a hogan, how to address the residents, how to talk to people, how to listen, and most importantly, how to wait.

"Silences are not readily accepted here, but there, to wait on each other is very important. Let the other person signal he is finished talking. Also, interrupting is not tolerated. If Grandfather were telling you a story, and you interrupted him, he would not finish."

"It seems there is a lot of respect for each other."

"Exactly! Be respectful, and you should do well."

Another problem was how to introduce herself. Navajo introduce themselves by listing their mother's clan and then their father's. Since she didn't have clans, they argued whether to just say she was not Navajo (his idea), or list her mother and maternal grandparents followed by her father and his parents (her idea). She thought she should come as close to their way as she could. He was afraid his relatives might think she was mocking them.

He had told her of his sister who had taken friends to visit the family.

She requested, "Call Bernadette."

"How's Bernie going to help?"

"She's been through it. Here, what's her number, I'll call her."

"No, I'll call."

He looked at his watch. He figured Bernie would be free now. If not, he'd leave a message. At any rate, he wanted to change the subject.

The phone rang a few times. He was about to hang up when it was answered, "Hello?"

"Hi, Bernie. How are you?"

"What do you want, Mark?"

"What makes you think I want something?"

"When else do you call? I'm in the middle of something. Either let me answer your question, or I'll call you back when I'm free."

He didn't want her to do that because she never called back— she was never free. He asked his question and got her not-very-helpful answer.

"Well?"

"She's tried both ways."

"And?"

"You're not being patient and waiting for me to signal I'm finished." Mark laughed.

"Sorry."

"Grandfather took it more in the attitude it was given. If the person was being disrespectful, he wouldn't accept either. If respectful, he would accept the person."

"Wow. Your grandfather sounds interesting. You said relationships are important."

"You have no idea!"

Another issue they disagreed on was what she would do there. "You are a guest. They wait on you."

"But I'll be there so long. Shouldn't I help wash dishes or something?"

"It would be rude."

"I would think it would be more rude to just sit around and do nothing."

"Talk with the Old One."

"All the time? Surely he has other things to do."

"Not usually."

"Okay. So I listen to Grandfather's stories. Does he have one for every day all day long?"

"All right. You've made your point, but be sure to ask first."

"Couldn't I go with you sometimes?"

"Sightseeing? Sure."

"How about hunting?"

"No. That's man's work. You would get me into a lot of trouble that way."

"And they talk of sex discrimination at college!" She laughed.

"We'll go sightseeing a lot." And he told her more of the things to see, which she might enjoy.

Language study was a continuing and, at times, very frustrating part of Jocelyn's training.

"That's what I said!"

"No, you said…"

Inflection, intonation, stress, and pronunciation—it seemed as if it was a constant battle. Jocelyn could not always tell the difference.

"Excuse me"—Robert knocked on the door during their first week of study—"Would my tape recorder help?"

"Hey, that sounds good. Then it wouldn't be your word against mine," Mark enthused. "It will also give you something to work with when I'm not here. Thanks, Robert."

"Yeah, thanks. You're a great brother."

"I just don't like to hear you two arguing. It's hard enough to concentrate on my own studies with you talking all the time."

"Should we move? We could go downstairs somewhere."

"No, it's okay. Maybe I can go with you next, Mark. I've already had the training." Robert laughed, but there was a hopeful look in his eye as well.

"Why don't you go with us this time?"

"Would it be all right? Shouldn't you ask first?"

"You're very welcome. I'm sorry, I didn't realize anyone else would be interested. But if anyone else wants to go, someone is going to have to sleep out in the arbor."

"Would it really be okay for others to go?" Jocelyn asked.

"Maybe we need to talk to Father first." Robert cautioned. "I don't think it would work if all of the Meyers clan went."

"Father is home. Let's go ask him now."

They chatted excitedly as they went downstairs to Father's study. Phillip listened to Robert's suggestion then requested that he have a private talk with Mark.

"Sure, Dad," Brother and sister agreed and left the room.

"Mark, I never thought that any of the other children would be interested in going. To be honest with you, I was surprised Jocelyn was. But I don't want you to feel pressured to take even Robert, let alone any of the other children. You said that the summer hogan is not very large and water is a luxury. Please don't overburden your family on our account."

"My family would welcome your whole family if you all wanted to go. I was planning on installing a new water tank, anyway. We could have more water delivered. That is not a problem. The problem is in your family believing me about the details of our life. Even with this training, it will be a cultural shock for everyone who goes. The men, and sometimes the women, often sleep in the arbor on hot nights. I told Jocelyn to bring a ground cloth and sleeping bag. Where we put them down is of little consequence. Is there anyone you would rather not go, that might not do well under our conditions?"

"I feel at this point we should limit the invitation to just the boys."

"And Suzanne?"

"She's too romantic. Her comfort level is just too high, but she doesn't realize it. I'm afraid she would make everyone miserable." Mr. Meyers went to the door. "Robert, would you bring in your brothers?"

"Sure, Dad," Robert said as he spun on his heel to find them.

After a lengthy discussion, all three wanted to go, but Matthew was not sure he would be free. He would need to consult his adviser as he was studying to become a medical doctor. He thought the experience would be very valuable to his training, so hoped his adviser would agree. The class of two became a class of five that night. They had to find another classroom as Jocelyn's study was far too small to comfortably fit all five.

Jocelyn began to appreciate her brothers even more as the pressure to learn the relationship rituals and the complicated language spread over all four. Mark also appreciated the men's questions in their quest to learn. As they studied, they also realized it helped to have the extra sets of ears to hear the subtleties of the language. The rest of the family tolerated the noises they made, but they seemed to find more activities away from the room they were using. Matthew's adviser also thought the experience would be good for him, especially if he could observe at a medical office while he was there and report on it.

All too soon, Mark had to leave on his submarine patrol, but when he returned, they would take their trip. The four siblings continued their studies together, including research on their own, the results of which they shared. They had always been close, but this experience bonded them even further. They all had their schoolwork and classes to attend, so they busily and eagerly awaited Mark's return.

When he returned, the whole family met Mark. His shipmates teased him about it, but he just laughed. He quickly did all he needed to for his job and then went with the family to their house. He would spend the night with them, and then early the next morning, the adventurers would start the first leg of their journey.

It was hard for Jocelyn to relax to sleep, and then suddenly her radio came on, signaling it was time to get ready to leave. She must have slept. She felt rested, but she had no memory of it. Soon she was surrounded by her sisters who were laughing, teasing, hugging, and giving last-minute advice.

"Hey, traveler," Father knocked on her door. Brianna opened it. He stuck his head in and said, "Anything else to go?"

"Just my grooming case."

"I'll carry it," Suzanne offered.

As they moved into the hall, Jocelyn heard her brothers in the foyer. "Where's Mom, Dad?" she asked.

"With your brothers. Let's go."

When they joined the rest of the family, he checked on everyone's tickets.

Amazingly, everyone, with their excitement overflowing, fit in the van. The short trip to Trumbull Airport was the first leg of their all-day journey, followed by the short hop to Kennedy Airport in New York City, then Chicago's O'Hare, and on to the Albuquerque Sunport.

As they flew southwest, the window-seat occupants began pointing out the landscape changes. The captain told the flight that they were going to go north over Las Vegas and around the Sandia Mountains to avoid turbulence. Mark explained that he meant Las Vegas, New Mexico, and pointed out the Sangre de Christo Mountains in that area, then the Rio Grande River, the Sandia and Monzano Mountains, and then the city of Albuquerque.

"Wow, it's larger than I thought."

"But it's as big as it can get with the Sandia Mountains on the east, Sandia Pueblo on the north, Isleta Pueblo on the south, and the volcanoes on the west."

"Volcanoes? They won't explode, will they?"

"No. They are all extinct. But the badlands, the Malpais, cannot be built upon."

"Why?"

"It is lava, unstable. There are holes, which would collapse."

The plane touched down, and Jocelyn realized the airport building was a lot different from the previous three. She commented on it.

"It is built in pueblo-style."

"What do you mean?"

"It is built in the style the pueblo people use for their homes."

It was time to get their carry-on luggage and deplane. When they got into the walkway away from the gate, Jocelyn realized the inside of the building was also different. They discussed this and the decorations as they headed toward the baggage-claim area and Mark's family.

When they passed the security barrier, Mark strode purposefully to a large group of people patiently awaiting his arrival. Jocelyn recognized his mother Rose and grandfather Roger from the pictures. The rest of his family was standing respectfully behind Grandfather.

She and her brothers hung back, waiting for Mark to greet his family first. Mark had said this was the first time he had been home since he returned to the mainland from Hawaii, so she guessed that everyone was eager to see him again. It was only when he introduced them that she realized that it was the Meyers family who was the main attraction, for there were so many of them who had made the trip to Albuquerque Sunport!

After greetings were over, the group slowly moved toward the baggage-claim area, and Jocelyn and her brothers were each claimed by different members of the family. Jocelyn was surrounded by females, and it seemed that Mark's cousin Angela was appointed spokeswoman as they would talk together in Navajo, and then she would talk to Jocelyn in English. Their first question was about her hair: why was it brown and curly? Jocelyn noticed theirs was black and straight.

"I don't know, just grows that way."

By the time her luggage arrived, there was a comfortable conversation between them, the women wanting to know about Jocelyn.

On the way to the parking lot, Jocelyn stopped Mark. "Do all these people live with your grandfather?"

"No, they are just here to greet you. Some are from the other side of the reservation, and some live here in Albuquerque. Only My Mother and one of My Sisters and her family live with Grandfather."

"That's a relief." She laughed, and he joined her.

The men were each guided to pickup trucks different from the one Angela guided Jocelyn toward.

"We are going to my house to feed you your last mutton-free meal before Grandfather's house." Angela laughed. Jocelyn noticed her easygoing personality was similar to Mark's and appreciated it. They all seemed to know where to sit in the pickup and guided Jocelyn to her designated seat in the cab as a guest.

Angela pointed out the sights as she drove to her house. She pulled into a driveway and past a solid plastered wall. There was a circle drive, which enclosed a grassy area. There were many large trees and a single-story house. Angela opened the door into a courtyard with the house rooms surrounding it and opening onto it. Long tables with chairs were set up in the courtyard with place settings already arranged on them. The women with Angela went into a room but had Jocelyn sit in a particular chair. Her brothers, Mark, his mother Rose and grandfather Roger were seated at the same table. The rest of the men sat down, and the women brought out bowls of food. They served the guests first, but soon everyone had their plates full. As they started eating, Jocelyn wondered aloud to Mark, who was sitting next to her, where the rest of the women were.

"They will eat later. Those who are going with us will eat in the kitchen. Your coming is a special event, remember?"

Jocelyn nodded and tasted the food on her plate.

"Do you like it?" Rose quietly asked.

"I'm not sure."

"They can get you something else."

"Oh, no. I think I'll like it as I eat it."

Rose seemed to relax some at her answer. Jocelyn realized, for the first time, that their coming was a very big deal for her and decided to enjoy everything about her stay for Rose's sake. Since Jocelyn rode with Angela from the airport, she had not gotten acquainted with Rose at all. But Rose seemed to be following everything Jocelyn said and did. She also decided to talk to her brothers about her discovery at the first opportunity. She found her chance with Robert when he went to investigate some plants growing in the courtyard. He said he would pass on

WANDA E. PALMER

the information that Mark's family was concerned about their reaction to them and their way of life.

Soon they were saying good-bye to Angela and the others who were not going out to the reservation with Rose and Grandfather Roger. Jocelyn and her brothers were again guided to specific seats. Jocelyn had headed to the back of Rose's pickup but was guided to the front.

Mark explained, "You're a guest."

As they headed west out of town, Mark took up the tour guide's role, pointing out the volcanoes and the lava flows called Malpais, along with other sights. After the Malpais, there really wasn't much to see until they entered the reservation and he pointed out the various places, giving the Navajo name, its translation, and the English name, if it was different.

"You said there wasn't much vegetation, but I couldn't picture this, even with your pictures." All Jocelyn saw was ground: dirt and rock formations. She did notice more vegetation in low areas and near houses, but the houses were far apart.

Soon they left the freeway and passed through a small settlement. You couldn't really call it a town as the buildings were scattered, with roads going off to each one. Mark pointed out a tribal council house, a medical clinic, a police station, and a trading post.

"What is a trading post?"

"A store. The people used to trade things with the owners."

"What would you trade?"

"Things we made or had of value."

They left the four-lane road for a small two-lane. The paving petered out. Then they turned on to a track, its roughness increasing and their speed decreasing the farther they went. The track led over a rise and then down an embankment. It looked like they were going along a dry river bed for a while and then going up out of it on the other side. Jocelyn learned later that this type of embankment and dry river bed was called an arroyo.

Jocelyn held her tongue as she didn't want Rose to be insulted, but Mark's description in no way really prepared her for *this*. Then it looked like they were headed into a rock. She knew they weren't going very fast, but she covered her mouth to keep from crying out. Mark patted her arm and smiled into her eyes. She hoped her smile was stronger than what she felt right then. They stopped.

Jocelyn moved to get out, but Mark shook his head. It seemed that some people were leaving them here, so there was some rearranging of passengers and good-byes. Then they started up again. They had to backtrack a ways, so Jocelyn glanced over at Rose and smiled and then looked ahead again. About the time Jocelyn felt that she would be better off walking (at least, she wouldn't be so jostled!), they topped a rise, and Mark pointed to a hut in the distance.

"Home," was all he said.

Rose looked at her as well. "Ah," was all she could manage with a smile.

Grandfather said something. Rose answered and then turned the pickup around. Jocelyn looked at Mark, her face full of questions.

"Grandfather reminded me that we need to pick up the mail, since we are out," Rose explained.

"Ah." The smile was weaker this time.

Grandfather said something to which Mark replied. Rose stopped the pickup again.

"Grandfather wants to know if you would rather stay here."

Jocelyn was not sure what to say. She was tired, but what would be least offensive? Her face registered all of this. Grandfather opened his door and got out, motioning for her to follow. Mark got out then went to the back of the pickup and opened the camper top and tailgate. He started unloading the bags and told her brothers to get out as Jocelyn stretched and Grandfather got back in. The rest of their luggage was quickly unloaded, and the five of them picked up their things as Rose drove off. Jocelyn and James started asking Mark if they had offended them.

"No," Mark said. "Grandfather thought you would be better off walking to the house while they went for the mail. He is putting his guests first, trying to think like you. But it is still his decision. He is the head of the family."

"There's a whole different thought process going on here," Matthew said, and his siblings agreed.

They discussed their first impressions of the new experiences as they carried the luggage the last two miles to the hogan. Jocelyn wondered if the entering ceremony was different if it was empty.

"We can't go in until invited."

"But it's your home," She argued.

"Not anymore. My home is in Groton."

"A whole different thought process!"

"We'll wait for them in the arbor."

"What's an arbor, anyway? I don't see anything like you described."

Mark pointed out things and answered questions about what they saw. There were questions about the hogan, and all near it: the flora (or lack thereof), the land formations, the sky, and the distances. He had told them about all of this, but at home they had nothing to reference his comments from; here they could see and register the reality. By the time they got to the arbor and found seats under its shade, the siblings had a new level of appreciation for all that Mark was trying to teach them. They were discussing some of the other aspects of his training when a large tanker truck topped the rise.

"Looks like you have company."

"Water man."

"And that shiny, new-looking tank is the new water tank of which you were speaking?"

"Yes, and here is the water to go into it."

All of a sudden, the siblings no longer felt so dirty or thirsty as they had. They watched as the water tanker lumbered its way toward them. Jocelyn thought it looked somewhat like an elephant as it lumbered along the track, slowly maneuvering over rocks and into potholes, one quarter up and another down. When it stopped at "a respectful distance away," they understood more of the instruction Mark had given them.

"I'd better go greet him so he can give us the water." Mark glanced at them. "By the way, remember to not be rude."

Eight eyes looked at him and then off in the distance past the water truck.

Mark greeted the man as he moved toward the truck. The quartet did not understand most of what was said but just enough to know they were introducing themselves just as he had taught them. They talked a little more, and then the water man moved the truck close to the new tank and hooked them together. After the water started flowing, he came toward the arbor. As he approached them, he greeted them in Navajo.

"My friends do not know much of our language," Mark explained in English. Then the hogan greeting ritual started in English. Jocelyn realized she needed to just remember what Mark had told them and quit being surprised when it happened.

Robert was fishing in his bags. After everyone had greeted the water man, whose name was Ben Tsosie, Robert said, "I'm sorry we don't have much to offer you except some water and some peanut butter crackers." He handed them each a package and a cup while Mark and Matthew went to get a pitcher of water from the old tank.

They discussed the weather, their families, and many news items as they ate their crackers and drank their water

Ben kept glancing at his truck then asked, "Do you want the old tank filled also?"

When Mark said, "Yes," Ben left to change the hookup.

"May I come with you?" James asked.

"I guess so," Ben shrugged. James started talking with him about what he was learning in some of his classes about water distribution and usage. As Matthew realized what they were discussing, he joined them.

Jocelyn also got curious. "Why did you get the new water tank, Mark?"

"As you can see, the old tank is small. The spring is giving less water. It barely gives enough to water the garden. Also, one of my cousins and her husband are talking about moving here. His job is not far, and she has helped Mother with the sheep since she was small. We all did, but she really enjoys it. She has become a good weaver as well. Her work sells at some of the better shops in Albuquerque and Santa Fé. More people need more water."

"When do they plan to move?"

"They have to build their house first."

"I see. Do we need to do anything about the garden and the sheep?"

"No. My sister, Jessica, and her son, Roger, stayed to take care of them, so Mother could take Grandfather to meet me...uh, us."

Jocelyn laughed, so Mark joined her, chagrined over his mistake.

"Will Jessica be back soon?"

"This evening. There's not a lot of grazing right here. Oh, the tank must be full. I need to pay him." Mark jumped up.

"We got it. After all, we'll probably use it all anyway," James said as they returned. "That's some garden your mother has down there. May we go look at it?"

Everyone wanted to go. Robert especially was tired of sitting. They went down the arroyo bank to the garden. They hadn't been admiring the garden long when a little boy challenged them.

"It's okay, Roger. Do you remember Mark?" Mark squatted down to talk with the boy in the Navajo discussion posture.

Roger squatted as well. "Mark? Did you come to visit?"

"Yes. How are you, Roger?"

"I am watching the garden for My Mother and Grandmother Rose and Grandfather."

"And a very good job you are doing. Will you show our guests your garden?" Mark introduced the guests. Roger went up to each of them and greeted them as he had been taught. When he came to Jocelyn, she asked if he were named for his grandfather. Proudly, he announced that he would carry on the name Roger for Grandfather.

He proudly talked about each of the plants. James asked if they had any problem with the garden getting washed away when it rained.

Roger said, "No."

Mark added that their garden was mostly protected by the arroyo wall, but there had been a few problems in the past.

Roger went to get a washtub. "I have to pick some things for My Mother to cook."

"May we help?"

"Sure." Roger told them what he needed, and soon the washtub was full. They all went back to the arbor.

Roger and Mark got a fire going, and the rest washed the vegetables and put them into the pots, which had been hanging on the arbor.

"I wondered what these pots were for."

"So did I," The rest agreed.

Things were cooking nicely when someone called, "Roger?"

"Yes, My Mother. We are cooking the vegetables like you told me," Roger greeted his mother.

"Jessica."

"Mark?" They greeted each other, and then Jessica greeted the rest. She checked the food, and then they talked about the weather, the garden, the flock, her son named for her grandfather, and the guests.

"Grandfather!" Roger spied the pickup lumbering its way to them.

Jessica and Roger greeted Rose and Grandfather. Jocelyn was surprised that the little boy did not run up to them but waited for them to come to him. There was so much she wanted to ask Mark; she got out her notebook and started writing down her questions.

Mark adjusted everyone to give Grandfather the seat of honor. Grandfather greeted everyone and sat down. Rose greeted everyone then went into the house to get some mutton stew to complete the meal.

Grandfather said something to Mark, and then all Navajo eyes were on Jocelyn. Because everyone else was looking at her, her brothers also did, wondering what it was all about.

"Grandfather wants to know what you are writing, Jocelyn?" Mark asked.

"Well, things keep happening that bring up questions for me. I decided to write them down so I wouldn't forget to ask you later."

Everyone started laughing, including Grandfather, Jocelyn noticed.

"What are your questions, My Child?" Grandfather asked.

"You know English?"

"Yes. But as the…" he said something in Navajo.

Mark answered him in English, "Patriarch or grandfather."

"As the grandfather, I wanted to check out your honesty, your sincerity. Come here, My Child, we will discuss your questions." Quietly, Jocelyn went to the place Grandfather indicated.

"May we join you?" Robert asked.

"I have questions I was saving for Mark too," James added.

"Me too," Matthew joined.

"We will talk. Jessica."

"Yes, Grandfather?"

"Let us know when the food is ready."

She smiled, "Yes, sir."

Their first question was, "How do you know English? We were told you only spoke Navajo."

"I learned English as a young man in school. That is why I was chosen as a code talker when I joined the marines."

"What is a code talker?"

"In World War II, the military needed a code to use so information could be transmitted without the enemy being able to break it. The Navajo language was chosen to make up that code, which even other Navajo would not understand. It worked very well and was never broken."

"So you know of the rest of the world, but came back here to live?"

"This is home."

It was like one of their training sessions with Mark, only now they were questioning their experiences. They talked through the meal and after. The others joined them as they were free.

Then Grandfather said, "Now, My Children, it is time to be grateful for the day and rest."

Mark and Rose had determined where everyone would sleep and had been putting out ground mats and sleeping bags. Roger wanted to join the men in the arbor, so his sleeping mat was moved. They wished each other good night and settled down.

Jocelyn had wanted to sleep outside as well, but did not say anything. She felt tired but was too excited to sleep. This was an adventure with real people and real places. As she wondered about Grandfather learning English, the thought drew her to him as a person. The questions started tumbling over one another.

Suddenly, she realized the ladies were getting up. "What's the matter?"

"It is morning." Rose laughed. "Nothing is wrong. We are going to greet the day. Would you join us?"

"Oh. The last I knew I had a million questions for Grandfather churning in my brain," she explained as she got ready for the new day.

"Grandfather enjoys your questions. He likes eager pupils."

When they finished dressing, and rolling and putting the beds away, the women went to greet the new day. Then Jocelyn saw the men were doing the same.

"Rose and Jessica, what do you want me to do?"

"You are the guest with a million questions. After your questions are answered, you can join us."

"I have a lot of questions for you as well."

"When you join us, we can talk as we work."

"That will be great. My father was afraid I would not like it here and want to go home early. Now, I'm not sure a month will be long enough."

"You are welcome to return. You can also write your questions in letters."

"Thank you so much. I would like to return. What can I carry?"

"May," Jessica and Rose said together.

"Oh. What *may* I carry?"

"We are used to correcting Roger's language usage. Please forgive us." Jessica looked unsure.

"Mother or someone would have corrected me at home. Thank you. I had thought of you as backward and ignorant. That's incorrect. You, your country, your way of life are just *different*. Like the Amish, or the hillbillies, or the Eskimos, you have a way of life that is different from mine, but that doesn't mean one is worse or better. Just different."

"Now you know why I wanted you to visit my home." Mark joined them as they took the breakfast to the arbor where the men had a fire going. "You were talking about going to college and going to work all in your area, within a few miles from your home. I wanted you to see that the world is full of differences, which are just as good as your differences."

"We wouldn't have known of our differences otherwise." Robert joined them.

"The things I was studying in my engineering classes make more sense to me now," James added.

"Speaking of differences," Matthew asked, "When would it be convenient for me to see the medical clinic? I would like to see it. Maybe even volunteer there while I'm here."

"I need to take Roger in for his school physical soon. I can take you in then," Jessica offered.

As they ate their mutton stew for breakfast, the discussion centered around where he could stay and how long.

"What happened to the rest of the vegetables?" Matthew asked.

"They are in the stew."

"Since you eat so much mutton, doesn't that deplete your herd?"

The discussion covered herd management and naturally led to the weaving that Rose did. The Meyers family asked to join Jessica when it was time for her to take the herd out. She counseled them on what to wear and bring as Rose prepared lunch for all of them to take.

Soon they were headed on the trail single file down the same embankment of the arroyo they used when they had gone to see the garden the day before. Roger went with them as far as the garden.

Jessica discussed the garden with her son. They talked about what needed water and what was ready to pick. Then she wished him a good day and headed up the arroyo. The others bade him good-bye and followed.

"Oh, look at those birds circling. Are they buzzards?"

"No. Those are eagles."

WANDA E. PALMER

They got a lesson on the appearance of eagles and buzzards flying on the way to the sheep pen, which was a cave on the other side of the embankment.

"The sheep are shy. Stay here. You can see everything, but they wouldn't come down if you were up there."

The family watched and listened as she climbed the trail to the cave, talking to the sheep as she went. She opened the gate in the entrance and walked back down the trail. A family of goats came first, then sheep after sheep, after sheep.

"I thought she had a few. Why, she must have fifty!"

"More, they keep coming!"

When Jessica got to the bottom, she stepped onto a rock by the trail. From this perch, she checked and talked to each one. They gathered at her feet. She seemed to have names for them. After she checked over the last one, she seemed to be calling for more. Three lambs came bounding out of the cave to her. It seemed like she was scolding them. She continued talking as she moved up the arroyo with the herd.

She began raising her voice and using English, "Please follow. You won't bother them now."

The four kept behind them, discussing all they saw. Jessica seemed to be giving commands to the goats, and the rest followed. At a fork in the trail, she gave a command, and they started moving into the left-hand arroyo.

After a while, James noticed that there was more vegetation growing beside the track. Soon they entered a valley carpeted in grass. James knelt down and checked the soil, grass, and other vegetation. "It's a coarse grass. It grows father apart and is perfect for this arid land," he commented.

"The bushes are good for the sheep as well." Jessica had returned to them. They continued to discuss the plants and sheep as they followed the herd farther into the arroyo.

"Why do you have the goats?" Robert asked.

"Many reasons. They are easier to milk than the sheep. My family milked the sheep for generations, but I like the goat milk better.

"They are more discerning of the plants. The sheep are natural followers. The goats avoid bad plants, so the sheep do also. I try to remove anything I see that is bad for them, but the goats are an additional safety factor.

"They do not overgraze, like sheep will. If you noticed, the sheep started eating when they first saw a hint of green. There would be nothing left in the entrance of the meadow if they were left alone, but the goats kept going to better pasture, so the sheep follow."

"Were you giving the goats commands?"

"Yes, and they listen and follow. The sheep would just follow me and my voice without the goats."

"I heard that shepherds had dogs to help them."

"Yes, most do. But back when Grandfather was in the marines, he was attacked by some mean dogs, so he does not think well of dogs. When he was convalescing in the hospital, he discussed with Grandmother, his wife, how the sheep must feel, based on his experience. After the war was over and they returned, they discussed it with Great-grandmother. She had taken all the sheep while her daughters followed their husbands to train for war. They decided to experiment on Grandmother's herd without the dogs. They seemed to be more calm but less controllable without the dogs. One of the aunties suggested goats. Once we learned how to work with the goats, the whole family began changing to goats for the sheep, although some like dogs better."

"So your family discussed this with your extended family?"

"And friends. When we get together, we discuss everything that we are doing. If I have a problem, someone else probably has a solution that worked for them."

"Wow! Community 101!" Matthew exclaimed.

"I don't understand."

"You live widely separated from each other, but everyone is important, and their ideas are important. So when you get together you present your problem and listen for a solution from the others."

"Exactly!" Jessica looked around, "Excuse me. I need to water the sheep now."

"How do you know? You didn't look at a watch."

"Have you heard of a sundial?"

"Yes."

"See the shadows? They tell me it is time to water the sheep."

"Would we bother your herd if we watch?"

"No, just don't get close. As strangers, you would be a distraction. Also, don't let them follow you."

"How do we manage that?"

"Let me know if you are going to leave."

"Excuse me, Jessica. Is there a bathroom?" Jocelyn asked.

Jessica waved her hand. "Pick a bush."

"Oh!" Jocelyn blushed. "It never dawned on me there would be no bathroom facilities."

"Come on, sis. I'll help you find some place. Did you remember your toilet paper?" James took her hand.

"Uh, no."

"Here's mine."

"Thanks." Jocelyn accepted the special camper's roll as the two headed toward some trees away from Jessica and the sheep.

Jessica headed toward a larger group of trees farther up the arroyo as she talked to her sheep.

"Look, Robert, the goats know where to go," Matthew said.

"I wonder if she told them, or they just knew."

"Another question! The vegetation here seems different from that at the mouth of the arroyo. Look at those flowers."

The two groups of siblings talked quietly as they went their separate ways. Jessica watered the herd then had them lay down to rest. When James and Jocelyn joined them, Jessica had everyone wash up in the pond then sit down for lunch.

When the conversation lagged, Matthew asked, "Do you have a siesta usually?"

"Grandfather does because of his age. I can't really because that would be an invitation to predators. My family will have more restful pursuits during the heat of the day. It is too tiring to do otherwise."

"You mentioned predators. What are they?"

"Coyote, wild dog, wolf, mountain lion, bear, and even eagle at lambing."

"Oh!" Jocelyn's eyes went wide, and she looked around. Robert said he had seen some tracks. They discussed this aspect of herd management and the wild country in which Jessica lived. She discussed each predator, where they lived, and how much of a problem they were.

After their rest, Jessica took the herd deeper into the arroyo. The rest noticed more about their surroundings than they had that morning. Jocelyn asked Robert to show her the tracks next time he saw some. She was worried the predators would attack them.

"Only if they are hungry," Jessica explained and then continued to tell them about the relatively small danger to people. The afternoon passed quickly, and soon Jessica had them head back to the sheep pen and the hogan.

Grandfather greeted them, "How was your day, My Children?"

"That's what Winnie and Mother always ask," Jocelyn said, noticing similarities as well as differences.

The talk again lasted until Grandfather reminded everyone to be grateful for the day and rest. Again Jocelyn wanted to sleep outside but thought it best to ask in the morning. The next night, they all went to sleep under the arbor because of the heat,

WANDA E. PALMER

but shortly before dawn, they had to move inside because of a thunderstorm headed their way. They stayed in until the storm passed. Jocelyn noticed that everyone had inside work to do, which kept them busy. Grandfather's job seemed to be telling stories. Jocelyn thought it was like having a radio program to listen to.

After everyone left, Rose stayed in as she had set up her loom indoors. The talk centered on her weaving, her patterns, her dyes for the wool, and her sales of the finished blankets.

"I would want to put them on the wall," Robert commented. "They are beautiful."

The rest of the Meyers siblings agreed. Jocelyn stayed near Rose, wanting to get more acquainted with Mark's mother. James wanted to go with Roger. Roger protested that it was not men's work. Grandfather talked with James, and learned his motive. Grandfather then explained to Roger in a way that made everyone understand that James only wanted to learn more about farming and water management techniques to add to his knowledge for his future work. Matthew wanted to stay with Grandfather to discuss healthcare issues.

~ 3 ~

Robert was at a loss, but he still followed Jessica, Roger, and James down the trail. He stayed with Roger and James for a time but found their discussion boring, so he headed up the arroyo after Jessica. He studied the floor and walls of the arroyo with mild interest. Finally, he came to the sheep pen and figured he could follow the tracks to the herd. After a while, he spied a large bird soaring overhead. He tried to remember Jessica's explanation on the differences between eagle and buzzard. When he rounded a corner, he could no longer see the bird, so looked down at the arroyo floor expecting to see herd tracks. There were none! The floor was sandy, so they should have been there, but what he saw that morning was not fresh. He even saw rabbit tracks across what was there. Rabbit would not be out here now. He turned back and studied the ground more closely. At the same time, he kept hearing something in the background. He kept wondering where the animals could have gone. They wouldn't just disappear!

Robert worked his way back toward the sheep pen, inspecting the arroyo bottom very carefully. Finally, he came to a point where the herd had gone up a side arroyo. Meanwhile, the background noise increased. As he started up the trail following the herd, he looked in the direction of the noise. A wall of water was rushing down on him!

In panic, he ran up the trail. He tripped and fell, and the water was nearly on him. He crawled, rose to his feet, and ran. The water caught his legs. There was a tree growing out of the arroyo side, and desperately, he lunged for it. He grabbed a branch, which was too small for him to hold on to.

He felt it bending. His feet were flailing at the bank. He grabbed another branch. His foot found a toehold on something. He got hold of another branch with his other hand and then turned loose of the first branch and reached for another. His other foot found something. He reached for another branch.

The noise seemed to be passing by him. His feet no longer felt pulled by the water. He looked down the arroyo to see the water level going down, the wall of water on its way toward the garden, toward Roger and James! He looked around for the path up. It was too far away. He looked for more handholds and toeholds. He frantically worked his way up, finally reaching a tree he could climb, which went beyond the top of the arroyo. Branch by branch he worked his way up, calling to James and Roger knowing he was too far away for them to hear him, but anxious for their safety.

When he got high enough to work his way to the arroyo rim, Robert realized there was someone reaching out for him. Hands clasped his arm, and he was pulled to firm footing. Someone also was on his other side grabbing that arm.

He kept repeating, "James, Roger, James, Roger. Got to warn them."

"Okay. It's okay. Roger knows what to listen for. They left the garden safely."

Finally, Robert understood what the other person was saying and stopped talking. He looked at the speaker and then the one on his other side.

"Jessica!"

"It's okay, Robert. You are safe. James and Roger are safe. They are the ones who warned us that you had come up the arroyo in search of me."

"Oh." Robert felt limp; the adrenaline all flew out with the sound. The man eased him to the ground, squatting to look in his eyes.

"Everything is okay now. Just relax. Here is some water."

Robert laughed weakly. "Water seems strange to me now. It has taken on a whole new meaning."

"I expect so," The man agreed, "But drink up. It will help calm you."

Robert obeyed. As he calmed, he focused on the man. "Thank you."

"You are welcome."

"Robert."

His head slowly turned to Jessica. "Yes?"

"I would like you to meet my husband, Abraham Chee."

"Good to meet you." Robert looked again at Jessica. "Husband?"

"Yes."

"Roger's father?"

"Yes."

"Good."

"I am glad you approve."

"Oh…Um…Well, you see. Ah…I was thinking…"

Abraham and Jessica waited in the respectful Navajo Way.

"I'm embarrassed to say. There is Grandfather and Rose and Jessica. But who was going to teach Roger to be a man and manly things? I'm not trying to be difficult. He's so young and so wants to be a man. Now he has you. Oh. He does, doesn't he?"

Abraham smiled. "Thank you for your concern for My Son. He has had me his whole life. You have not met me because I have been away in Albuquerque for a Federal trial. I am a Navajo Tribal Policeman. I helped to capture a criminal. I needed to give testimony at his trial. The trial is over, so I am back home."

"You live here with Jessica and Rose and Grandfather?"

"For now. When Jessica's cousin moves here, we will move closer to her work."

"But I thought the sheep were yours?"

"They are Mother's. I am an instructor at Canyoncito College."

"Then why are you here?"

"Mother had a bad fall. She still walks slowly, if you notice. She cannot care for the sheep, so I took leave to help her. We will build Mary Rose a house, and they will build us a house. We will all live here until the sheep get acquainted with her, then we will move into our house."

"Community! Does everyone come to build the house?"

"Yes. How did you know?"

"That is what the Amish do."

"Amish?"

Robert felt himself getting lost in the explanations.

Abraham said something, and Jessica answered in Navajo. To Robert, he said, "I think we need to get you back to the house. You may still be in shock." He helped Robert up and led him to a Navajo Tribal Police vehicle. Jessica gathered her sheep and took them back down into the arroyo where there were now many pools of water.

Abraham asked Robert about himself, which helped him to recover from the aftereffects of his near-drowning. When they got back to the house, sure enough, he had been the only one of the ten residents and guests in danger.

Abraham didn't stay long, as a call had come for him prior to their arrival at the hogan. The dispatcher first asked about Robert, who got very embarrassed by her concern. Abraham talked to him about community in Navajo country, "Remember, people are important to our people." He talked to Grandfather some in Navajo before he left to take the call.

Later, Grandfather took Robert aside for a talk. He was reluctant, but afterward was glad for the talk. Grandfather explained many things, which helped ease Robert's distress over the whole incident. He promised to never go off alone again as well.

The rest of the family discussed what to plant this late in the year to replace the garden washed out by the wall of water. When Grandfather and Robert joined the rest for supper, along with Abraham, it seemed all of Mark's family had flash flood tales, including now young Roger. Robert noticed they were not told in a spirit of one-upmanship but more in a spirit of camaraderie. Robert began to feel more like one of *them*.

When there was a lull in the conversation, after waiting for what she hoped was a respectful time, Jocelyn asked, "Where did all of that water come from?" Her siblings expectantly looked at Grandfather, also wanting to know the answer.

"From the rain." The eight eyes waited, but wanted more information.

Abraham said something in Navajo. Then in English, he asked, "Do you have severe storms in Connecticut?" They nodded their heads. "Where there is much water in a short time?" Again, heads nodded in agreement. "That is what happened last night. With a very heavy rain on dry ground, the water has to go somewhere. As it travels, it collects and becomes a flash flood rushing down the arroyo."

"But it didn't rain that much here."

"No, but if it rained hard at the head of the arroyo and kept it up in this direction that water is going to come down to the river. At times, we get a flood and no rain here. It is what happens there"—he gestured toward the head of the arroyo—"that determines what size the flood will be here."

"So it washed out everything to the river?"

"Yes."

"What about the meadow?"

"If it came that way, it would have destroyed it."

"Even those big old trees?"

"If they were weak for some reason. Actually, the small young trees are more vulnerable, because their root systems are not as strongly developed."

"That is why I always check the head of the arroyo and sometimes go different ways. If there was a storm in one place and none in another, I take the sheep where there was not a storm," Jessica explained.

James asked, "You keep saying storm. Are there gentle rains too?"

"Squaw Rains," Roger said.

"Yes, but we don't have many," Mark added. "If we did, it would be green here, like Connecticut." Many nodded in agreement.

Grandfather reminded them that it had been a hard day, so everyone needed to rest. The murmurs of agreement came from all parts of the arbor.

The next day, Mark suggested a sightseeing trip. He also requested that Matthew bring his things because they were going by the nearest clinic, which was near where some of his family lived. If it was okay with everyone concerned, Matthew would stay there for a week or so until he could be brought back. They also would take young Roger for his school physical as he no longer had a garden to tend.

They stopped at the clinic first. The doctor was pleased to have someone to help and requested that Matthew stay with him at the clinic. While Roger was having his physical, Matthew's things were taken into the clinic residence and good-byes were said. Matthew spent the rest of the day shadowing Dr. Andrew Pettijohn.

The rest, including Roger who proved to be an excellent tour guide, enjoyed their visit to more of the reservation. About the time the family became tired of sitting crowded into the cab of

Rose's pickup, Mark turned off at a scenic vista, and everyone got out and discussed what they saw.

At one lull in the conversation, Jocelyn asked, "Mark, if it's not too personal or rude, where were you yesterday?"

"Remember, I told you my family would arrange a cleansing ceremony for me to bring me back into harmony with the world?"

"Yes. That's where you were? So is it a private ceremony?"

"Yes. Just you and the singer."

"Singer?"

"Yes. That's the best translation for his title."

"Does it make you feel different?"

"In a way, yes, and in a way, no. I feel more relaxed, more at peace. Afterward, I can enjoy all of this"—he waved his hand to include all they could see—"much more."

"I kind of assumed it would be something your whole family would participate in, since that is how you do so much."

"There are other ceremonies, rites of passage, marriage, and such where that is true."

"When will you build the houses for Mary Rose and Jessica?"

"Would you like to participate?"

"Yes," the three Meyers siblings agreed in unison.

"I will talk to Grandfather."

"But what could we do?" Jocelyn asked.

"You would help cook and serve. The men would help carry and whatever they can."

"We've never built anything. Not even a doghouse." James laughed.

"You follow instructions well. You would be a great help. Mary Rose's house will be a traditional hogan. Jessica hasn't decided yet. Where she will be living, there are more winter houses, but she and Abraham would like to be more traditional. I think they will end up with a hogan as well."

They discussed traditional hogan building off and on for the rest of the day.

"How about lunch?"

"That'd be great."

"I could do with something."

"May we have Navajo Tacos?" Roger asked.

"What's that?" The siblings queried.

"Next up, Navajo tacos, one each."

"I…uh…I'm kinda hungry." James tried to be polite as he expressed his need of a real meal, not just a snack.

"You're thinking of tacos like those at a Mexican food restaurant. Roger might not be able to finish this."

Everyone looked at Roger and thought how much the young boy could eat.

"Okay. I guess we could order more if we need to, right?"

"Of course!" Mark and Roger laughed, as Roger knew what a Mexican food taco was like as much as the Meyers family did.

Soon they were pulling into a large trading post, which had a café in it. They went in and were seated at a round table with enough room for all. A Navajo woman waited on them. Even here, Mark and Roger greeted her with the Navajo greeting, which Mark enlarged to include the Meyers family. Then he requested Navajo Tacos for everyone, and each gave their drink order.

"Mark." Jocelyn got everyone's attention. "Would you greet someone in Albuquerque the same way?"

"Of course."

"Even in a business like this?"

"Unless it was very busy, and the boss was harried. This is our way."

"I guess I'm having trouble accepting that your real way of life could be so different here, and yet away from here you're so much like us. It's almost like you are two different people."

"I've been wondering about that too," Robert said. "It's like you're different, but you blend in. I noticed that in Abraham too. He acted like an EMT, yet he's a policeman. At the same time, he had that patient, waiting attitude. I don't know...so much the same and yet so different too."

"Perhaps," James said, "it's a different way of looking at life. I have seen teasing but no ridicule. I have seen patient acceptance, like over the loss of the garden, but a desire to do what needs to be done, like the discussion of what to plant next."

"Or Jessica," Jocelyn said, "taking leave from her job to take care of the sheep when your mother got injured, until Mary Rose could get her family moved here. I don't see people at Groton doing that sort of thing. My friend's grandfather had a heart attack. Her dad didn't take leave from his job to take care of his store. He wanted to sell it and move his parents to a retirement home. That's a more self-centered, selfish way. Yours seems more people-centered, but accepting of what is."

"And yet you get the job done in an easygoing way," James added.

"This is a lesson in more than just climate. It's also a way of life," Robert concluded.

Before Mark could respond, their platters of food arrived. The three siblings stared at them wide-eyed and then looked at Mark with wonder.

"Navajo Tacos, one each. Enjoy." He and Roger started eating. The rest tasted, picked, dissected, and discussed the food.

"Taco meat."

"Lettuce and tomato."

"Big as the platter."

"Tastes like a taco."

"Except for the fried dough thing on the bottom that is like an elephant ear from the fair."

"Yeah, it doesn't crunch."

WANDA E. PALMER

"James, do you think you'll need another one?" Mark asked. There was a smile on his voice and face.

"Probably not," James laughed.

"You can have whatever I can't eat," Roger offered.

"Thank you, but let me get around this first." Everyone laughed then.

Mark led the conversation off onto the Four Corners area where they were headed. He explained that it was the only place in the United States where four states met. He also talked about what they would see there—the monument, which had been placed first, and the commercial side and how it had grown over the years.

"What are the four states?" Robert asked.

"New Mexico, Arizona, Utah, and Colorado," Roger answered.

"I don't usually think of Arizona and Colorado together, and I have no idea of Utah," Jocelyn said.

"Just like you had no idea of New Mexico when we first met, remember?" Mark mentioned.

"So this trip is a geography, lifestyle, cultural odyssey," Robert said.

"With some food and storm issues to liven it up," James added. Everyone laughed.

When it was obvious that everyone was about finished with their platter of food, the waitress started clearing their plates. "Would you like some fried ice cream?"

The 'you are kidding, right' stares prompted Mark to tell her to bring one and plates for everyone. After she left, three pairs of eyes focused on him. "You dip hard frozen ice cream into a batter and quick fry it so it doesn't all melt before you eat it."

"What was that about food issues?" Everyone laughed.

When they finished the fried ice cream, Jocelyn moaned. "Is it within walking distance to the Four Corners? I'm so full I need to walk this off."

"How long do you want to take? Remember you can walk anywhere. It just takes longer than riding. We'll walk around at Four Corners."

On the way, Mark encouraged them to see the monument first and look at the vendor's wares later. The family took pictures of each one standing in four states at once and four standing in a different state while holding hands. Before they left the marker, Jocelyn asked if the merchandise was all made by Navajo.

"Mostly, sometimes a Hopi will come but no other people."

"But nothing mass produced in other countries, is there?"

"Definitely not."

"Good, I don't want to get something mass produced in another country, which I can find in Groton for less money.

The men were standing in front of the truck talking when Jocelyn finished looking.

"Did you find something?" James looked at her empty hands.

"Not really. I wanted a gift for Mother and something small for a few of my friends. But...I don't know..."

"What were you thinking about?" Mark asked.

"Maybe a necklace, or pin, or a vase. There just wasn't..."

"Would you like to visit a jewelry maker or potter?"

"Maybe."

"I'll see what I can do."

"Where to now?" James asked.

"The trading post and then home. It will be dark before we get there as it is. Let me know if you need to stop for anything else."

"I'm on sensory overload," Robert said.

"You might not be over your fright completely."

"I feel the same way, and I wasn't scared like that. Maybe that's why I couldn't find anything I liked," Jocelyn commented.

"Could be, because I don't think I could take in any more new things either," James added.

They all got comfortable in the cab, and Mark sped off. Suddenly, he stopped the truck on the side of the road. "I know you said you were tired, but would you like to see a rattlesnake as long as the road is wide?"

"I would," James requested. "Where is it?"

"We just ran over it." James opened the truck door to go back to see the snake.

"No, we'll drive. It may not be dead yet. You really don't want to add snake bite to your experiences."

"If it is dead, may I get the rattles? They must be large too," Roger asked.

"Let's go see." Mark turned the truck around and drove slowly back to where a rope looking thing was stretched across the road. He stopped a few feet away and pulled a big knife out from under the seat. James opened his window but not the door. Mark got out and walked across the road after looking at the end of the snake in front of the truck. He cut something off on the other end but left it. He returned to the end in front of the truck and carefully removed something from it.

"Roger, is there a sack in the truck?"

"I'll see." Everyone started getting out.

"James, keep looking for another one. They sometimes are in pairs."

Startled, James scanned the roadside for another snake. Roger did not find a sack, so Mark put the snake rattles and the knife in the back of the truck. They all wanted to see the rattles until Mark said it wasn't safe there.

Robert laughed. "And I thought I was on overload before!"

Snakes and other common unpleasant inhabitants of this arid land were the main topic for many of the miles back toward the trading post. Jocelyn was less sure of sleeping under the arbor after that. Robert and James agreed with her, but Mark pointed out that there wasn't enough room for everyone to sleep inside and such creatures rarely came where people's homes were. That was why the first snake they had seen was away from any habitation.

Mark pointed out more of the landmarks and told stories and legends about most. As the sun fell toward the west, they noticed the change in colors. "Is the land colored differently here?"

"Yes and no."

"That doesn't make sense."

Mark laughed. "Let me explain. The mineral content of the earth colors the land, as you put it. But also the light from the sun is colored by the atmosphere, which puts its color onto the land. Remember I told you that the Sandia Mountains were called 'watermelon' because they often look like a broken open watermelon in the setting sun?"

"Yes. It was curious to me," James said, and his brother and sister agreed. "They didn't look watermelon red to me."

"You did not see them in the setting sunlight. You saw them in the noon sunlight."

"We haven't seen any sunsets since we have been here."

"Because of our mesa on the west, tonight you will see a great sunset. There are some clouds to increase the beauty. Look at the sky. See how it is darker in the east than in the west? Look at the mesas to the east and then the ones to the west."

Their excited comments filled the cab, often overlapping each other.

"Eastern mesas look golden," Jocelyn said.

"Even that red one has a gold tinge to it," Robert exclaimed.

"That cloud has turned golden," James added.

"That one is turning pink," Robert pointed out.

"Look west. There is a pink glow with the gold," James offered.

"The pink is deepening, what would you call that color?" Robert asked.

"Magenta?" Jocelyn offered.

"Look at that purple over there," James stated.

"This is even better than the sunsets at home," Jocelyn affirmed.

"There is more red there," James agreed.

"This is more golden," Jocelyn said

"Here is more purple or..." Robert hesitated, not sure what to call the color.

"Yeah. What would you call it?" James asked

"There is more blue mixed in. Even the purple is more lavender than red," Jocelyn stated.

"Look back east now. The sky is a dark blue," James pointed out.

"The pink in the east has deepened also," Robert agreed.

"Look at the owl beside the road up here," Mark suggested. The owl watched the pickup as it passed, turning its head to keep the vehicle in its vision.

"Hey, there's a deer over there," Jocelyn said.

"That's no deer. Look at the antlers," Robert noted.

"There's more of them," James added.

"Antelope," Roger said.

"Wow, and I thought I was on overload before," Robert lamented.

"But this is different somehow," James added.

"More restful," Jocelyn agreed.

"Wow. Look at the size of that moon!" James exclaimed.

"I don't remember a moon rise at your house," Robert questioned Mark.

"We were always too busy talking," Mark explained. The visitors watched in awe as the world again changed under the moonlight.

"Mark," Jocelyn got his attention.

"Yes?"

"Thank you for asking us to come," Jocelyn quietly said, and her brothers agreed.

James elaborated, "Hearing about it and living it are two different things. I had studied water usage and conservation in my courses, but I really had no clue until I saw the reality, lived the reality here."

"That is why we pretty much ignore most of the 'experts' who come here from BLM and BIA, because they really don't know. They have never lived here. We have centuries of experience. We know what works. Sometimes we will try one of their suggestions, which sounds like it will work, and sometimes it really does work."

"I assume you discuss it with your neighbors first," James asserted.

"Of course."

"What are BLM and BIA?" Robert asked.

"Sorry. BLM is Bureau of Land Management, and BIA is Bureau of Indian Affairs."

"Right now, I think it would be easy to get used to this way of life," Robert commented.

"But would you be willing to give up everything you take for granted?"

"Right now, I think so."

"What are you studying?" Mark asked.

"English."

"Maybe you could teach in one of the schools," Mark suggested.

"That's a possibility," Robert agreed.

"What were you planning to do?"

"I don't know. Maybe teach in a college. I don't want to put up with bratty kids who don't want to learn. But…I'm not sure how to say this…I don't want to put it badly."

"Just say it. We're friends."

"Are all the kids respectful like Roger?"

"No. Some are just as bratty as you are used to. But I think most of the parents would support you. Roger, what do you think?"

"What does bratty mean?" Roger asked. Mark discussed it in Navajo with him. "Okay. Robert, the ones who are not respectful are sent to the principal's office. Does that answer your question?"

"Yes, Roger." The two discussed school atmosphere for a long time.

Mark pulled up to the trading post. "I need to get the mail and a few things for Mother. They have a restroom, if you need it. It'll be about an hour to the hogan."

Jocelyn followed Mark into the building. "Mark, what would be a good thank-you gift for your mother for having us?"

"Um, I'm not sure. Let me get back to you on that, okay? What kind of cost were you thinking about?"

James had followed them and answered, "As much as she and your grandfather have done for us, let's not put a limit on it."

"Okay. A helicopter…"

"Within reason!" Jocelyn shook Mark's arm as they all laughed.

Mark went to the post office window and talked with the lady there. He bought some stamps then pulled out a key from his pocket and went to the bank of mailboxes and emptied his mother's box. He then consulted a list, which she had given him. The five took turns refreshing themselves in the restroom and helping to gather the needed items on the list. As they scoured the shelves for the list's items, wants were also spied. The pile grew.

"Hey, remember we have limited space in both the truck and the house," Mark pointed out as he pulled out his wallet.

"I'll get this." Robert pushed Mark's arm away.

"Maybe that's a thought for a thank-you gift," Jocelyn said.

"Supplies?"

"Well, yes, but what I was thinking is storage space: shelving or storage bins, or something like that."

"Okay. I'll ask her," Mark agreed.

"It's supposed to be a surprise, silly."

"But what if there's something that she really wants and keeps putting it off?"

"I know something like that," Roger interjected.

"What?"

"One of those things that goes in the back of the truck to put things so the groceries don't roll all over."

The lady behind the counter spoke up, "Aren't you Mark Denton, your mother's Rose and your grandfather is Roger?"

"Yes."

"Well, she's got one of those things Roger is talking about on order."

"Oh. What we want is a thank-you gift for her for letting us visit her," Jocelyn explained.

"Well…The one she has ordered hasn't been paid for. There are a few other things she has talked about. You were mentioning storage. She has wanted something to put staples in that would keep the varmints out. How long ya gonna be here?"

"Three more weeks."

"Oh. We got plenty of time. That thing for the truck will be in next week."

"How much is it?"

"Let me look here." The lady thumbed through some papers. "Here it is: $142.56, with tax."

"Do you take traveler's checks?"

"Sure." The Meyers family pulled out their traveler's checks, and each came up with a fifty-dollar check.

"That gives you $7.44 left over."

"Apply it to this stack, and I'll pay for it," Robert said.

"Y'all having a good time?"

"Yes, we are."

"By the way, this is Robert Meyers and Jocelyn Meyers and James Meyers, and you know Roger." Mark pointed out the members of the group standing around.

"Sure do. Glad to meet ya. I'm Susan Sommers. My husband's Jason."

"Where are you from, Susan?" Jocelyn asked.

"Oh, we're from the Mobile, Alabama area. We had a store there. Somethin' like this. Then that gamblin' moved in. Got to be too many riffraff, so we sold out and took a trip. Got out here and had a flat. The people were so nice we looked for a store. This one was falling apart and most empty. Got it reasonable. Been here now a long time. They's a few riffraff here, but mostly good, honest people. Trying to pick up the lingo but not doin' too good. They talk English, so's we get by. Now, that truck storage bin will be on the Tuesday truck. Anythin' else you need, we order Saturday and get it Tuesday. That'll be $98.23. Now, aren't you Robert? I'm pretty good at names, but just remind me if I get it wrong. Y'all have a good time, ya hear." Susan greeted another customer, and the group carried their bundles to the truck.

"Whew! She's quite a talker," James commented.

"Yes, but she fits in here," Mark stated.

"That's what I'd like," Robert asserted.

"To fit in here?" Mark asked.

"Yes, but to be useful to people who would appreciate it."

"If you're really interested in teaching here, we could go visit my teacher. He taught somewhere else first, and he says he likes us better," Roger added.

"Mark, do you suppose we could try?"

"Sure. Our list of people to see is growing: Roger's teacher, a jeweler, and a potter. Anyone else?"

"I'd like to know more about water usage, gardens, and things like that. Do you know someone who really knows?" James asked.

"Mother and Grandfather, and what they don't know they are more likely to know who would really know."

"Mark, one time you talked with me about ceremonials. Will there be one while we are here?"

Mark said something to Roger in Navajo. Roger said to Jocelyn, "There is a ceremonial coming to which we were planning to take you."

"Oh. Thank you."

"Mark, don't forget to ask about us helping to make the house for Mary Rose."

"I'm going to have to make a list!" The conversation lagged as everyone settled down to their final leg of the day's travel.

~ 4 ~

The next morning at breakfast, Mark discussed the house for Mary Rose. The building had been planned to start after the guests left. Rose and Grandfather argued that they were guests, but when they understood that the Meyers family wanted to help, they agreed to see about starting it earlier.

Mark asked about Robert visiting Roger's teacher and Jocelyn a jeweler and a potter and then brought up the subject of thank-you gifts. Rose didn't know what to say when she learned that her truck storage bin had been paid for. This discussion took some time, but finally Rose understood.

When the rest went off to their tasks, James stayed to talk with Grandfather. Rose, Roger, Jocelyn, and Robert went to the garden area to work on it.

"Hey, not everything is washed out!"

"That's why we plant where we do, protected by the arroyo wall that sticks out here."

Rose directed the work, and soon the new rows were planted.

As soon as they were not needed, Robert and Jocelyn went to Mark and asked when they could make their visits. Mark said they could go now and asked Robert to learn if Roger wanted to go with them. The boy wanted to visit his teacher, so soon Mark, Jocelyn, Roger, and Robert were on their way with the understanding that the ones they sought might not be home.

The first place was the teacher, who lived in the government-supplied housing near Roger's school. Roger led the way and rang the doorbell as Mark explained that a house to live in was one of the incentives to get teachers for the schools. The door opened.

The teacher's eyes moved down the group to Roger and lit up. "Roger, how is your summer?"

"Fine. My friend Robert wants to talk with you," Roger grabbed Robert's arm as he spoke. "This is his sister Jocelyn. This is my uncle Mark. This is my teacher Mr. Kant."

"Thomas Kant," he said as he shook everyone's hand. "Come in. Sit down. I'll get some more chairs," Thomas said as he brought kitchen chairs into the living room. "Let me turn my music down."

"Wagner."

"Yes. The *Ring Cycle*. Not my favorite, but I enjoy it as well."

"What's your favorite?"

"Chopin. Some of his piano pieces are like liquid silver."

"Do you play?"

"No. I'd like to learn. I have more time to practice now that I have the summers free. Enough about me, Roger said you want to talk with me, Robert?"

"Yes. I have been visiting with Mark and Roger and would like to discuss teaching here with you. Would this be a good time for a detailed discussion?"

"Sure."

"Before we get into that, my sister wants to visit some artists to see about gifts, so she and Mark want to go on."

"Sure. It's nice to meet you, Jocelyn and Mark. You go on. The three of us will talk school until you get back."

"Thank you, Thomas. We'll be back after a while."

"Have a good time looking." Thomas escorted them to the truck.

Jocelyn and Mark got in and headed to the home of a potter. Soon, they were off on a track into the wilderness, slowly working their way along.

"I just had a thought. What if I don't have enough cash? Do you think they'll take traveler's checks?"

"I don't know. But you don't have to buy anything today. You could even order it today and then bring back the cash when you pick it up. Don't feel you have to buy until you are sure."

"That would work."

Mark asked what she had in mind. They discussed possibilities as they drew closer to a group of buildings.

"Do they have a store?"

"I don't know," Mark answered as he stopped the truck a respectful distance away.

A door opened to one of the buildings, and a woman stepped out and came to the truck. She greeted them in English but in the traditional Navajo Way. Mark handled the greeting and introduction then expressed interest in the pottery he had been told she made there.

"I do not make all of the pottery. Most of my family also make things."

"Do you sell them here?"

"We have some to sell here. We just returned from Albuquerque where we sold much of what we had. You are welcome to see what we have left."

"Is your work only decorative, or is it functional?"

"Both. My Daughter makes bowls and cups for eating. I make more decorative pots. My Son makes more pots to cook in. Get down and come in."

"I'm looking for gifts for my mother and sisters, and am traveling by airplane, so am limited on what I can get," Jocelyn explained.

"We can ship your purchase to your mother."

"That would be helpful. Do you take traveler's checks?"

"Yes, we can."

"You said you don't have much, could she order things?"

"Yes. When do you leave?"

"Three weeks."

"That is plenty of time to make some things for you, if you like. Come into our workroom."

They stepped through the door, and Sarah Etcity introduced them to the various people working there, including her mother and husband, Marvin Etcity. Marvin said that he didn't make pots, just dirt, and laughed. Then he explained that he brought his family the clay and other supplies they used. The shelves where they kept their finished work held a small variety of items. They discussed the kinds of things in which Jocelyn might be interested, as well as the costs.

"I had no idea of all of the possibilities. I need to think about this. Thank you for your time." While they were headed toward the next place, Jocelyn thought out loud about the things she had seen. Suddenly, she looked at Mark. "This must be awfully boring for you. I'm sorry to put you through this."

"This is another cultural difference: I enjoyed sitting there and listening to you talk with the Etcitys. I have often heard non-Navajo talk about being bored. I just relax and enjoy whatever it is: whether it is hard work, or flying across country, or watching my friend find the right gift for her mother and sisters. I don't really understand this idea of 'nothing to do'!"

Jocelyn looked at him thoughtfully, "Major cultural difference."

"This is Samuel Nakai's place. He makes jewelry," Mark said as he stopped a respectful distance from a place that looked much as Rose's did, except here was a chicken coop and a dog, which barked at them and lay back down.

A man was working under his arbor. He carefully set down on the fire a pot from which he had been pouring a silver liquid out into what seemed to be a mold. Mark and Jocelyn waited and politely watched him from the side. Mark had told her to not look directly at someone unless you were talking, but you can look near them and still see them out of the side of your eyes. The man had to move some things he had around him so he could stand. He also cleared a place for his guests to sit before he made his way to the truck. When the greeting was over, Mark said that he had heard that Samuel made jewelry to sell.

"Yes. I was pouring some melted silver into a mold when you arrived. Get down and come see what I have. I will get it from the house."

They talked as he led them to the places he had cleared for them, then he excused himself. When he returned, he had a tray with cups and a plate of cookies in one hand and a basket on his other arm. He sat the basket down carefully first. It seemed quite heavy. He then handed them plates and let them select a cookie from the tray. He went to his fire and poured coffee from a pot setting near it into the cups on the tray and gave each of them one. They had been talking about the weather and their families. When those topics were well-covered, he asked if there was something specific they wanted to see.

Jocelyn started to say something at the same time that Mark said, "No. I'd like to see all you have."

Samuel took bundles one by one out of the basket and opened them so they could see the contents. Mark seemed to be watching Jocelyn's reaction to what Samuel displayed more than the jewelry. It was obvious she liked what she saw. Mark asked the price of most items so that Samuel started telling it first. There was a squash blossom necklace with earrings, which Mark asked Jocelyn to put on, where it remained. Jocelyn saw a belt buckle, which she wanted for her father for whom she had not thought of getting a gift, but realized it was perfect for him.

"Do you want a pin for your mother, which is very similar to the belt buckle?" Samuel asked.

"Oh, that would be nice."

Samuel got out several bundles of pins to find the one just like the belt buckle. Jocelyn saw three pins, which were similar to each other. "I would like those three."

"For your sisters?"

"And Marcie."

"What about Winnie?"

The three pins were placed with the belt buckle. In the third bundle that Samuel opened, he found the pin for which he was searching, and Jocelyn agreed that it would be good for her mother.

"Anything else, Jocelyn?"

"No."

Samuel started to put everything away, but Mark stopped him.

"I would like to look at rings."

"Men or women?"

"Both." Samuel removed several bundles and returned those he had out.

"Do you have any man and woman rings that match?"

"You look at these." Samuel looked at tags on the bundles, searching for a particular one. "Ah. What do you think?"

Mark looked at each pair carefully and asked Jocelyn if she liked certain ones.

"Uh. Yes."

"Here, put this one on."

"Okay?" Jocelyn put on the ring and held it out for Mark.

"Would you wear it all of the time?" Mark asked.

"Is it for me?"

"Yes."

"May I choose?"

"We are."

"Oh?" Jocelyn looked more carefully at the ring. Then she looked at the others Mark had indicated. She then looked carefully at the rest. "But, Mark, these are like wedding bands!"

"Mmm."

She took off the ring and handed it back to Samuel.

"I really can't choose now. May we talk later?"

Samuel looked carefully at her and then at Mark. He said something in Navajo and started putting the rings away. Mark said something, and the two talked. Jocelyn removed the necklace and earrings Mark had put on her and also handed them to Samuel. Mark said something, and Samuel handed them to him. Jocelyn got her wallet out and roughly figured what she owed. Samuel put the purchases into individual cloth bags and figured the cost on his receipt pad and then told Jocelyn the total. She handed him the money; he put the small cloth bags into a larger paper bag and counted out her change. When her transaction was done, Jocelyn told Samuel that it was good to meet him. She then got up and moved to the truck. She sat next to the passenger door, confusion clouding her mind and face. Mark said nothing when he got in; just started the truck and drove off.

"Do I need to tell Sarah that I found something else?"

Mark said nothing; he just looked at Jocelyn and then drove on. Then he stopped the truck in the middle of nowhere. There was no road, but there was a nice view. He reached over and took Jocelyn's hand. She looked at his hand and then his eyes, confusion still clouding hers.

Mark took a deep breath and said, "Jocelyn, I have very much enjoyed getting to know you and your family. I told you I wanted you to come here so you could see this country. There's another reason. I wanted to see if you could accept my family as I have accepted yours. Jocelyn, I love you very much. I have liked you and enjoyed you, your company, your friendship since that first night at the party. Something more has been building in me.

Today, there with the Etcitys, I realized that I want you to be my wife. I want you and need you. The world is so much better where you are. Jocelyn, will you marry me?"

Jocelyn looked at the mountains in the distance, then at his hand, and then at his face. "Oh, Mark, I don't know what to say. I enjoy your company, but I have never thought of getting married. Oh, maybe someday. I'm not one of those girls who think all of the time about getting married. I'm not saying no. I guess I'll have to think about it."

"Did I make you angry over the rings?"

"No, not angry, just confused. I never thought of our relationship as more than friendship."

"Is there someone else?"

"No, no," Jocelyn laughed, "Did you ever meet Michael Johnson?"

"No."

"He has asked me to go steady every year since the third grade. I'll tell you what I told him: 'I'm not ready to settle down.'"

"I see. You want many men."

She laughed very hard. "I don't want 'men' plural. I have a good friend Stephen with whom I do things, but we've never had a date, even though I went to the Coast Guard Academy Ball with him. And you—you've never asked me out on a date. We've been very good friends and have done many wonderful things together, but I really haven't thought beyond friendship. Mark, I'll have to think about it." Then she remembered something. "Okay, maybe this will help. Remember when we were headed to Four Corners, and I said I'd never thought about Utah, and you said that I'd never thought about New Mexico until Penny's party?"

"Yes."

"This is the same thing. Please give me time to think about it. Also, please don't say anything to anyone else. Is that acceptable?"

"Yes. May I talk with you about it?"

"Yes. But remember how stubborn I can be if I think you're pushing!"

"I understand. I think maybe if I were to 'push,' as you call it, I would push you away."

"Quite possibly."

"Then will you accept the necklace and earrings as a friendship present from me? No strings attached other than as a token of how much I value our friendship?"

"Yes. Normally I would say no. It's too much. But maybe it's just right. Now if I seem to be off doing other things, please don't think I'm avoiding you. I really don't want anything to change in how we treat each other. Will that work?"

"Yes." Mark's hand started toward the keys to start the truck.

"May we sit here longer?" Jocelyn asked.

"Yes."

Jocelyn stared off in the distance, not seeing anything before her. *What is it like to be in love? Do I really want to spend the rest of my life with Mark? I enjoy him. Am I ready to commit to him?* Questions flooded her. She looked at Mark. He looked at her and then back out the front window.

"Mark, what did you and Samuel talk about?"

"He asked me if I had talked with you. When I said no, he said that the man usually asks the woman first before coming to see him. He said I put things badly."

"You put the cart before the horse."

"Yes, that is what I did. But I did think you were thinking something more. I really thought you were interested in more than just friendship when you visited me in Hawaii. Then when you agreed to come here, I thought you had to be interested, or you wouldn't have come."

"You didn't think this is just an opportunity to see the world? Your world, yes, but just that? I never thought beyond friendship to some other possibility. I'm here because a friend asked me to come. There was no other motive. I guess you had another motive though."

Mark did not answer for a long time. Finally, he turned to look at her, leaning against the truck door and pulling his knee onto the seat. "Do some girls, uh, women…" He looked at his hands.

She waited a long time. When he said nothing else, she asked, "Are you finished?"

He nodded his head, yes.

"Some of my friends greet each new acquaintance as a potential husband, weighing, sorting, comparing, and trying them. When they meet someone they think fits the bill, they go after him with everything they have, plotting and scheming to get him. My parents taught us differently. Mother said that when the right man comes along, wait to see what develops. Don't manipulate. They advised to just be friends. The best marriages are between good friends, so be friends. If something more develops, fine. At least, you have a good friend, and you can never have too many friends. I count you as my best friend. I have never thought beyond that until now."

"And now?"

"It's too soon to say. My mind's a whirl of questions."

"What kind of questions? What would you like to know?"

"Things like: What does 'in love' mean? Or 'am I ready to commit my life to him?' Or…" She laughed. "Mark, you look scared to death. Why are you so serious?"

"We say that the other is holding my life in your hand. I *am* serious. I *am* scared. I'm putting this badly." He turned, opened the door, and ran off to the edge of the mesa.

Jocelyn watched him go, wondering what it would be like to not have him in her life. It was easier to think without him right next to her. She looked off in another direction, but her eyes kept moving to him. She thought about what he had said. *Is my life in his hand? Do I think of Mark Denton in that way? Do*

I want to spend the rest of my life with him? Right now, the idea was too new.

She looked out the side window and saw a storm moving their way. Then she looked toward Mark. He wasn't there! She opened the door and stood on the running board. She got out and started calling, telling him a storm was coming, as she moved to where she had last seen him. She found where he had been and then followed his tracks down a trail. She rounded a curve and saw him in a cave, and then raindrops hit her. She called him again. He yelled for her to run back to the truck. He was running along the path now. She made it to the top before the deluge hit, but she was soaked by the time she got to the truck. She got in, started the motor, and moved the vehicle near the trail so Mark could get in sooner. She turned on the heater to warm up from the cold rain and then moved to the other side of the seat as Mark rushed into the truck.

"Which way did the storm come?"

"The south."

"Good, then we won't have to wade." He turned the truck around and headed back toward Thomas Kant's house.

"What do you mean 'wade'?"

"If the storm had come from the west, the direction we are going, there might be water in some of the arroyos, which we would have to wade. Since I do not know these well, it would be better if we didn't, because I would not know what is under the water."

They rode in silence for many miles. "Mark?"

"Yes?"

"Please wait for me."

"I am so embarrassed."

"Don't worry about it. Just wait."

"But I have messed everything up."

"No. Forget it. Later we'll talk about it."

When they pulled up beside Thomas Kant's car, they were both lost in their own thoughts. They both got out and made their way to the door. Mark rang the doorbell. They stood there, looking at the door, when Jocelyn heard familiar voices that seemed to be coming from outside. She turned toward the side of the house and made her way to the back. There was a large garden, in the middle of which was her brother who was bent over a plant.

"Robert," she called as she made her way toward him.

"Jocelyn, doesn't Thomas have a nice garden?"

"Yes, very nice. What are you picking?"

"Okra."

"What is okra?"

"One of the main ingredients in Cajun Cooking," Thomas answered.

"Are you Cajun?"

"Yes."

"That must be quite a switch, from Cajun to Navajo."

"Ah, yes, but it pays the school bill."

"I don't follow you."

"My student loan. They forgive a big chunk of it every year I teach here. I did not know it when teaching in the other school system and about went bankrupt with bills until someone told me. So here I am, and I love it, especially the kids." He looked at Roger and smiled. "I feel like I am about to drown when I go back to the Louisiana humidity and feel like I'm becoming a prune when I return, but I am thinking of this as home and that as my parent's house. Who, by the way, think I am crazy. Ah, well."

"May I finish picking the okra?" Robert asked of Mark.

"Of course," Mark said. "May I help too, Thomas?"

"Why, thank you. I haven't looked at the tomatoes and squash yet. There are baskets and bins in the shed."

Jocelyn turned toward the shed as well. "Mark, do you have a knife?" she asked.

"Yes."

"Why don't you do the squash, and I'll do the tomatoes?"

"Okay." He did not look at her until she had a bucket and headed back to the garden. He sighed, picked up a basket, and went to find the squash.

When the garden was picked and they were in the kitchen, Thomas invited them for lunch. "Won't be mutton or fancy, just a fresh vegetable frittata."

"Thank you. How can we help?"

"May I have some water first?"

"Sure. Here." Thomas pulled a pitcher out of the refrigerator and put it on the counter, then opened a cabinet and got out a glass, filled it, and handed it to the nearest person. When everyone had a glass, he refilled the pitcher and put it back into the refrigerator.

"That's a fancy pitcher. Is it a filter?"

"Yes. I had a hard time getting used to the taste of the water until I got that. Now sit at the table and cool off."

"Are these places furnished?" Robert asked.

"No. But used furniture works fine, if you're not too picky."

"Mark, may we go to the Board of Education Office this afternoon?"

"Sure."

Thomas got up and pulled out a package of thin rectangular white things, which he spread out on the table. Then he put knives on them. He picked out some squash, washed them, and placed them on the table. "Slice them very thin. I need to get some spices." He picked up a pair of kitchen shears and a small basket and went outside. When he returned, he placed the basket of sprigs and leaves on the table and said, "Chop these very fine."

"Uh. Thomas, may we have a cutting board?"

"That's what these are"—he indicated the rectangular white things—"see?" He proceeded to slice a squash. "They are cutting mats. They work well and are inexpensive, so when one gets ruined it's okay to throw it away and get another."

"Ingenious."

He then put a large skillet on the stove and turned the heat on. He put some butter in it and with a large plate got the squash slices to put in the skillet. He chose a very ripe tomato, washed it, and requested for it to be sliced thin.

"The spices are chopped."

"Good." He sprinkled them over the squash in the skillet. He then got a bowl of eggs out of the refrigerator and another bowl and whip. "Here, whip these up. You can put the shells back into the bowl." He turned the frying squash and then got the cheese out. "Chop this into small pieces." When the eggs were whipped, he added them to the squash, topped with the tomato slices and cheese.

"What do you want to drink? I have iced tea and water." He got a jar of tea and the water pitcher out of the refrigerator. "Someone please get the rest of the tea off the back porch. We'll need some ice. Who'll fill up the glasses with ice? Plates are right here. Please hand them around. Napkins on the table. Salt. Pepper. Oh, forks! They're here. What else?" He looked over the table. "That seems like everything. If I've forgotten something, just holler. I don't have guests every day. In fact, you are the first I have had." Thomas laughed nervously. The rest smiled and filled their glasses.

"Please pass the sugar," Mark asked and then put some in his tea and started to stir it with his fork.

"Oh, I have iced tea spoons! Any one else need one?" Everyone else shook their head no. He handed one to Mark, put an extra by the napkin holder, and one by his plate. Then he sliced the frittata, put a pot holder on the table and the skillet on it. "Ah.

There. Please hold hands while I say the blessing." When he was done, he asked them to hand him their plates, placed a large piece of the frittata on each of them, and handed them back. After he had served himself, he said, "As you can see, there is more. Help yourself to seconds when you are ready.

"Mmm. This is delicious. What are the spices?"

"Oregano, basil, and chives."

"Do you like to cook?"

"I had never tried until I came here. As you can see, there are no fast food places and just a few restaurants. So I asked Mom for some of her recipes and planted a garden. I also got some recipes from the internet and got a cookbook."

"You have internet here?"

"Not at the house, but at the school."

"Can you go to the school in the summer?"

"Sometimes. They use the building for other activities too. But I have been here several years, so I have built up my supply of favorites."

"It seems to live here you have to be self-sufficient."

"That is a good way to put it. Say, there is a piece left, someone want it?" Robert and Mark looked at each other. "Here." He cut it in two and gave half to each.

Jocelyn picked up her plate and asked Roger if he was finished. He handed his to her and poured himself some more water. She took the plates to the sink.

"Just leave them."

"But you have all these vegetables to care for. It won't take us long. Where is the dish soap, washrag, drain board, and dish rack?"

Thomas got them out, and Robert picked up the dish towel. Quickly, the kitchen was cleaned up and the floor swept.

"Thank you, Thomas, for a good morning." Robert reached out to shake Thomas's hand. The rest added their appreciation.

"What are you going to do with all those vegetables?"

"Gumbo."

"What?"

"I will make gumbo. It's a Cajun stew."

"Oh, well, thanks again." They all got into the pickup and headed toward the road.

"Mark, please remember the Board of Education Office," Robert said.

"I remember."

"Well, Jocelyn, did you find any gifts?" Robert turned to his sister.

"Yes." She explained about the belt buckle and pins. "I take it your talk with Thomas was informative."

"Yes. Very. I have to do an internship and then write my Master's thesis. I'm going to see if I can do the internship here. That will give me the opportunity to learn if I would really like teaching and living here before I commit to a contract."

"That sounds wise."

"The contracts are for only one year though," Mark commented.

"Yes, but I have to do the internship anyway, so might as well kill two birds with one stone."

"Why are you going to kill birds?" Roger asked.

"It's a saying my grandmother had. It just means accomplish two things at one time. She had many sayings—one for almost anything that happened. I just wish I had written them down before she died. I didn't realize how apropos they are."

"What does 'apropos' mean?"

"Pertinent, appropriate, just right. See, that's why I think I would like it here. I can be myself, and the kids will ask if they don't understand."

"But I wouldn't ask if you weren't already my friend."

"Then I will need your help to make friends with the children."

"Maybe if you ask if everyone understands after you say something and then just answer as you did to me, it would help them to understand. When someone puts us down, we don't ask again."

"That's true anywhere. Have your teachers treated you badly?"

"Not me, but some do."

"Will you let me know if it happens again?"

"What can you do?"

"Encourage them to treat you more positively. No one learns well when treated like that."

Mark interjected, "People with an inferiority complex try to build themselves up by putting others down."

"So do people with a superiority complex, but that doesn't make it right."

"No, but don't get discouraged when the system doesn't change with your one-man attack."

"What do you mean?"

"You are not a minority who looks different, talks different, acts different. Many people treat us as subhuman. That is why I visit your family so often. There I am treated as an equal. Most whites don't treat us that way."

"Oh. I didn't know."

"What is that quote about don't judge someone until you have walked in their shoes?" Jocelyn asked.

Robert and Jocelyn looked at Mark with new understanding and greater respect. Jocelyn wondered if this had some bearing on Mark's regard for her. She decided she would ask him about it the next time they were alone. Since they had not traveled this way before, Roger started pointing out new sights. He also had some interesting tales about many places. Mark added some as well.

"Robert, you said Master's thesis. What about college level? With a Master's degree, you could teach college."

"Yes. But I understood that they were under the Board of Education also."

"Maybe so. Why don't you ask while you're here?"

They all got out and went in the front door. At the receptionist's desk, Mark greeted her as Laurie, whom he knew. Then he turned the conversation over to Robert, who explained his interest. She seemed very pleased and then seated the rest before she led him down the hallway, discussing Robert's qualifications and answering his questions.

Jocelyn studied Mark. When he glanced her way, she asked, "Remember what we were discussing when we left Samuel Nakai's house?"

Glancing at Roger, he hesitantly said, "Yes?"

"Is it in any way related to how you feel about my family?"

"Some."

"Umm," She continued studying him, but said nothing more. Mark realized what she was asking but did not want to discuss it in front of Roger. He looked at Roger and then away.

"I understand. Roger, tell me about your teacher. He seems like a nice man."

Roger gladly told her about Mr. Kant and was describing one of their experiments when Laurie returned.

"This may take a while. May I get you something?" Laurie offered.

They all said, "No, thanks."

Roger added, "We were visiting Mr. Kant. He gave us a good lunch from his garden."

"Mr. Kant is a good teacher and seems like a nice man."

"He is. He has a big garden. He let us help him pick the ripe vegetables."

"That's nice, Roger. I have some work to do. Please let me know if you need anything."

"Thank you," they all said. They settled down to wait. Mark stared off in the distance, Roger and Jocelyn talked some, but after a time, their conversation slowed, and Roger seemed to settle against her. She looked at him and realized he had fallen asleep.

She moved him so his head was in her lap, and then she too stared off into the distance. Occasionally, she glanced at Mark, who didn't move. She reviewed each of her questions and tried to honestly evaluate the situation. Everything seemed to boil down to one question: How important is Mark to me? She looked at him out of the corner of her eye. Then slowly her head turned so that she was studying him fully. He didn't seem to notice, but she thought he knew.

When Robert returned, he seemed excited with all he had learned. He had a folder of papers and talked all the way back to Rose's house.

As they pulled up to Rose's parking place, Jocelyn laid her hand on Mark's arm. "May we take a walk?"

"Yes." When they got out, Mark led Jocelyn on a path she had never taken. They walked silently to a big rock where he sat her and sat beside her. Again he stared off into the distance. Jocelyn studied him and noticed a slightly pained expression on his face. When she spoke, he flinched slightly like he expected her to strike him.

"Mark, please look at me."

Slowly his eyes moved toward her feet and up her legs, took in her hands calmly laying on her lap, moved up to her arms and her neck, and rested on her mouth. She reached out to move his chin up, but his eyes stayed focused on her lips.

"Why are you afraid to look into my eyes?"

"I don't want to know what is there."

"I haven't made up my mind."

"Why have you been staring at me?"

"I'm trying to answer my questions."

"Are the answers written on my face?"

"Yes."

His eyes jerked up to hers, "Where?"

"Everything about you: the way you look, the way you hold yourself, the way you sat there all of that time and never moved tells me about you. Mark, I really want you in my life. But I need you to wait for me. I want to finish my education and work at Baker's to find the cure for the cold. That has been my dream, my life, for so long. It's going to take time to consider your proposal. It's so different from my plan. But while you're waiting, please don't lock me out."

"I bared my heart to you."

"And I'm baring mine to you."

He looked into her eyes. "You are not saying no?"

"I'm not saying no. I'm saying, 'wait.' You're racing ahead of me. Please stop and let me catch up."

Hope flamed in his eyes. The dejected body perked up. It was a very small change. He didn't show his emotions, but she could see it. She realized how much she knew him already.

"Mark?"

"Yes."

"Remember what you said about being a minority and enjoying my family because we treat you as an equal?"

"Yes." He looked off in the distance. "Yes, it does have a bearing on how I feel about you."

Jocelyn watched him. It seemed painful for him to talk about this, but he continued. He explained how people treated him. He described his pleasure at meeting her and her acceptance of him, her family's acceptance of him, his loneliness for them and for her when he was stationed in Hawaii, how her trip to see him in Hawaii had encouraged him, and how he believed she must love him back because she had accepted his invitation. Then the waiting until he was with her again, the joy at being stationed again at Groton, and now her coming here. He turned toward her and took her hand.

"I guess I had a pipe dream about you, but it really wasn't you. It was my dream of you."

He looked at their hands. He placed hers back into her lap and turned away.

"Thank you for telling me. May I give you my side of the story now? Maybe I can alter your dream to include the real me."

Mark looked at Jocelyn with an odd mixture of hope, resignation, and fear in his eyes. She started with her friend's death and her dream of developing a cure so no one else would have to go through that horror. She explained her plans of making that dream come true. As Mark began to really understand the importance of Jocelyn's dream to her, a change came over him, a feeling that their worlds could never join. She continued on to her meeting him and the joy she had in their friendship. She explained her reasons for visiting him in Hawaii and coming here.

"Mark, I really do think of you as my best friend. I treasure the great times we've had together, but there have been no shooting stars over seeing you or doing things with you, more just quiet pleasure."

"Shooting stars?"

"Isn't that what love is? Shooting stars, earth shake, that sort of thing?"

"Not for me."

"Oh? What is it like for you?"

"Quiet pleasure, joy, anticipation of seeing you again, sitting there at the Etcity's pottery shop and watching you as you tried to find gifts for your family. I don't want a future without you."

Jocelyn looked at him and then off in the distance. Mark watched her, realizing for the first time the age difference between them. She was just beginning her adult life. He was ready to settle down.

"Jocelyn."

"Hmmm?" Her eyes returned to his.

"I think you are right."

"Hmmm?"

"You need time to consider all of this. I have rushed into this, and you weren't ready. Will you forgive me? We can go back to before."

"No. We can't go backward. But maybe we can be more honest with each other."

"No more pipe dreams?"

"No more pipe dreams. I'm not sure what mine was about you. Maybe that we would be best friends for the rest of our lives," She laughed.

"I can accept that."

"Can you really? Even if I say no to marriage?"

"I'm not sure I could go that far, but if you're my best friend I still have a chance of more."

"Hope springs eternal."

Mark thought a while. "I think so."

"Can we change the subject a little?"

"I guess so."

"You seem to know some nice Navajo women like Laurie. Why haven't you considered any of them?"

Pain crossed Mark's face. He looked away. "Laurie is not nice. I'm a half-breed."

"I don't understand. Your people seem so understanding."

"When I introduce myself, I don't have a father's clan. In high school, no one wanted to go out with me. The ones who did were, uh, were not, uh…"

"Were not the kind of girls you really wanted to spend your life with."

"Yes. I dated Laurie and a few others. But they were all over me. They only wanted one thing."

"Now I wish I hadn't asked."

"Why?"

"What you're saying is no one else wants you. That really puts the pressure on."

"Oh, Jocelyn. I didn't mean to…I don't want to…Please…"

"It's okay, Mark. We're being honest and open, remember? Maybe I shouldn't ask so many questions. I really don't like the answer to that one!"

"You don't think I was pushing, do you?"

"Don't worry. Why, you're trembling! You thought you had blown it."

"Yes." Mark's voice was squeaky scared.

"This isn't going to work. You can't be walking on eggshells if we're going to be open and honest with one another."

They both stared off into the distance for a long time.

"Mark?" He sighed a huge sigh and looked at her. "This is a beautiful view."

"I come here to think."

"Okay. Think on this." She took his hands in hers. He watched her, and she waited until he again looked in her eyes. "Let's promise that there will be no sudden decisions. We need to be free to learn more about each other without the fear of the other one not liking what they hear. In olden days, there was something called a courtship. It was a period of getting acquainted, of exploring the possibility of a future together before engagement. What about if we say that's where we are? No walking on eggshells. No fear of loss, just getting to know each other better. If an upsetting revelation is made, we agree to discuss it. So how does that sound?"

"You really don't think I was trying to push you?"

"No. You were just answering my question, and I was responding to it. Mark, before today you wouldn't have gotten scared so easily."

"I need to put my emotions back away."

"Maybe not. After all, I don't like to be manipulated. Now I know an area where you can easily be manipulated, so I need to be careful to not do so."

Relief seemed to flood him. "Is that what you meant about walking on eggshells?"

"Yes. You shouldn't be afraid of my reaction so that you watch what you say. That wouldn't be open and honest."

"You really want to talk about us, about you and about me?"

"Yes, I do."

"Okay." He held her hands more firmly and searched her eyes and face. A confidence seemed to flow from him to her. A contented sigh settled a small smile on his lips. "May I kiss you?"

"Not yet. I made an agreement with my parents that my first kiss would be at my wedding."

"Oh!"

"By the way, you haven't answered my question."

"What question?"

"What about courting?"

"I said okay."

"When?"

"Before I asked to kiss you and after you answered, 'Yes, I do.'"

She laughed. "I thought you were just commenting on my answer."

They sat there for a time.

"Jocelyn?"

"Yes."

"The necklace and earrings."

"Yes."

"In my culture, that is a sign of engagement."

"Like an engagement ring?"

"Yes." She just looked at him, wondering what he was trying to say. She could tell he was searching for the right words, but she didn't know what to say either so she just sat there holding his hands and looking in his eyes. Finally, he took a deep breath. "Jocelyn, would they be okay as a courtship gift?"

"No. You don't usually give a courtship gift. I'll give them back, and you can save them."

"No! I gave them to you as a friendship gift."

"But so much has changed. That was premature. Let's wait and get everything back in the right order."

"Put the horse back in front?" A smile played on his face.

"Definitely!" It was Jocelyn's turn to breathe deeply. "I'll give them back, and I promise to not think of you as an Indian Giver."

Mark roared, and Jocelyn joined him. The weight of the day evaporated.

When they calmed, she said, "That's the first time you have laughed today. I like your laugh."

"It was a tough day, but with a good ending. Let's promise that we clear up tough days."

"Yes. With laughter."

Mark looked beyond her and then back to her face. "It's late. Are you hungry?"

"Now that you bring it up, I am."

She looked beyond him and realized also that it was dark. "Oh, everyone will be wondering where we are."

"Probably not, Grandfather knows we went off. He has been talking with me about you."

"What do you mean?"

"He knows I love you and talked with me about it."

"You told him?"

"No."

"How did he know?"

"The way I am around you and the fact that I asked you here."

"What has he been talking with you about?"

"Would I stay in your world, or would you come here to my world. That is why he talks with you like he does. He wants to know if you could live here, or if I would have to live there. Now I know I would have to live there so you can follow your dream."

"Would you really do that?"

"I have thought of it for a long time. Remember, this is not completely my world any more than yours is."

"What would you do there?"

"I don't know. My military training doesn't really prepare me for a civilian job there any more than it does here."

"What was your degree in?"

"History."

"What did you plan to do with it?"

"Be an officer in the navy."

"Really?"

"Yes. If you have a college degree you can go into the navy as an officer where the pay and benefits are better."

"I guess you could teach."

"But I don't have a master's or teaching certificate. I could be a policeman. My training could be used that way."

"Okay. Let me get this straight: You want to get married with no job or prospects of a job?"

"I have a job—a very good job with good pay and benefits!" Mark sounded hurt.

"Then why are you talking about something else?"

"I have to be away from you and have to move regularly. Your job would be in Groton. The two don't go together."

"You would leave your Naval career for me?"

"Yes, Jocelyn, I would. That's how important you are to me."

"Oh!" Her mind reeled with the recognition of the depths of his love for her. Then a new thought assailed her, *Can I return such enormous commitment?* She wondered if she would be willing to live here with Rose and Grandfather, with no water, with gardens washed out, and with all the other things she had encountered here in Mark's world.

"Jocelyn?"

"No."

"What?"

"I don't know if I could give up my world for yours."

"You don't have to decide tonight."

"But no water and the insects and the long distances…"

"Jocelyn, you are now thinking like I have been for months. How about if we go visit some of my relatives who don't live in traditional hogans? Their homes are not much different from Thomas Kant's rental house."

"Oh, Mark, it's not just that. As you said, you've been thinking about all of this for months, years actually. But I'm just starting to think about it."

"Jocelyn, we can't decide anything tonight. Let's go find something to eat and sleep on it."

"I'm not sure I'm hungry. I'm not sure I can sleep either." He helped her up and then turned to go, but it was too dark for them to see the path.

"Children," Grandfather called from a long way off.

"Yes, Grandfather."

"Do you need some light?"

"Yes, Grandfather."

"I am coming." They watched as the lantern slowly got larger.

"Mark?"

"Yes?"

"What do we tell him?"

"The truth, he already knows. He has been asking me for days what I'm going to do."

"Do you feel pressured?"

"Yes and no. He doesn't pressure."

"But you felt pressured enough to want to buy the rings before asking me."

"Yes."

When Grandfather arrived, he held the lantern so he could see Mark's face and then Jocelyn's. "So now Mark is calm and Jocelyn is upset. Why is this?"

"Because I had my life all planned, and now I have to rethink everything."

"Let us talk as we walk. An old man needs his rest."

"You're not old."

"Almost ninety."

"Oh!"

"So, what is this plan?"

"When I was little, I had a friend who died from a common ailment. In my town, there's a pharmaceutical company named Baker. They make things like penicillin. They have a research department that searches for medicines to combat common ailments. My goal has been to work for them and find medicines to prevent such tragedies."

"And when you met Mark?"

"He's a friend—someone nice to do things with."

"Like go to Hawaii and come here?"

"He said he wanted to expand my world, and he has. I really appreciate all he has done for me, but I wasn't thinking about getting married."

"But he was. Here. Sit. I have food."

He handed them something to eat, and then turned to Mark. "You had not talked with her about your feelings for her?"

"No. I just assumed that she did all of these things because she was interested in a future together."

"Did you talk of this?"

"No." Mark was glad it was dark, so the others could not see his embarrassment.

"Did you know of her dream?"

"She told me that night at the party, when we met."

"How does her dream fit into your dream?"

"I assumed that I would have to get a job in Groton near her work."

"Grandfather?" Jocelyn asked

"Yes, My Child."

"Do the rest know?"

"Yes."

"Then the pressure is on for me to decide."

"No. They all want what is best for you and Mark."

"I always thought I would get my doctorate and work a while before I got married."

"Why should that change?"

"Uh. Well, I don't know. That's about five years away."

"Mark, is that a problem?"

"No. It would give me time to save up and look for a job in the Groton area."

"Are you finished eating, My Children?"

"Yes."

"Yes."

"Good. Jocelyn, do you still feel pressured?" Grandfather asked.

"No. Mark, are you really willing to wait for five years?"

"Yes. First, I will wait for you to decide about marrying me. If you decide you want to, I will be glad to wait for you."

"Good. Now, My Children, to bed. It is a short night." Grandfather led Jocelyn to her sleeping bag, did the same to Mark, and then he lay down and put out the light.

Jocelyn really didn't think she would sleep, but when she awoke, the sun was up, and no one was around. She put her sleeping bag away and found Rose under the arbor, weaving.

"Here is some food. You had a long day."

Jocelyn sat down near Rose and started to eat. They discussed how Rose knew that Mark's father was the man for her. They went on to many topics that Jocelyn had been wondering about. When they stopped to fix lunch, Jocelyn felt she not only knew Rose better, but also Mark and their culture. She spent the afternoon with Grandfather, again gaining understanding of what a future with Mark might be like. During supper, she watched Mark closely. He seemed embarrassed by her scrutiny. When the meal was over, he asked her for a walk. Grandfather handed him the lantern without comment.

She laughed. "What's the matter? Don't you like coming to look for us?"

"An old man needs his rest. Young people need to talk. Good night."

Mark thanked him and again took her to his rock. They discussed a possible future but agreed to wait for definite plans. They discussed the view, his life here and in the navy, and her plans.

The next day, Rose announced it was washing day. Jocelyn said she wanted to help, so she was given baskets in which to gather everyone's dirty laundry. Behind the hogan, she found Rose and Roger had strung out hose to the garden from an old wringer washing machine to use the water from washing to water the garden. Rose explained how she sorted the clothes by color and by soil level. Jocelyn gathered the least soiled white clothes for the first load. Rose explained that they washed and wrung out all of the articles, changed the water and rinsed them, and repeated the process until all were clean. Then she hung them on the lines she had strung to dry them. It was all new to Jocelyn, who had never done more than throw the clothes in the washer and dryer and put them away. Actually, Winnie, the housekeeper, did it all most of the time. They talked, laughed, and enjoyed the time.

"Excuse me, ladies, lunch is ready," James told them.

"Who fixed it?" Jocelyn asked.

"Robert, Mark, and I. There's not much to putting a pot on to heat and cutting the bread. By the way, do you need help making more bread?" He asked Rose.

"That is woman's work!" Rose answered.

"Sure, but since we eat most of it, the least we can do is help make it," James assured her.

"Okay. I was planning on doing that tomorrow."

"It's a date then." James held Jocelyn back as Rose went on to the arbor. "Sis, you doing okay? Do we need to talk?"

"How about this afternoon after the laundry is done?"

"Fine." They joined the others for lunch. Again, Jocelyn watched Mark. He seemed more relaxed than he was the night before. She noticed each of the others more than she had previously, and she began to realize what a self-centered existence she had led. That led to memories, some of which caused her to smile. Then she realized that Mark had been watching her for some time. She smiled at him and started gathering the bowls to clean up.

When she headed back to the laundry, Mark joined her. "You okay?"

"Yes. Thank you for your concern. I was thinking about my life and realized what a self-centered life I have led. My memories were funny and embarrassing."

"That's why you were smiling?"

"Yes." She chuckled.

"Can we talk again this evening?"

"Actually, James wants to talk first. Okay?"

"Sure. We can talk tomorrow."

"May James and I go to your special rock? It will be as soon as I finish the laundry with Rose."

"Oh, I guess so." Mark did not seem pleased.

"If you don't want us to, we can walk another direction. That's not a problem."

"Would you mind?"

"We'll walk down the road."

"Thanks."

"Sure." Then she turned to Rose. "Now what do I need to do, Rose?"

"We need to take down and fold the dry clothes so we can put up the rest of the wet ones." By mid-afternoon, all of the clothes were dry and folded. Jocelyn remarked that it would take much longer for the clothes to dry in Groton. Then they got off onto what Groton was like, and Jocelyn invited Rose to visit her family there.

When they were finished, James and Jocelyn walked down the track while she explained what she had been doing, thinking, and feeling the last few days. They returned in time to finish supper preparations. James and Rose discussed what was required for baking the bread.

Jocelyn again watched Mark. When he looked her way, she asked if he wanted to talk.

"No. I'm not ready. We'll go tomorrow."

"After bread-making?"

"After supper."

"Okay. But I need to give you something."

"The necklace?"

"Yes."

"Tomorrow."

"Okay." Everyone sat around and talked after cleaning up from the meal until Grandfather announced that it was time for bed. The next morning, it seemed that everyone was busy. Robert and James were making a fire in a mound shaped thing as Rose directed them, which turned out to be the oven.

Jocelyn and Mark fixed the meal. After cleaning up, Rose brought out the ingredients for making bread and a large flat board and gave Jocelyn a large bowl like hers. Jocelyn mimicked Rose, measuring, stirring, kneading, shaping, and preparing the loaves for the oven. Rose checked the oven and directed the men how to clean out the fire, sweeping all of the coals out and away from the front. She explained that the bread rested on the floor of the oven where they had built the fire and that no one liked ashes in the bread. When the oven was ready, they hauled all of the loaves over, and Rose carefully placed them to be sure they would all fit. Then she put the door on the opening and piled rocks in front of it to keep it closed.

Then they made some more dough. Rose explained that the loaves would not be ready for lunch, so they would have tortillas. Jocelyn thought making bread had been fairly easy for someone who wasn't a cook. But tortillas! That was another matter. She followed Rose exactly, but her dough was not as elastic as Rose's. Then rolling them out! A few rolls of her rolling pin and Rose had nice neat rounds. Jocelyn had lumpy ovals! Rose cooked hers on the large piece of metal she had placed on the fire under the arbor and encouraged Jocelyn. Rose moved very slowly and described each step in detail. Jocelyn tried, but the results were so bad that she wished that Rose had a dog that she could feed them to.

Grandfather said something, and Rose answered and told Jocelyn they would try fry bread with her dough. Jocelyn was sent to get the bottle of oil, and when she returned, Rose was doing something with her dough.

"There, try that. Remember, you have to press hard, but fry bread doesn't have to be nice rounds. You can even do it with your hands, like this."

Jocelyn felt more successful with the fry bread. She asked, "Is this what Navajo tacos are made of?"

"Yes, this is the base. But we don't have the rest of the ingredients."

"That's okay. I was just asking, as it looks the same."

Before the fry bread was all cooked, Rose put the pot of stew on and some vegetables from the garden. Then she called everyone to refresh themselves for the meal. As they were getting ready, Abraham drove up and joined them.

When everyone was finished greeting him, Abraham addressed the Meyers siblings, "I understand you want to help with building Mary Rose's house."

"Yes, we would, if it works out," Robert answered.

"They will be here this afternoon to talk about it."

As they started eating, the talk focused on what needed to be done to prepare for the house. Abraham looked at Rose when he realized the fry bread was tough but said nothing.

"Jocelyn has made her first fry bread. She also made her first bread." Rose smiled at her.

"Mmm. Good," everyone commented.

"You are really making yourself at home. That is good," Abraham added.

Grandfather changed the subject, and Jocelyn looked at Mark. He mouthed, "Later," and then looked away. Jocelyn could hardly wait until cleanup was done. She looked everywhere for Mark but couldn't find him. She was upset. She had asked that he tell no one, but everyone seemed to know.

"Grandfather, have you seen Mark?"

"No. Come sit with me and talk."

"About what? It seems everyone knows my business except me!"

"People are not blind. People have minds. Mark is not the only one who assumes that a girl who would go to Hawaii with My Son and come here to meet his family is interested in more than just being good friends. Men are good friends like that. Women are good friends like that. But a man and a woman? Everyone assumes that more has to be there. My people are wondering if you are just playing with My Boy: get what you can out of him and then leave him high and dry, a wreck. They have seen it happen before, so they are curious about you. They want to know your motive. Rose and I were afraid of this also. And you,

you are not really sure yourself, so don't get upset at others when they voice their thoughts."

Jocelyn sat there in shock. She felt very naive. "I see. I guess there's much I don't know." She looked over at the oven. Rose was talking with James and Robert. "I think I need to go talk with my brothers."

She got up and went to her brothers and asked Rose if she needed them right then. When she said no, Jocelyn asked them to walk with her. When they were out of Rose's hearing, she told them what Grandfather had said and asked them what they thought about it.

"Sorry, Jocelyn, but that thought crossed our minds also. Not that we think you would be mean on purpose. That's one reason we wanted to come along, besides the experience. We wanted to be sure you weren't taken advantage of, nor you taking advantage of Mark. Dad said that he wasn't sure you were mature enough to handle the boy-girl relationship, since you'd never had one. He was also sure you didn't realize this side of the whole thing." James explained.

"So what should I do?" Jocelyn asked.

"Go slowly. Don't promise anything. You said you hadn't thought along the love and marriage path," Robert advised.

"Right."

"Don't give an answer until you're sure, and you've talked it all over with Mom and Dad. This is your future. You're better off being too cautious than not," James added.

"I feel as if I'm five years old, just learning how to ride a bicycle—all awkward and useless."

James put his arms about her, hugged, and rocked her.

"How have you guys dealt with this?"

"Uh…Not well. I have to get a good job first," James said.

"I feel I have lots of time. You and Mark do have a good friendship going for you. That's good," Robert suggested.

"Like Mom and Dad say, the best marriages are between friends," James added.

"But what if this ruins our friendship?"

"Then maybe it wouldn't have been a good marriage," James said.

"I think I need to talk to Mark about all of this. Then explain that I can't give him an answer one way or another until I have my doctorate. Also, that he should not wait for me, but he should date others," Jocelyn decided.

"What about you?"

"I'll be too busy. Besides I really don't like to date."

"Okay. But talk to Mom and Dad when we get home," James concluded.

"Do you think we should leave early?" Jocelyn asked.

"Not unless you get really uncomfortable. So keep us posted, okay?" James assured her.

"Okay."

"I think Rose is taking the bread out. Do you need me anymore?" Robert asked.

"No. You both go on. I'll be along in a bit. I have a lot of thinking to do."

Both brothers gave her a hug and told her they loved her. Then they raced back to the oven. Jocelyn sat down on a rock and thought about all she had learned the last few days. Later, she saw a truck making its way toward her. She guessed that they must be Mary Rose and her husband. She got up and started walking back toward the house. The truck stopped a little way off, and Jocelyn looked at it. The woman looked familiar.

"Jocelyn, would you like a ride to the house?"

"Mary Rose?"

"Yes."

"You came to meet us in Albuquerque."

"Yes. Do you remember my husband, Joseph?"

"Oh, yes."

"You have a good memory. There were so many of us." Everyone laughed.

"My Mother, may we get out?" One of her children asked.

"Not yet. I'll let you know."

On the way to the house, Jocelyn and Mary Rose talked about what she and her brothers had been doing. Joseph stopped the truck a polite distance away, and they all waited until someone came to greet them. Jocelyn was surprised that they didn't all get out since Rose's family had been expecting them. Even the children waited until Mary Rose went to the back, opened the tail gate, and helped them out. The rest of the family waited to greet them at the arbor. It wasn't until after greeting and Roger had asked permission that the children ran off to play.

After the adults had been served coffee and fry bread, Rose again commented that it was Jocelyn's first batch. The conversation covered the weather, the health of relatives, and the activities of the guests before starting on the new house. They talked about where it would be placed and what outbuildings would be needed, as Mary Rose had chickens. Joseph's supply of building materials and what was still lacking were discussed. Then Grandfather got up, and the men followed him to check out the possible building sites. The women discussed the food that would be needed and Mary Rose's supply of staples and frozen food. Jocelyn began to realize that the house-building was a ceremony itself, especially when they began to discuss the singer they had hired to bless the construction. Mark had talked about traditions; this whole process, every aspect, was based upon tradition.

Jocelyn also began wondering who owned the land. Did it belong to Grandfather? If so, how much belonged to him? The new house would not be next door, like in the city. It would be quite a ways away. She would ask later, as her questions were not pertinent to the discussions taking place.

She looked toward the men and noticed that they seemed to be marking off something. Her brothers seemed to be gathering rocks, which Mark was placing where Joseph and Grandfather indicated. Then Grandfather led them down into the arroyo.

Jocelyn was forced back to what the women were saying when she heard her name. The women seemed to be waiting for something from her. Rose said something, and Mary Rose repeated her question, and Jocelyn entered their conversation.

~ 5 ~

The family stayed until after supper and clean up. As they left, Mark picked up a lantern and asked Jocelyn to walk with him. She went with him down the path to his special place. They were almost there when she remembered the necklace. They turned back toward the hogan. He went inside with her to get it and took it from her immediately.

They didn't really talk as they walked. Mark seemed very grave; Jocelyn was curious but figured she would learn soon enough what it was all about. When they got close to the rock, Jocelyn realized that Mark had decorated it. He had a fire prepared and a pot with something in it on the fire. There was also a container and a mug. He led her to a pile of pine boughs and had her sit on it.

He sat at her feet and began to ask her about her parents and grandparents. He asked her about her life growing up and her hopes and dreams. Even though he knew some of the information, he asked probing questions and wanted in-depth answers. He asked about her plans for marriage and a family. Did she want children? How many? She didn't feel threatened, but at times, she felt like he was grilling her.

He had lit the fire after she sat down. Now he poured the hot liquid from the pot into the mug and tore some bread off of the loaf in the container and ceremoniously offered them to her. The liquid was some kind of tea, which she had not had before. She ate some of the bread and drank some of the tea. He took the mug and also drank from it and ate the rest of the chunk of bread.

He replaced the mug then sat back at her feet and began to tell her the same kind of information about himself. He told about his father and his dying and their moving back to live with Grandfather. As hard as that had been, it was not as hard as being labeled half-breed with the taunts of the other boys that first day of school. Some things helped her to understand him better, but some were just cruel and embarrassing. He told of his loneliness growing up and of his desire to get away. He told of his rejection by both the Navajo and white girls. He even told about the things the bad girls, Susan and Laurie, had done to him. He told of his college years and his hope for the navy, but even there, he was treated as subhuman, even though he had the highest grades in the class. Then he told of the impact of meeting her and her family, and how their treating him as an equal helped him. That was why he had paid her way to Hawaii. He had been so lonely and longed for the comfort she supplied. He told how her letters kept him going and how he read them again and again, the first ones practically in rags from so much reading. He shared about requesting Groton for all three of his choices when it was time to be transferred. Then he also spoke of his desire for her to visit his family to see if she could accept them and his pipe dreams.

"Jocelyn, I respect your desire to wait. I will wait. But I request the honor of courting you and dating you and of getting better acquainted with the real you."

At this point, he got up and poured more of the tea into the mug and tore off another chunk of the bread. He drank some of the tea and ate some of the bread then offered the rest to her. She drank and ate and handed the mug back to him. After he sat the mug down by the fire, he got out the necklace and earrings. He repeated his request to court her as he tried to put them on her. She took his hands.

"Mark, I can't accept these. We're not engaged as your people would view this gift. But I also feel that I can't accept your request for courtship until I talk with my parents. I talked with James and Robert today as well as Grandfather. I was very naive. They all pointed out that a man and woman are thinking about marriage when they give and receive gifts like the trip to Hawaii, or your invitation to meet your family. Now that I think of it, meeting the prospective in-laws is a part of the engagement process. I like you very much. I consider you as my best friend. But I meant it when I said that I want to wait until I work a while after my doctorate. I think this is too much for where I am. It's still too soon. All my questions about love and commitment are still there. I don't want to break our friendship, but I have to ask you to take back the necklace and earrings until such a time that engagement is proper for me, for us."

He looked at the jewelry. She raised his chin, as she wanted to look in his eyes. She searched in them for the fear and defeat she had seen before.

"Are you all right with this?"

He nodded yes.

"Mark, this is very romantic. This is a side of you I hadn't seen. I like it."

"This is an engagement ceremony with a small omission."

"What omission?"

"I did not take you."

"Take me?"

"Yes. Make love with you to see if we are a fertile couple."

"Mark?"

"Only fertile couples marry."

"Mark!"

"I will not take you until we get married, I promise. I'm only half-Navajo."

"Thank you." Relief filled her. "Mark, I think you're the better half of a Navajo man."

"I'm glad you liked this ceremony. I guess we'd better go now."

He wanted to kiss her, but knew he couldn't, so he got up instead and suddenly realized how dark it was; the fire was almost out. He lit the lantern and wrapped up the jewelry, while she picked up the bread container, the mug, and the pot.

"What shall we do with the rest of the tea? It was good."

"Here." He took the pot and poured the leftover tea on the remaining embers of the fire. "We don't need a fire hazard."

He picked up the lantern and led them back to the house. He took her to her sleeping bag and then went to his and turned out the lantern. Jocelyn lay there and thought about everything she had learned of the lonely man she called her best friend.

The next day started with Joseph bringing a load of building materials. Rose asked Mark to go with him for the next load and stop by the trading post for the mail and some supplies. Robert and James were asked to go along; even Roger was asked, but not Jocelyn, and she didn't know whether to be glad or sad about it. Then she thought that this must be man's work, so she helped Rose as much as she could.

The men brought load after load of things, and one time it looked like a load of dirt. At noon, they looked tired and hungry. Rose had fixed an extra pot of stew and as much vegetables as she and Jocelyn could find in the garden. She had Jocelyn prepare mugs of cold water for each one and then started dishing out the stew and vegetables. When all of the men had a bowl, she had Jocelyn offer them coffee. Some wanted more water, so she got a pitcher of cold water and refilled those mugs. Jocelyn noticed that Rose did not eat with the men, so she did not get any for herself. She listened to them talk though. Even her brothers sounded like they had enjoyed themselves.

After lunch, the men sat back and relaxed, planning the afternoon's work. Jocelyn was amazed at all that was required to get ready to build the house. It seemed that Joseph had the singer scheduled for the next day to bless the building site, so everything needed to be present to receive that blessing. When the talk went off to other subjects, Mark went to Rose's truck to bring her the mail and groceries she had ordered. James realized what he was doing, so he went to help, as there were some large items like fifty pounds of flour.

After the men left and she helped Rose put the groceries away, Rose dished up bowls of stew for them. Rose explained more of what would happen the next day and the things they needed to do to get ready, one of which was to make more tortillas. Jocelyn laughed and told Rose that maybe this time she would just cook them. Rose laughed with her and agreed. Jocelyn asked about the fry bread the day before. Rose looked away and said something about practice. Then Jocelyn asked about the bread she had made. Rose said that was what Mark had taken with them the previous night. Jocelyn said that she would need a lot more practice before she could make it on her own.

While they talked, Rose was busy making tortillas while Jocelyn kept the fire going, turned the tortillas, and put them in a basket when they were cooked. At one point, Jocelyn got the fire so hot that a few burned, and she said they would be good for a dog. Rose said they could give them to the birds, so the burnt ones went into a pile for that purpose. The afternoon seemed to fly by, and the men were washing up for supper. Joseph had gone home after the last load, so it was just Rose's family and the Meyers.

When they were finished, Mark asked Jocelyn to go for a walk with him. She agreed. Instead of taking her to his special place, he showed her where Mary Rose, Joseph, and their children would live. He told her where each of the buildings would be and then took her into the arroyo to see where their garden would be. He then walked down the arroyo while he explained about the blessing ceremony for the following day. She asked if this was the ceremony Roger had told her about, and he told her that was something else and that this had been planned for after they left, but then rescheduled to an earlier date so that they could be present. Jocelyn was struck again with how kind and considerate Mark's family was. When she mentioned it, he looked away.

"It's what you do for family. They all think you are my wife, so you are my family."

"Oh!"

They walked quietly for some time before Jocelyn asked, "Mark, you have a cell phone. Why don't the others?"

"Mother and Grandfather couldn't afford one. Also the mesa would give too much interference. There aren't many towers out here either."

"But what about Abraham? He has a link with his office."

"His is a special police radio."

"But he had to come all of the way out here to give Grandfather and Rose the message about Joseph and Mary Rose coming."

"That's part of his job."

She laughed, "I get it. He's a glorified messenger boy for your family and gets paid by Navajo Tribal Police to do it."

"No! But he does carry important messages to people."

"Like, 'Be prepared, your family is coming to visit'?"

"Jocelyn!"

"Okay, okay. It was just a joke. But doesn't seem to be a joke, does it?"

"Well…"

"Did you bring the lantern?"

"We weren't going to be gone that long!"

"It seems a little dark down here."

Mark looked around for a way back up and turned them back toward the hogan.

"Jocelyn! Mark! Where are you?" James called. About that time, they saw a light at the arroyo rim.

"We're down here, James."

"Okay. We're coming."

Mark guided them toward where Jocelyn's brothers were coming. It was much harder in the dark.

When the four met, James chided them, "Look, you two, you have to take a lantern with you. Grandfather said he couldn't come to get you because the trail is too rough."

"I was just showing Jocelyn about Joseph and Mary Rose's house and garden."

"That's quite a ways from here."

"James, are you angry?" Robert asked.

"Yes. They could be more considerate."

"I can remember nights when Mom and Dad stayed up late for you, James."

"That's different."

"How?" The two argued and stomped on toward the hogan.

Mark had to hold onto Jocelyn to help her keep up. "Look, men, could you slow down a bit? Jocelyn is having a hard time keeping up."

James turned on him, "What intentions do you have toward my sister?"

"To wait for her until she's ready to get married."

"You know that will be years. She wants her doctorate and to work for Baker first."

"I know."

"Then you'll bring her to this dry and barren land."

"No. We'll come to visit, of course. But we'll live in Groton, because that's where her work will be."

"Can you keep your hands off her till then?"

"I have so far. I've never even kissed her."

"You haven't?" Robert asked, surprised.

"No, Robert. All we've done is talk and hold hands."

"James."

"What, Jocelyn?"

"This is what we have agreed to. Why are you so angry? Mark has always been a gentleman to me, and he will always be a gentleman." Then she turned to Mark. "Won't you, Mark?"

"I love your sister very much and promise you I will always treat her like the lady she is."

"What are you always going off and doing?" James charged.

"Walking. Talking. How do you think we got where we were? We didn't fly there." Mark's attempt at levity made Robert laugh, but James was still angry.

"Come on, brother, you've made your point. By the way, Mark, if you ever hurt her, you'll have three angry brothers on your tail. You understand, don't you?" Robert warned.

"Yes. I understand. But she is too precious for me to ever hurt her. Do you understand that?" Mark held out his hand to the others. Robert readily shook it, James more grudgingly. Mark also promised to always carry a lantern with them when they went for a walk.

Jocelyn's last thought that night was how cherished she felt. All three were ready to fight for her. The next day, the men were building a new fire pit where the sheep that Abraham and Roger had butchered for the ceremonial feast would be roasted. Jocelyn was sent to pick vegetables. When she returned, she asked Rose how many would be there.

"Only about twenty, but we'll need the meat and bread to feed the workers. The big feast will come when we dedicate the house. Then there will be fifty or more. Joseph and Mary Rose will supply most of the food."

Soon, the others arrived. More cooking pots were brought by the workers or their wives and put near the fire. Then the fire was banked so everyone could attend the ceremony.

Mark had the Meyers stay back and off to the side some so they could hear and see, but he could translate for them what was happening. After the ceremony was over, he asked James to take a walk with him. Robert took Jocelyn back to the arbor with him, telling her that his job today was wood boy—to supply both fires with the needed fuel.

Robert soon realized that he would need to cut up a lot more firewood, so he got out the wood holder and saw, put a log on the holder, and started sawing it into small pieces for the arbor cooking fire. One of the men noticed what he was doing and came over.

"Hi! Aren't you one of Mark's in-laws?"

"In-laws? No, just friends. He and my sister aren't married."

"Oh, well, I'm Ben Begay, one of Joseph's cousins. Here, let's put several logs on and get this pile built up." They went to get another log. Ben kicked the pile.

"Why did you do that?"

"To scare off the scorpions and black widows that like to nest in the log piles. See, like this." He stomped on a spider.

Robert saw another one and stomped on it. "Why are you killing these? I've just been shooing them away."

"Well, black-widow-spider-herder, you can keep them as pets at your house, but around here we stomp them. Like this."

"Those are black widows? I thought there was some red something to identify them."

"There is, see?" He turned one of the dead ones over and showed Robert the red hourglass on its underside. "I don't have to turn one over. See the body is a glossy hump?"

Robert spotted another one, "Yeah," He stompe
then turned it over to look at the red hourglass. "I
guess we're stomping my herd to death."

"You can collect another at your house."

Both men laughed, made sure nothing was on a log by kicking it and hauled two more to the holder. Ben took one handle of the crosscut saw, while Robert took the other. The sawing went much faster.

"By the way, I'm Robert Meyers, Jocelyn's brother, friend to Mark Denton."

"Good to meet you. What do you do?"

"I'm working on my Master's degree in education. I'd like to come back for my internship. I'll fill out the paperwork when I get home."

"What's your major?"

"English."

"Oh, no. Have to use proper grammar around you." They laughed again.

"What do you do?"

"I teach math at the high school. Algebra, trig, stuff like that."

"So, are you counting the pieces we're getting out of these logs?"

"Sure. I like multiplying by threes better than counting by ones though." The two men laughed and talked while cutting up many logs. Soon the piles of available cooking wood were large.

"See how much faster it goes with more logs?"

"And another man and fun conversation. I hope we see each other more and get better acquainted when I return."

"When will that be?"

"January, I hope."

They shook hands. "See you around."

"Sure."

The day was very busy, and it was almost dark before Jocelyn saw Mark or James again. "Jocelyn, can we talk a little? We won't go far."

When they were out of earshot of the arbor, Mark briefly told her of his talk with James—that he understood his concerns and renewed his promise to care for her.

"You actually said, 'Like one of my sisters'?"

"Yes. What's wrong with that?"

"That's kinda how I've felt about you all along, like one of my brothers. Do you really think we can continue being good friends?"

"That is my desire."

"Oh, thank you, Mark. I could hug you for that."

"Uh. Maybe that wouldn't be such a good idea."

"Probably not, but it's okay to want to, isn't it?"

"I guess so. Let's go back now. I don't have a lantern."

"I think that will be a joke for us."

"I think you're right."

They walked back, both feeling lighter than they had for days.

The next day they started working on the house. James hauled logs to be used for the uprights on the hogan walls and bundles of sticks for in between. Robert cut some logs for firewood and some of the other wood for the house. That night, everyone's muscles were sore.

"I've never worked this hard," Robert said.

Abraham said he hadn't worked that hard since the last house-building.

Grandfather said, "Then, My Children, let us be grateful for this day and rest. Tomorrow will be another hard day."

"And all of the tomorrows until we are done," Abraham added.

The next morning, there was a larger crew there, but some who had been there the day before were not there. Jocelyn got acquainted with more of the women. Everyone was related, but she didn't always understand the connection. She did understand that some of the people were related to Joseph and Mary Rose by marriage.

Everyone seemed interested in Jocelyn. Sometimes, she felt that Rose answered their questions in Navajo. They asked her about her life growing up and seemed to accept her all right.

The days seemed to fly by. Some days there were a lot of people, some days just a few. One evening about a week later, James asked when the house would be done.

"Next week we should be able to start plastering and start working on the other buildings and the arbor. But it won't be finished until after we're gone."

"Oh. You don't suppose they could take some pictures for us, do you?"

Mark answered, "No one has a camera, but they can tell me about it, and I can tell you."

"Sure. That'll work."

"There's a ceremonial tomorrow, so no one will be here. It's the ripened corn ceremony. If our other garden had not been washed out, our corn would be harvested by now. So we celebrate. We'll be over where Matthew has been so we'll see if he is ready to come back here."

"Probably not, since he's been living in the lap of luxury!" Robert laughed.

"You want to go join him?"

"And miss all of the sore muscles? Naugh." And he laughed harder.

Everyone got ready for bed. As Jocelyn lay there awaiting sleep, she had a hard time believing the month was almost over. She had learned so much, almost as much about herself as about Mark and his family.

The next thing she knew, it was morning. Everyone was washing up and putting on their best clothes. Rose was wearing the squash blossom necklace she wore when she came to meet them, and Jocelyn was curious if Mark's father had given it to her on their engagement. She realized that her questions had changed to more personal ones— -ones she was not sure she should ask. She dressed in her skirt and blouse she had brought for a special occasion and then went to help with breakfast. After cleaning up, Rose gave Mark a blanket to put in the back of the pickup so the nice clothes would not get soiled from whatever was left there from hauling building materials. Then Grandfather told each one where to sit.

Jocelyn realized they were going a different way, but some things looked familiar. Mark explained that they had come this way when they had taken Matthew to the medical clinic. He talked more about the ceremony than what they were seeing on this trip. The first stop was at the clinic, but it was closed with a note on the door stating that the doctor was at the school where the ceremony was being held. So they headed to the ceremony. Everyone got out, and Mark directed the Meyers family to a place where they could watch the dancing. When there was a break in the dancing, Mark pulled Jocelyn away to get a drink. They sat down in the shade of a tree to cool off.

"Mark?"

"Yes?"

"Your mother's necklace, was that her engagement present from your father?"

"Yes."

"And these other necklaces?" Jocelyn swept her hand in front of them, indicating most of the women at the ceremony.

"Yes."

"I think I was right to say it isn't time for that."

"You're right, but I can dream, can't I?" Mark laughed.

"Another pipe dream?" She laughed.

"No, the same one."

They talked about other things. Then there was an announcement that the three-legged race would be run soon at the high school track.

"Oh. Let's go watch it."

"I was hoping you'd want to. Are you finished with your drink?" She gave him her paper cup, which he put into his and threw both into a trash can on the way to the track. "Mary Rose's son, Edgar, may be running with Roger. Let's look for them."

"That makes it more fun when you know someone. Oh, is that them over there?"

"Yes. Go, Roger! Go, Edgar!" Mark's call alerted the boys to their presence, and they all waved.

When the race started, the roar of encouragement from the crowd was almost as exciting as the race.

"Who won?"

"I'm not sure, but it looks like Roger and Edgar."

Sure enough, they were announced as winners. Mark moved Jocelyn to the location of the next event, which was an all-girls cross-country run. He explained about the event and told about two of the racers he knew. After the race started, he mentioned casually that if they had a traditional Navajo wedding, she would participate in a race. Jocelyn was incredulous, but since he had never lied to her, she accepted what he said with reservations. She would have to see what he meant.

"Well, if she won't run for you, I would, Mark," was said seductively by a woman about his age, who took his arm and seemed to rub herself against him.

Anger flashed from Mark, "Go away, Susan," He jerked himself away and pushed her.

"Why don't you introduce me to your girlie, Mark?"

"I said go away!"

"Ahw, come on, Markie, I can still show you a good time. Remember?"

"I call that rape" He took Jocelyn's arm and steered them toward the food. "Come on. How about a Navajo Taco?" He again pushed Susan away.

WANDA E. PALMER

"Is there a problem here?" Abraham and another policeman converged on them.

"Susan's stoned," Mark charged.

The other policeman took Susan's arm. "I told you I'd lock you up if I caught you making trouble again. Let's go."

"You two okay?" Abraham asked.

"Yes."

"Yes."

"Sorry about that, Jocelyn. Susan's always been a troublemaker."

"It's okay, Abraham. Mark told me about her."

Abraham gave Mark a startled look.

"Did you see Roger win the three-legged race with Edgar?" she asked, trying to change the subject.

"Yes, I did." The proud father smiled. "You two have a good time." Abraham looked at where the necklace would have been on Jocelyn and then away. "See you later."

Mark and Jocelyn moved to a food stand, and he asked her what she wanted to drink, gave their order, and paid. They carried their plates off to a table by itself in the shade.

"Jocelyn, I'm sorry."

"Mark, it's her fault. I think it's easier to understand what you told me she did to you now that I've met her. People here are just as varied as they are in Groton."

"I never saw anyone strung out on drugs there."

"They are there though. Maybe I should look for an inoculation against drug abuse. By the way, was Abraham surprised you had told me about Susan?"

"Yes. Men don't usually tell their…uh…"

"Girlfriends?"

"Is that what you are?"

"We're friends. You're a boy…uh, man…and I'm a girl. So we're girlfriend and boyfriend, okay?"

"Okay, but that seems like more commitment than you wanted. Are you sure?"

"Oh, this is getting too complicated. Why don't I just kiss you and get it over with?"

"No!" Mark jumped up and knocked his plate on the ground.

"Here, share mine, you still have your fork."

"What's going on, guys?" James asked, walking up.

"Hey, did you see Roger win the race?" Robert asked.

Jocelyn forced Mark down at her place, picked up his paper plate and food, and took it to the garbage can. When she returned, they were talking about Matthew, and then Robert and James went to get some food. Mark looked at her sheepishly and started to apologize again.

"Oh, lighten up. It's been a great day. What do you want to do next?"

"I don't know what's next. They haven't announced anything. Uh…Did you notice Abraham looking for your necklace?"

"Does he know you bought it for me?"

"No. Grandfather knows."

"And my brothers. So let them look. We'll get it all straightened out when we're ready, boyfriend. Oh, did you bring the lantern?"

"No, they have lights here, and it's midday."

"So let's relax and enjoy ourselves, boyfriend."

He looked at her for a long time. His reverie was broken by an announcement of the next event. "Shall we go, girlfriend?"

"Yes."

"Hey, are you leaving?" Robert asked as he and James brought their food to eat.

"See you later." Jocelyn waved at them.

"Do you want to go by and see Matthew?"

"Lead on, boyfriend. Whatever you want."

They went to the clinic booth.

"Hey, Jocelyn, Mark."

"Hey, Matthew. How have you been?"

"Great! This has been interesting. I can't believe how much I've done in such a short time. I've had fun too. The hard part is coming up. I have to write a paper on this experience. Some of it is going to be hard to put into words."

"You'll do fine. You express yourself well. How have you been, Jocelyn and Mark?" Dr. Pettijohn asked.

"I'm glad I don't have to do a paper on my experiences," Jocelyn laughed.

They all discussed some of their experiences when suddenly Dr. Pettijohn launched himself out of his side of the booth and Matthew out of the other. Mark and Jocelyn turned around to see the two men bending over someone on the ground with others standing near.

Matthew called back to Mark to bring the stretcher rolled up at the door. He found it and brought it to Matthew, who helped him unroll it and place it beside a young woman on the ground. The doctor and Matthew helped her onto it, picked up the ends, and carried her into the booth.

"Why don't we go on, they're busy," Mark said.

"Where's that next activity?"

The loudspeakers blared again, and Mark guided them on. They had a good time, but they were ready to go by mid-afternoon. They were the first ones to reach the truck, so they sat in the back and talked.

"Jocelyn, I like calling you 'girlfriend.' That's what I've called you in my mind for a long time, but I've never used it out loud before."

"What did you call me?"

"Jocelyn."

"Even when you talked about me to the men on your ship?"

"I didn't talk about you to them. Did you talk about me to the women at your college?"

"Not really, or just called you Mark when I talked about coming here, but I really only talked with one close friend about coming, and then only about coming here, not about you. Hey, I've thought of something you could do: be a politician like my father."

"A politician? My mother's a politician, not me. Is that what your father does? Here, it's what the women do."

"Your mother's a politician? Why is it women's work?"

"They are the ones who like to talk all of the time. Besides, we have a matriarchal society. The women are in charge."

"Come on, I've seen you with the men building the house. All of you are talking all of the time."

"Then who's listening?"

"You know what I mean. But with your honorable qualities, you would make a good politician."

"How could I get the people to look past my skin to vote for me?"

"You're friendly, honest, and hardworking. Talk with my dad about it when we get back."

"I have a lot to discuss with him as it is. I will bring this up too."

As they talked, they both were getting sleepy. When she mentioned it, he suggested they lie down and take a quick nap. Both of them were soon stretched out asleep.

"Hey, look here, you guys," Matthew said.

"Leave them alone. I wouldn't mind taking a nap myself," Robert said.

"Why are you all so tired?"

"We've been building Mary Rose's house."

"What?"

Robert and James told Matthew about the sore muscles from the house-building. As they talked about their experiences, the brothers sat in the shade of the pickup.

Later, a man came by looking for his truck. "Hey, English, how you doing?"

"Hey, Math, good to see you. I'd like you to meet my brothers, James and Matthew, and this is Ben Begay."

"I met James at Rose's, but I don't think you were there, Matthew."

Matthew explained that he had been helping at the clinic with Dr. Pettijohn.

"Well, nice to meet you. See you in January, English. Keep working on that stomp."

"You need to come back to Rose's and check my technique, Math."

"No, they'll make me work!"

"You can help me saw again. How else will I perfect my stomp?" They laughed. Ben shook hands with all three brothers and moved off.

"Stomp?"

"Perfect your technique?"

Robert explained about the black widow spiders in the wood pile. Matthew was explaining about some of his experiences at the clinic when the rest arrived.

"Children, why are you not in the truck?" Grandfather asked.

"It's occupied."

Grandfather looked in and shook Mark's boot and Jocelyn's running shoe.

"Children, it is time to make room for the others so we can all go home."

Jocelyn sat up. "I really fell asleep."

"Yeah, you've been out for well over an hour," Matthew stated.

"Really? We were just going to nap for a minute."

The sleepers moved over so the rest could get in and there would be space for Matthew's bag.

"I wouldn't mind stretching out on the way home," Robert said.

"What do you mean? You've only been sawing logs," James charged.

"We can trade if you like. I'll teach you the stomp."

"Okay, tomorrow I'll saw, and you can lug and hold and whatever."

"It's a deal."

"If you're so tired, why don't both of you stretch out?" Mark suggested.

They followed Mark's suggestion and were sound asleep before the truck got out of the parking lot.

Over the following days, the number of people coming to work dwindled to one ragged old lady. She had no jewelry on, and even her truck looked old and covered with dirt. In the back was a load of dirt, which she began to unload by the previous pile. The men joined her, and she got down and got a bucket out of the cab. Rose left Jocelyn to finish cleaning up from breakfast and told her to come as soon as she was finished. Rose got two buckets, filled them with water, and joined the lady. Jocelyn then noticed that Rose was also wearing old clothes. The two women seemed to be making mud and hauling it to Mary Rose's house where they proceeded to fill up holes in the walls. Jocelyn joined them, and they showed her what to do.

"This doesn't look like your house."

"We have to fill the holes then we can start plastering. After four or five coats, it will be the same."

"Then it won't be finished until after we're gone."

"No. We have worked hard, but each part takes time."

"What if the men help?"

"This is women's work."

"Oh. Rose, Mark told me yesterday that you're on the council. Tell me about it."

"Each clan has its council, then each area has its council, and then the tribe has its council. We are the governing body for our people."

"Are you voted to your position?"

"Yes."

"How long have you been on the council?"

"I was voted on to my clan council many years after I came back to live here. Several years later, I was voted to be on the area council. I have recently been voted to be on the tribal council."

"So you're a politician. My father's also a politician. He's in the State Senate. He used to be in the Federal Senate. Have you ever thought of running for state or national positions?"

"The tribal council is talking about getting on the state legislatures of our respective states."

"You should so you can be better represented. My father thinks all people should be represented."

"Would you like to know that Miriam Nakai here is vice president of our tribal council?"

"That's good to know, Miriam. Would you two explain to me what Mark meant when he said you have a matriarchal society?"

The three talked as they applied the mud to the outside of Mary Rose's house. Jocelyn was getting tired when Mark came to them with a bucket of clean water; Robert had a basin and soap, and James had a stack of towels. They washed up and went to the arbor where there was fresh coffee and a snack prepared for them.

Jocelyn pulled Mark aside. "Is it okay for the men to do this?"

"Yes, when the women are plastering, the men cook. We will have lunch ready for you when that time comes. This will go on until the plastering and any other women's finishing touches are done."

"Mark, how long have you had a democratic government?"

"Always."

"You didn't learn it from white people?"

"No. We were democratic when you were still feudal."

"You mean kings and queens, lords and ladies?"

"Dark Ages. There are some things the white men could learn from us."

"I see."

"No, you don't, but come eat anyway." He led her back to the others and got her food.

That night, Robert complained with a laugh that everyone's job had changed, but he was still getting firewood and stomping spiders. Over the following days, many final things were done to the outbuildings while the women plastered the house.

Soon, it was time for Mark and the Meyers family to leave the following day. Grandfather talked with each one during the day. Late that afternoon, Mary Rose's family came to thank them for helping.

After they left, Mark asked Jocelyn to go for a walk. James had purchased a lantern from the trading post and had it engraved with Mark's name and presented it to him. Each one asked if they had the lantern with them, even though it was obviously in his hand. They went to his rock and agreed they would miss it. They watched the sunset then went back to their final night before going back to her world.

The next day, they loaded up by sunrise to meet the plane. They would again have a long day of travel, and it would be late before they got back to the Meyers' house. Rose had packed them each a lunch. When Jocelyn hugged Rose good-bye, she repeated her invitation for her to visit the Meyers family in Groton, Connecticut. Mark spent that night at Jocelyn's house as he wanted to talk with her father.

~ 6 ~

The next morning Jocelyn awoke in her own bed to the whispering of her sisters outside her door. She got up, went to the window, and greeted the new day as Rose had taught her before going to the door to invite her sisters' curiosity in. They talked as she got dressed, and they all went down for breakfast.

When Mark and Jocelyn saw each other, they drank deeply from each others eyes. At breakfast, the travelers thanked Mr. and Mrs. Meyers for the opportunity to go. The conversation covered many things they did. At a lull in the talk, someone would say, Remember . . ." and they would be off talking about another aspect of their adventure.

When Mr. Meyers got up from the table, Jocelyn asked to talk with him. "Quickly, I have an appointment."

"I need to talk with you and Mother soon."

"Let me check our schedules and get back to you on a time."

"Thank you, Father, for letting me go. I don't think I can ever explain how much I learned by this trip," she said, as she gave him a big hug.

Next, she went to find Winnie and found Robert just leaving. "Next!" Winnie called. "You're the last to tell me how much you appreciate all I do."

While giving her a big hug, Jocelyn said, "After cooking over an open fire and having to cut up the wood first and doing laundry in an old wringer washer and hanging the clothes on a line and sleeping on the ground in the same sleeping bag for four weeks and whatever else, I appreciate you a whale of a lot more."

"Hoo wee! That sounds hard. But did ja have a good time?"

"Oh, yeah. I learned about making bread and tortillas and fry bread and mutton stew. But it will be some time before I want any more mutton stew."

Mark entered the kitchen and overheard the last. "Oh, come now. That's what I was going to make you on our date."

"Oh, Mark, you're such a tease."

"Mark, I have your clothes ready."

"You didn't ask her to wash your clothes, did you?"

"No, I told him to let me."

"And I have a thank-you gift for all you've done for me." He handed Winnie a wrapped box with a bow.

"Now you kids go on. You don't have to give me gifts."

"Would you open it now?"

"If you really want me to."

"I really want to see your face when you see it."

All three sat at the kitchen table. Mark and Jocelyn watched Winnie carefully remove the gift wrapping. There was a nice box. When Winnie opened it, she cried, "Oh!" and put her hand to her mouth.

"Let me put it on you." Mark took a pin out of the box and pinned a submarine insignia to her lapel. "Now, I officially declare you a submarine mate." Then he hugged her, as tears covered her face.

She hugged him back. "Oh, Mark, thank you so much. You don't know how much this means to me. Now you two go on so's I can wash up and get busy."

When they neared his car, Jocelyn asked, "Mark, may I drive?"

"If you really want to."

On the way, Mark explained that Winnie's boyfriend had been in the submarines but had died before they got married.

That was why she insisted on doing his laundry and always had food for him when he left Jocelyn's house.

"I never knew that. I'm realizing that there's a lot I never knew. But this I do know. This is my special place to come and think." It was a small picnic area overlooking Long Island Sound.

"Hey, this is nice. Let me get my blanket out and let's talk," Mark said as he opened her door for her, helped her out, and then went to the trunk. "Those guys!"

"What?"

"Your brothers put the lantern in here with a big bow and note, 'Don't forget me!'" He laughed.

She joined in. Sometimes they talked. Sometimes they remembered. Sometimes they looked off in the distance, lost in their individual thoughts. Sometimes they drank in the depths in each others eyes.

That afternoon, Jocelyn met with her parents. She explained what she had learned about herself and Mark. She shared about her self-centered life and him awakening in her the desire to be more aware of those around her. She also told of his assumptions and proposal, and her goal and reluctance. She told them of her talks with Grandfather and her brothers.

Phillip and Mary asked questions to clarify things but mainly just listened. They were grateful that she was talking with them, but they also wanted to learn how she felt about it all. Their little girl was growing up, a little slower than the boys, but was gaining a maturity they were not sure the boys had.

They each tried to explain how they knew they had found the right one when they were dating. Jocelyn gained assurance that earth shake and shooting stars were not usual for people to know they were in love. Mary said that there was a comfortable peace in and about Phillip that drew her to him. She had enjoyed his presence so much that she could not imagine a life without him. The details were different for Phillip, but the essence was the same: a desire to spend the rest of his life with her. Jocelyn said that was the way she felt about Mark. Her parents suggested that she not say anything to Mark because it would be such a long time before she and Mark got married.

That evening when Mark arrived, her heart skipped a beat, but she was not called. Then she remembered that he wanted to talk with Father first. She sat there looking at her book, but never turning the page. Her thoughts were in Father's study and on what Mark was talking about. Every time they had a long talk, her world changed. She wondered about the changes coming now. When Brianna called her, she ran downstairs.

"Yes, Dad," Jocelyn entered the room.

"Please come in. Oh, Brianna, please ask Winnie to bring the flowers to Mark." Then turning to Jocelyn, he said, "Jocelyn, Mark has asked my permission to court you. What do you think about that?"

"It was my idea. I need time to think beyond being good friends to marriage. Mark, did you tell him how long we talked about waiting?"

"Yes, and I told him I am willing to wait for you until you are ready."

"Then I consider you a couple. Please continue to be good to one another. Ah, Winnie, please give the flowers to Mark."

"Do I ask her now?" Mark asked.

"Now."

Mark got down on the floor at Jocelyn's feet. "Jocelyn, your Father has given his blessing for us to court. Would you be willing for me to court you until we are ready for further commitment?"

"Yes, Mark."

He handed the flowers to her. "Jocelyn, would you go on a date with me for lunch and a drive tomorrow?"

"Yes, Mark."

Mr. Meyers said, "Breathe, Mark. She said yes."

Jocelyn watched as it looked like he almost passed out, and Father kept telling him to breathe. She saw the nerves and fear in her very controlled, very proper, very Navajo Mark.

The next morning, he was getting nervous. He wanted their first date to be special. He had watched closely as Mr. Meyers escorted Mrs. Meyers. He had practiced before his mirror in the bathroom. He hoped he was ready to perform.

He went by the florist to pick up the corsage he had ordered. As he drove to her house, he kept hearing in his mind Mr. Meyers telling him, "Breathe, Mark, breathe." He took a deep breath, picked up the corsage, went to the door, and rang the bell.

"Hey, Mark, why didn't you come on in?" Robert asked.

"I'm here to pick up Jocelyn for our date."

Robert took in the suit, the corsage, and the nerves. "Come in, Mark, please be seated. I'll get Jocelyn."

When he found her, he told her to change from her jeans and T-shirt to a nice dress and told her the color of the corsage. He also told her Mark was very nervous. When she was getting ready for their date, she really didn't do much except earrings and a dab of perfume. She snagged Brianna to help her fly into a fancy dress and heels to coordinate with the corsage Mark brought.

"Brianna, help me get dressed up, fast. Please!"

They worked as quickly as they could. Robert tried to distract Mark, not very successfully. Mark's eyes were glued on the spot where he would first see Jocelyn as she descended the stairs. He rose as he saw the top of her head over the banister. As she came downstairs, she saw the fear and nerves overpowering him and wondered what to do to help him. She tried hard to not laugh as Robert and Father tried to help him, but she was hurting at the same time that he so wanted to do it their way.

Father kept saying, "Breathe, Mark, breathe." Mark was distracted enough to take a breath and then watched Jocelyn float down the stairs. He met her at the foot of the stairs, holding the corsage out in front of him. She opened it and asked him to pin it on. Father saw the panic in his face and stepped up to instruct him in pinning on the corsage. The boutonniere fell out as he picked up the corsage. Robert retrieved it, put it back in the box, held the box until the corsage part of the pinning was completed, and then held out the box so Jocelyn could get the boutonniere and pin it on Mark. Mark stood there, his eyes glued on her.

Robert and Father gently helped him turn around. From behind, Robert helped him lift his arm so he could offer it to Jocelyn. She took it, trying hard to not laugh. Robert had to push Mark some to get him started toward the door. Mark seemed to come back to life but seemed uncertain how to proceed. Robert stopped him while Father and Mother demonstrated how to escort her through the door. He followed their example, Jocelyn helping all she could. He successfully took her to his car and helped her in.

Father told Robert, "He asked me to help him. We'd better plan some lessons. If he's going to do it our way, we need to teach him how. We have twenty years of training to cover in a couple months before he goes to sea again."

James and Matthew came up. They readily agreed to help Mark become a Meyers gentleman as quickly as possible. Jocelyn coached him when he was unsure what to do and kept praising him on his choice of restaurant and the meal. She tried every way she could to help him understand that she liked him as he was, that he *was* her kind of gentleman. They drove up the coast.

"But you expect me to be like your father and brothers."

"Pipe dream. No, Mark, I expect you to be my best friend, Navajo Mark. I don't expect you to be Matthew, or James, or Robert. You couldn't. For one thing, you're a lot shorter." She laughed.

He deflated.

"Mark, I like Mark as Mark is and as Mark does. I like the way you talk, I like the way you think, I like the way you laugh. I like *you*."

"But how do I get you to love me?" He pleaded.

She was exhausted by that time. She was not going to tell him for years. Then it quietly came out in a whisper. "I do love you."

Mark pulled in to the state park, found an overlook with a nice view, parked, and helped her out.

"Jocelyn, what did you say?"

"I do love you, Mark. But we have years to wait before we get married, so just relax, be Mark so I can be Jocelyn. Do you realize I had to change clothes after you arrived because you were all dressed up? Maybe tell me what to wear, let me in on your plans a little more so I'll be better prepared."

"Am I too short?" he asked in a small whisper.

"Nope, you're just right. I'm too tall in these heels, but I don't like to wear heels anyway."

"Do you really love me?"

He couldn't seem to take it in. When he finally accepted it, everything about him changed. It was like turning on a light. He did a Navajo dance, shouting to Long Island Sound.

Then the light switched off. He put her into the car and drove off.

"Jocelyn, we'd better not be alone anymore. I may not be able to wait until you're ready to get married."

"What do you mean you're not able to wait?"

"Jocelyn, I want you."

"You have me."

"I want to…ask your mother. She's had six children."

"You want to make a baby?"

"And everything that leads up to that."

"Oh. Birds and bees."

"Rams and ewes."

"Are you the ram and me the ewe?" She laughed. "We're humans. We can control ourselves. We can wait."

It was a nice drive. Fall color was starting to show in places. He talked about everything but them. He made a date for the next Saturday, telling her his specific plans. When he drove back into the Meyers' avenue, all four men came out, telling him they would teach him to be a Meyers gentleman. They had Jocelyn wait in the car to be removed and seated several times. They taught him how to guide her between the cars and through the house doorway. After a time, they dismissed Jocelyn and talked with Mark, covering topics far beyond his conception of a gentleman.

They also demanded that he get a tuxedo made. He thought it an unnecessary expense until he went with them to his first symphony with Jocelyn. He thought he might grow to like her fancy dress-up music programs.

All she wanted to do was to go to her room and think, but her brothers and Father insisted on gentleman lessons for Mark. Then she was dismissed like a servant! She went to talk with Mother. What she learned there was worse. Mother was pleased with Mark and started explaining some things Jocelyn really did not want to hear about a man.

She went to her room angry and certain she didn't like this turn of events, but facts started crowding her prejudice. Mother and Father had been married a very long time. Maybe Mother knew this stuff from experience. She also explored her physical reaction to Mark. When she got lost in the deep black pools of his eyes, something happened in her. What if what Mother and Mark said was true? What if she had condemned them to years of waiting to satisfy this desire she felt growing inside of her? Was this love too? She began noticing her reactions to Mark and then his reactions to her. She talked more with Mother. She found this side of love confusing. She felt joy and pleasure at seeing him and then embarrassment at the desire overtaking her. He started seating her in a single chair and himself a separate chair. Then they began to spend less and less time sitting alone talking except on the phone. Five years? How would they ever make it?

When he told her his boat was going in the Groton Shipyards for overhaul and that he would be around for a couple more years, she was not sure how to handle it.

"Mark, we need to talk."

"Sure. Where?"

"I don't know. Maybe the phone."

"Is something wrong?"

"Yes. You know why we don't let ourselves be alone and don't sit next to each other?"

"Yes."

"Mark, I was looking forward to you being gone to regain my equilibrium."

"I will go one more time. Then when the boat's in the yards, I will have duty often."

"We only see each other once a week as it is. Maybe we should go ahead and get married."

"How would that help? It would relieve our desire for each other, but what about your studies? What about saving the world? What if the babies start coming? That is the result of our desire: babies. I think if we went ahead and got married, it would sacrifice your dream on our lust. That is not right or best. You might begin to resent me and our babies, because we get in the way of your dream. No, we will wait. Lust is destructive. It is selfish. It is putting me before you. Love does not force its way in. Love is gentle and kind. Somehow we need to change this lust for love and respect. What did your parents do?"

"They didn't have to wait. They were married young and had Matthew seven months later."

"Are you sure they didn't conceive Matthew before marriage?"

"Of course not!"

He calmly looked at her. "They are ram and ewe. I'll ask your father."

"No. I'll ask Mother."

"I can make it sound better. Sometimes you can be too direct."

"Oh, but…"

He waited. She realized that it didn't matter.

"We don't need to know that. All we need is how to focus lust into love."

"You are right. Maybe we need to talk about it more. I really don't want to hurt you, which is what lust would do."

"It would hurt us. Maybe we need this talk whenever it's getting too strong. We want our love to protect us from our lust."

"Yes. Right now, I want so much to hold you."

"I know. That's why you leave suddenly. But you're not a ram going after the ewe. You're my noble Navajo Mark. We can do this. What do your people do?"

"Remember the engagement ceremony? They don't wait. The first babies are conceived before the wedding. Roger was for Abraham and Jessica. Then Abraham agreed to put her through college. Now that she has her degree and is working, they are trying hard to have more babies."

"How do you know?"

"We all sleep in the same room."

"They're doing it right there in front of you?"

"We're asleep!"

"Then how do you know what they're doing?"

"I think we need to change the subject, or I will end up showing you."

"Either you go home, or we find someone to be with."

"I will go." He sat on the floor at her feet. "Jocelyn, you are my Little Flower. I do not want to force you in any way and cause you to be any less than the full flower you are to be. I will protect you by leaving."

He stood, turned, and left. She watched him go, full of love and respect for her Navajo.

Mark often called her to vent his frustration over his captain's demands.

"Mark, you keep calling me all upset over this. What did you do about your frustrations before?"

"Before?"

"Before you started calling me about things."

"Go work out or work out here in the apartment."

"I wonder if that would work for me. Would you show me some things you do?"

"You can't come here!"

"What about the gym, or the workout room here?"

"You have equipment there?"

"Yes."

"Do you have a treadmill or something like that?"

"Yes."

"That will work for your legs. It also helps to take the heat out of the anger. What about your arms and chest. Is there something for that?"

"I can ask my brothers."

"But I don't want you all hard with muscles. I like you soft and curvy."

"Mark!"

"Yes."

"I think I'd better go. You're getting worse. You're supposed to be helping."

He started using Navajo.

"That's not fair. I don't know what you're saying."

"You will one day."

"Teach me."

"Not those words."

He gave her a word. When she said it to his satisfaction, she asked what it meant. He laughed and hung up.

He learned of his promotion. He could choose where and when he could receive his commissioning.

"What about the Meyers Mansion ballroom?" he asked Captain Spencer.

"Denton, if you get the ballroom, I want to know who you know."

"The owner. As for time, I want to bring My Mother and Grandfather, so how much notice would you need?"

"At least a week, two would be better. How do you know Senator Meyers?"

"My Navajo good looks. May I be excused, sir, to go call him and make arrangements for My Mother and Grandfather to come?"

"Do you think you could introduce me? Maybe get me an invitation to a party? What do you need to get your parents here?"

"Transportation from their house."

"Where is it? I'll arrange it."

Mark gave their Navajo address. The Captain called the Motor Pool and asked for their commanding officer to send someone over as he needed a VIP picked up for a ceremony.

"But, sir, I need to make arrangements with them," Mark said.

"Call them."

"They don't have a phone. I'll have to call My Brother-in-law through the Navajo Tribal Police Station and make arrangements to have them there so I can talk with them."

"Is he in jail?"

"No. He is captain of the Canyoncito Police Station."

"Here, call. You want him to come too?"

"No. My Sister, his wife, has to take care of My Mother's sheep. But My Uncle would like to come."

"Who is he?"

"Lieutenant Colonel Raymond Pinto, US Marine Corps, Retired. Grandfather is a code-talker, Master Sergeant Roger Pinto, US Marine Corps, Retired."

"You have quite a military history, Denton."

"Yes, sir."

"Here, call."

"Thank you, sir."

Mark got Phillip Meyers' number from his phone.

"You have his phone number in your phone?"

"Yes."

"Hello, Meyers' residence, Winnie speaking."

"Hello, Winnie. This is Mark Denton. May I speak to Phillip?"

"Sure. Hold on."

"Hello, Mark. How can I help you, son?"

"I have received a promotion to Lieutenant Commander. I want to know if I can have the commissioning ceremony in your ballroom?"

"I'd be honored."

"Thank you. I would also like to bring some of my family for the commissioning to stay with you, if I may."

"When do you want them to come and have the commissioning?"

They discussed dates.

"Congratulations. You might make Captain before Jocelyn gets her doctorate."

"I'm trying. I need to call My Brother-in-law Abraham Chee to see when he can get everyone together so I can talk with them. Thanks again, Phillip. Let me call Captain Chee."

Using English, Mark told Abraham his good news and his desire for Mother, Grandfather, and Uncle Raymond to come for his commissioning ceremony. They set a time the next day for Mark to call them.

The transportation officer came in. Mark told him how to adjust his picture to get to Grandfather's house. He also asked how much notice was needed to bring his family and was told that it would take a week.

Mark and Captain Spencer discussed dates for the ceremony. Then Senator Phillip Meyers talked with Captain Spencer about arranging dates and times for the review of the ballroom and the commissioning ceremony for Mark, plus a date for the Captain to talk with the Senator privately.

Mark saluted at the end of the conversation. The Captain returned the salute, as if he were an Admiral. After work, Mark went home, showered, shaved, put on his full dress uniform, and checked it carefully in the mirror. He had always taken Jocelyn's home for granted. That was where she lived, as he lived in a hogan. He looked at the three floors of the large home built in the 1600s carefully as he drove up, parked, and approached the door. He admitted it was "white man" impressive for Captain Spencer and his hero worship. It was the first time he had really considered Jocelyn's father as a Senator. If his Captain, who was impressed by very little, could fall all over himself by just meeting a politician, maybe Mark should consider Jocelyn's idea of him becoming one.

Mark talked with Winnie about his three relatives coming for his commissioning ceremony, the ceremony itself, and her fixing something for it as she prepared supper. He went to see Phillip. They discussed the ceremony. In the ballroom, they planned the placement of the furnishings. Phillip had chairs for the guests and tables for the refreshments. When they finished, the family was assembling for dinner. Phillip asked for their attention, being sure Winnie was in the dining room.

"Ladies and Gentlemen, Lieutenant Mark Denton, US Navy, has an announcement."

"I soon will be commissioned as Lieutenant Commander Mark Denton in your ballroom."

"Hear, hear." Phillip led a toast.

The family gathered around Mark, congratulating him.

"I have another announcement. I will talk with Mother, Grandfather, and Uncle Raymond about coming for my ceremony."

"They will stay with us," Phillip added.

Robert proposed another toast. They finally adjourned to the back parlor so Winnie could clean up. Brianna suggested a photographer. Suzanne suggested the newspaper. The Navajo reservation did not have a newspaper, but Mark could send a news release to the radio station, although he figured the gossip line would spread the news much faster. Jocelyn's family wanted her to be in the ceremony. Both Jocelyn and Mark refused. She did all she could to make it a success but looked forward to Rose and Grandfather coming more. Everyone was reluctant to go to bed, but finally Phillip broke up the party.

The next day when Mark called Abraham, both his captain and Abraham put the call on speaker so everyone could hear. In Navajo, Mark's family went through the Navajo greeting with Mark. Mark formally requested Mother, Grandfather, and Uncle Raymond to attend his commissioning ceremony to Lieutenant Commander. Grandfather requested that four other uncles come, who were also retired military.

In English, Mark made the request to Captain Spencer. By the end of the conversation, Mark had seven family members, six decorated veterans coming. Mark then called Senator Phillip Meyers.

Captain Spencer was suitably impressed that a simple phone call could so easily enlarge the guest list with Senator Meyers. He was even more impressed as the Yeoman told him more information on each of the military men coming. He told the Yeoman to contact all the stations with the information and asked Mark for the media in his area. Mark gave the Navajo radio station and the Albuquerque TV stations.

As soon as he was free, Mark went to the mansion, not even going home to change. He went in the kitchen door, knowing Winnie would be somewhere near. He explained that the three visitors had more than doubled to seven. She assured him that the rooms were ready, even the bathrooms. He read something in her face.

"Winnie, what is it?"

"Oh, I was just dreamin'."

"Tell me."

"You'll have your mother and Jocelyn to do it."

"You want to have a part in the ceremony." It was a statement, not a question.

"Maybe just a small one?"

"Jocelyn isn't my wife. We're not even engaged. Winnie, you have been like a mother to me in this strange land. Would you please take part in my ceremony? I'll hire someone to do your job for the day. I want you to sit with me and be served. Are you free right now?"

"Yes. How long you need?"

"At least an hour."

"It will be tight. You got one of those alarms on your watch?"

"I'll set the alarm on my phone. There. Let's go. Where's the nicest dress shop in Groton?"

"Dress shop? Don't you want a men's shop?"

"Not for me. We're going to find *you* two new dresses, one formal for the ceremony."

"Mark, you don't have to."

"Yes, I do. Come on."

He took her hand and led her to his car. They spent the hour finding the right dresses for her special day and securing the services of a chef to take her place for the day. When he took her packages into her rooms in the mansion, he gave her a big son-to-mother hug.

Phillip came home soon after, and they found all of the bedrooms and bathrooms working fine. Mark was concerned that his grandfather, and maybe even his mother, could not climb the stairs. Phillip showed him the elevator his grandfather had installed, which was in excellent order.

They determined who would sleep where. Then Mark told Phillip about Winnie, her replacement for the day, and her participation in the ceremony. Phillip was again amazed at Mark's knowledge and thoughtfulness. He liked this man both for his daughter and for himself. He started teaching Mark about his job as a politician.

"I have another request: No liquor. Not even wine. We don't hold it well."

"You do okay."

"No. I never take a sip of the wine. I use the water or tea."

"I never realized that."

"We Navajo don't do well. I drank once. I ended up naked, raped, and sick. I vowed never again to touch the stuff. Even at the military parties I only drink the water or the tea."

"Even wine or champagne?"

"It was wine, and I only had two glasses." Mark looked directly at Phillip, a challenge in his eyes.

"Very well. I'll tell Winnie."

"I know it would change things for your family, but would you not have it available, especially at the table? At least one of My Uncles doesn't know he can't handle it. He would be so ashamed the next morning."

"Certainly."

Phillip wondered what he would do if he had an alcoholic child. They discussed Mark's family, their arrival, sightseeing, and the actual ceremony. Phillip was impressed with Mark's organizational skills.

Mark and Jocelyn were talking about the ceremony and his family coming. She was surprised and pleased that Mark was including Winnie in the ceremony. They had been like mother and son since he had been coming to Jocelyn's house.

She wanted to get Rose something special to commemorate the commissioning. "Mark, you know that pin you got Winnie like your submarine insignia?"

"Yes."

"Does your mother have one?"

"Yes. I got her one right after I got mine."

"Oh. I wanted to do something special for you and for Rose."

"Just be your wonderful self and make her feel at home. Jocelyn, you don't know how much you have helped me by letting me sound off when I get frustrated. Let me continue to do that, please?"

"That's nothing. Am I really helping you? I can do that anytime."

"You are really helping. How are your workouts coming?"

"Fine. The treadmill does help when I'm upset or overwhelmed by you. But how do you know I'm soft and curvy?"

"Some of your clothes reveal more than they cover."

"Oh. Sorry. Please tell me, okay?"

"Yes. We'll get you looking like a dowdy old maid, and I'll have you all to myself."

"You do anyway, even with the swimsuits and show-off clothes."

"Okay. Subject change. Five of my uncles are coming. These men are My Mother's brothers. All were in the military. They're not impressed by your house, but they need your respect as my family. You met some of them. Just treat them like My Mother and Grandfather, please."

"Okay. I guess I won't have as many friendly chats with Rose or Grandfather."

"If the conversation lags, ask what one of them did during the war. Choose a different one each time. That will help me."

"Yes, Mark. Anything else?"

He said the Navajo word he had taught her, laughed, and hung up. She repeated it several times, determined to learn its meaning.

When the Captain and the set up crew rode to see the ballroom, Mark sat with the driver and directed him. Captain Spencer noted that Mark had them go directly there, not by the main roads. Mark noted the comments of the men as they saw the house exterior and interior. Phillip and Winnie showed them the setup and where everything was stored, emphasizing that the house and furnishings were over three hundred years old, and requested special care of the items.

Mark talked with Winnie about her part in the ceremony. "You will stand here and pin my new insignia on my collar. It will be tight against my neck, so you will have to turn that part of the collar over. Then you will put on the shoulder board. My Mother will be doing the same thing on the other side. Do you want me to bring it all to show you on the uniform?"

"Maybe so. Where will these things be?"

"The Yeoman will hold them for you."

The Captain balked at a servant being included.

"Captain, who's ceremony is this?"

"Uh...well...yours."

"Then Winnie and My Mother will do this, understand?"

The Captain backed down. The others were impressed.

"Anything else?" Mark asked Captain Spencer.

"Uh...no..."

"Then we're finished here. Thank you, Phillip and Winnie."

Mark shook hands with them and led the group out to the van. On the way back to the Sub Base Mark discussed the arrival of his family. Later, he talked with the Yeoman.

"Lieutenant Commander?"

"Yes, Yeoman."

"May we talk privately?"

"Close the door."

"You know Captain was getting angry."

"Yes, but I had two things in my favor. It is my ceremony and my family, and he wants something from me. I get along, cooperate, and coordinate until it is something very important. I will fight for my family. That is what I was doing. If we didn't follow the greeting ritual, my family would not get off the plane. They are coming for me. By the way, have you emphasized no liquor on the plane, even beer or wine?"

"Yes, sir. And Winnie?"

"She has been like a second mother to me since Sub School."

"The Senator?"

"He has been a father to me for the same time."

"They're married?"

"No, Winnie is the Meyers' housekeeper."

That evening was spent with Mark explaining the greeting ritual to Winnie and the four Meyers who had not been to New Mexico with him. Matthew was working, and the other three cleaned up after supper. Phillip decided Winnie needed a vacation to be with Mark, so he had hired the chef for the entire two weeks the company would be there. Mark also told Phillip that he was right that Captain Spencer wanted an appointment for his son to the Naval Academy in Maryland and the agreement they had made.

"Mark, you really would make a good politician."

Mary Meyers told Mark that she was excited to meet his family. Privately, she asked how everything was going between Jocelyn and him. He briefly caught her up.

Toward the end of the week, Phillip asked to go along to meet the plane. Captain Spencer agreed, hoping to get to talk with him. When they arrived at Trumbull Airport, they were directed away from the terminal building and to the side of the tarmac. Mark placed everyone according to rank and importance, like in a normal hogan greeting. As the stairs were placed by the opened door, Mark mounted them, entered the cabin, and froze. He requested a wheelchair. Then he turned on the attendant.

"Why were my instructions regarding no liquor not followed? You want to care for him as he gets sick? You and he will be last off. Try to get him as cleaned up as possible during that time."

"Yes, sir."

Mark then greeted his grandfather, asked about his health and his trip then escorted him off the plane, backing down the stairs in front of him. Mark escorted him to their host, Senator Phillip Meyers, and introduced them. Phillip thanked him for coming, for bringing his family, and for having Phillip's family visit last summer. Captain Spencer blanched at that. Mark interpreted each thing said and then went to Captain Spencer and made the introductions and the interpretation. Each person present was introduced, including the Yeoman and bus driver, and then Grandfather was seated in the place of honor.

Mark repeated the process with each of the people, ending with the drunk uncle, Hector Pinto, in the wheelchair. The steward manned the wheelchair and went along to help the man, promising Mark that he would be on the return flight to be sure it would not happen again.

At the Meyers' mansion, the process was repeated for all of the guests and people there. Jocelyn noticed Mark had a special word for each of them. James' word sounded like what Grandfather called him. When it was Jocelyn's turn, she heard the word Mark had taught her, and she knew. They were alone for a moment.

"Little Flower."

He said the word, laughed, reached his hand out like he was going to touch her face, flushed, turned, and then entered the room with everyone else. The Captain obtained temporary duty for the steward to stay with Hector Pinto. Mark apologized to Phillip, who said that having additional guests was just like old times. At dinner, Phillip told them about having house parties with two to four guests to a room and having three sittings for dinner. He and Mary enjoyed it. Jocelyn was not sure she liked all of the strangers around and then realized that four Meyers siblings had descended on Rose the same way just a few weeks before, so she changed her attitude. The steward was amazed. Phillip invited him to stay the whole two weeks with the family, giving him a room of his own.

"By the way, what's your name?"

"John Howell."

"Where are you from, John?" Mary asked.

"Los Angeles."

"Where all have you been?" Grandfather asked.

"I didn't know you speak English, sir."

"We all do for those who prove themselves worthy. So where have you been?"

"Only boot camp and here, sir."

Mark asked, "Would you like to do something besides steward?"

"Yes, sir, but my grades weren't good enough."

"Keep studying. What would you like to do?"

"I'd like to at least see a submarine."

"I'll take you. Mine is not in right now, so I'll have to make arrangements."

"Mark, if you can get him on a submarine, do you think you can get us on too?" Uncle Raymond asked.

"I'll see what I can do. There are seven of you and nine of the Meyers family, seventeen is a lot to ask."

"Mr. Senator Phillip Meyers, thank you for having us, but this old man has had a long day. I am tired. You young people can stay up. Good night."

"My Father, I am tired too," Rose Denton said. The others agreed.

"Grandfather, I have to go to work tomorrow morning, so I won't see you until later in the day. Have a good night," Mark said. He then shook hands with each person and wished them good night.

The Meyers family also had school or work the next morning, so they were ready to retire. The next morning, the guests were waiting at the elevator for Grandfather. It took two trips, but soon Grandfather's family and John were outside the front of the house when Robert came out.

"Grandfather, good morning. East is this way."

He led the group to the terrace at the rose garden. Each of the Navajo had a small leather bag of corn pollen. Robert joined them in greeting the new day. John watched, amazed.

Robert led them directly to the dining room. The butler helped them with breakfast. The rest joined them by ones and twos.

When everyone was present, Grandfather rose, "My Son has something to say."

Hector rose and addressed Phillip, "I am so ashamed for my behavior yesterday. Please forgive me."

Phillip accepted the apology, stood and said, "I would like to introduce my oldest son Matthew, who is learning to be a doctor and had duties yesterday related to his training."

Matthew stood, and Grandfather introduced his six children who were present. At lunch, Mark told everyone of the tour of the Submarine Base and one of the submarines. The sightseeing proceeded at a leisurely pace with Winnie and Rose getting acquainted. Rose thanked Winnie for her care of her son.

The morning of the Commissioning Ceremony, Mark joined his family and those who had accompanied him to New Mexico for greeting the day dressed in his full dress uniform. After breakfast he showed everyone what was expected of them. The

Meyers family, dressed in tuxedos and formal gowns, gathered in the entry—Mr. and Mrs. Meyers to escort the Captain and their children to escort their guests.

Winnie returned to the ballroom in her formal. Mark hugged her then pinned her corsage (mentally thanking Phillip for the lessons) and a submarine insignia on her. He did the same for his mother when he found her in the parlor where he had escorted Winnie. His family was wearing all their turquoise jewelry in honor of the occasion, waiting for him to escort them to the ballroom at the start of the ceremony.

James started the music. At the appointed time, Mr. and Mrs. Meyers escorted Captain Spencer into the ballroom. He gasped at the transformation, with all of the gilt furnishings in place and lights on. Mark escorted Grandfather as the Yeoman announced him, giving his full rank, name, and military accomplishments; the crowd clapped. He went out to escort his uncles, eldest to youngest. The Yeoman announced each one; the crowd's enthusiasm increased as they recognized the military expertise and heritage of this family.

When Mark escorted Winnie, he told her to be prepared for a surprise. The Yeoman announced her as a submarine widow and gave the information on her boyfriend. She looked wide-eyed at Mark, who smiled at her and squeezed her hand.

Then he went to escort his mother. With her introduction as his mother, the Yeoman included Mark's record. The commissioning went smoothly.

The afternoon was spent in reliving the day, war stories, and watching the movie *The Hunt for Red October*, which Mark told everyone was part of the foundation for his desire to be on a submarine.

Jocelyn sat next to Mark on a couch with Rose on his other side. In Navajo, Rose asked how his relationship was progressing.

He caught her up on his request for courting and the Meyers Gentleman lessons. He laughed at his mistakes.

Rose patted his hand and said in Navajo, *"You are doing well, my son, she likes you more."*

"We have many years to wait," Mark replied in Navajo.

Hector said, *"Why don't you just take her and be done with it?"*

Mark went after him. The uncles kept them separated and escorted Hector out, telling him they would kick him out of the house, and he would have to find his own way home. They took him to his room.

Mark had gone outside. Jocelyn, James, and Robert joined him. At first, he stomped around the garden, ignoring her questions. Finally, he calmed enough to explain what was said. The four talked. Mark explained that he was also the uncle who had gotten him drunk and let Susan abuse him. James and Robert were embarrassed, but Jocelyn knew about it, so she was concerned for Mark and his relationship with his uncle.

"I shouldn't have let him come. He was probably high on peyote or something."

Mark had to explain what peyote was. The men tried to change the subject, amazed that their sister already knew so much about Mark. They told each other that they would never tell their girlfriend such things. It took some time before the subject could be changed.

Raymond told his father what they had found on Hector and in his baggage then introduced Matthew's idea in English. Matthew explained about the drug treatment program at a certain veterans' hospital and what it would take to have him committed. Matthew could not answer all his questions. They had to go to the Submarine Base Naval Hospital. There Hector saw a doctor who determined to commit him to the drug treatment program.

A male nurse went into the room, and Grandfather left. He went to the receptionist's desk and got a brochure with the address of the place where Hector would be as well as information about it. When told about the brochure, Matthew asked if they could have a few more for their doctor to have and hand out. She gave him several dozen, which Raymond took to give to Dr. Pettijohn.

"Does John Howell have to leave?" Grandfather asked Mark.

"No, you have him for your return flight, and we have him until then."

"I like that young man. You take care of him."

"I'll try."

On the way home, the uncles teased Mark about Jocelyn and why he had not given her a necklace.

Grandfather said, "They are not ready. She wants to finish her schooling, and he wants to make Captain. They are doing it their way."

Raymond charged, "Mark was always different. Rose married a foreigner, and Mark has foreign ways."

Grandfather said something in Navajo, and the subject changed to the weather. When they got to the house, the uncles cleared Hector's things out of the room and then told the butler that it would not be needed anymore.

The women gave Rose some pants to wear under her full skirt for the trip to the submarine where they were served dinner after their tour.

All were impressed with Mark's knowledge of the submarine, knowing more than their seaman guide. Jocelyn's family was more impressed with how he handled the people: gently correcting the seaman, greeting each member of the crew, asking how they were and about their job. He knew a few, and he added questions about how their training was progressing.

Jocelyn enjoyed the visit with Rose and Grandfather more than the commissioning ceremony. Mark's family stayed for almost a week after the commissioning. Everyone enjoyed the sightseeing including a trip to the ice cream parlor, the fall colors, and sailing on Long Island Sound in the Meyers' sailboat. One evening at dinner when everyone was present, Rose said she had a presentation to make.

"I want to thank you for your care of My Son. Winnie, this is for you."

Her brothers brought in a blanket, which they held up for all to see, then folded it, and gave it to Winnie. Everyone commented on it, and Winnie hugged Rose and thanked her profusely.

Rose did not sit down but said, "Jocelyn, this is for you."

Rose's brothers brought in another blanket, held it, folded it, and gave it to Jocelyn.

"Oh, Rose, it's beautiful. Thank you so much."

She hugged Rose tightly and thanked her again. Rose still did not sit down.

"Mr. and Mrs. Meyers, this is for you."

Her brothers brought in a larger blanket, displayed it, folded it, and gave it to them. Jocelyn's parents thanked Rose profusely for the beautiful blanket. They kept assuring her that it had been a pleasure to have Mark in their home.

All too soon, it was time for the Pinto family to leave. Only the driver and yeoman came to escort them to the plane. Mark placed everyone, including the butler and other help, John, the yeoman, and the driver, for the leaving ceremony. The youngest uncle started, thanking each person and saying good-bye. The rest followed, with Rose and Grandfather last. Since John was also leaving, he too thanked each member of the Meyers family and help. He especially thanked Mark and promised to keep in touch.

~ 7 ~

Not too long after Mark's family left, he had to leave. Jocelyn was both sad and glad to see him go. Sad because she knew she would miss him and glad because she could concentrate more on her studies. At this point, she had a 4.0 average. The spring semester would be her hardest, because Mark would be back, but he had said he would not be free like he usually was after he returned.

She got busy studying. She was a little behind because of her guests, but she was quickly catching up. Then came his first phone call.

He used a lot of Navajo words and laughed when she asked what they meant. He told her what Scotland looked like and promised to take her there when they were married. He asked how her studies were going and praised her then started using the Navajo words again and sang his favorite lullaby, which also had the words in it.

"Terms of endearment!" she said.

"Yes. *I love you,*" he said in Navajo.

There was loud banging and yelling.

"I have to go. Someone else wants to call home." Then in Navajo, he added, "*Little Flower, I love you and miss you.* Bye."

"Mark."

"Remember our hand signal? I love you. Bye." And he was gone.

As he turned, the one who had been pounding on the door saw his rank on the drab blue submarine uniform they all wore and recognized who he was. He saluted and apologized profusely. Mark laughed and took off running. The other man watched open-mouthed until he was shoved into the phone booth.

"Hey, don't you know who that was? Commander Denton. He's got a girl."

"He's only Lieutenant Commander and hurry up. We ain't got all day."

But some of the men watched him as he charged up the nearest hill. His legend grew as he exulted in his *Little Flower*.

Jocelyn was left a wreck. She wandered in a fog. Somehow she ended in the exercise room, turned on the treadmill, and charged up her own hill.

She studied hard. She not only caught up, but was ahead in some classes. Mark called again.

"Mark, you're not being helpful. You left me a mess. I have trouble concentrating when you do that to me."

"I'm sorry, Little Flower. I guess I'm a mess all of the time. I'm going to wear out the exercise equipment on the boat. I've run these hills every chance I get. How are your studies going?"

"Does the running help you to calm down?"

"Yes."

"Maybe you should run before you call. My studies are going very well. Thank you for not using the cell phone. We would talk all the time that way."

"I know. I'm planning our trip here to Scotland. This is rugged country like my home but green like yours. They have their own language. They raise sheep also. It's like a very wet, green Navajo land. How's your family?"

"They are well. Everyone sends their love."

The Navajo terms of endearment started pouring out.

In a faint voice, she complained, "Mark, please stop."

"Yes, Love. You know my plans for seeing New England when I get back?"

"Yes?"

"I'm going to have to postpone them. I may not be very free. We'll see it together one day. Maybe after we're married," he rattled on.

She enjoyed the sound of his voice. What he was saying really didn't matter.

"*Little Flower*. Little Flower. Jocelyn!"

"Yes."

"Where are you?"

"I haven't accepted your necklace."

"But you love me. It's a mere formality."

"Like our wedding. Does that mean you'll take me?"

"Of course not! For us, that's after the wedding. I'm only half-Navajo, remember?"

"The best half. Oh, Mark, I miss your black eyes. They are deep rich pools for me to dive into."

"Jocelyn, finish this year. I'll be at your graduation. I'll take time off if I have to, but I'll be there. Then your master's, doctorate, work, and me. I promise I'll wait. I won't touch you until your mother gives you to me."

"Why do you keep saying Mother? Father will give me away."

"In my culture, it's the mother. What if we have them both do it?"

"Mark, you already—"The line went dead.

"Jocelyn. Jocelyn."

"This is the operator, sir. Your time is up."

"Here. Here. Don't cut us off." Mark frantically put all his change in the pay phone.

"All right, sir. Sir, I have her again."

"Thank you. Thank you."

"Mark?"

"Jocelyn. *Little Flower*, I wasn't ready to leave you."

"I'm here."

"What were you saying, love?"

"Well, I was surprised that you're already planning our wedding."

"Yes. Wedding. Yes. I have my speech ready."

"What speech?"

"The one where I pledge myself to you."

"Do I need a speech?"

"Aren't you going to pledge yourself to me?"

"This is different from what I'm used to."

"Oh. We'll talk of this together. I was thinking of combining the best of your wedding and mine."

"Does this mean I'll have to run like you told me is part of your wedding ceremony?"

"Only if you want to. We can sit down and discuss it when the time comes. This is a beautiful sunset."

"It's raining here. How can you keep talking without someone banging on the booth?"

"I found one on the other side of town, away from the harbor. I panicked when we were cut off. I miss you."

"I miss you too."

"You're the sexiest girl I've ever known."

"More than those in highschool who—"

"Much more."

"Mark, you cut me off."

"You're teaching me your foreign ways." They laughed. "From here you can see the waterway out to the sea. It's almost like Long Island Sound. Maybe I'll let you teach me about your boat."

"One minute, sir."

"Operator, please don't just cut me off. Let me tell her good-bye."

"I promise. Here she is again."

"Jocelyn?"

"I heard."

"For our honeymoon, I'll find us a private place where you can teach me all of those things."

"And you won't get embarrassed."

"You don't want to see me blushing all over."

"Mark!"

He started singing her a lullaby.

"Sir, it's time," the operator cut in.

"Bye, Jocelyn, Love, Little Flower, *Little Flower*." He hung up, crying.

He charged up into the hills. Later, he had to ask directions from a lonely house. They drove him back to the base. He tried to give them some money, but they refused. They remembered being far away from each other.

Jocelyn went to the exercise room. Mark was right—it did help, but it didn't help the dreams. She wondered what blushing arms and legs looked like and then wondered what his arms and legs looked like. Were they much lighter than his hands and face? She thought she would ask him then decided she'd better not. She changed the program on the treadmill to rolling hills. Soon, she went to the other machine Robert had shown her. She began thinking chemistry.

After the next call, Jocelyn realized it had almost been two weeks since that last one. She had been busy. Her classes were doing well. Her workout was getting more regular, at times more aggressive than others. The next call came just a few days later.

"Remember our hand signal? I'll start using it when I spot you. I've made arrangements for you to watch. Are you okay?"

"I'm fine. I miss you. You're right, the workout helps. My classes are doing well. I know I'll ace most of the tests. Robert's talking of leaving for New Mexico soon. He talks like it will be before Christmas. I don't know how he could leave before Christmas."

"I don't think of him like I think of his sister. Mm. Where will he live?"

"He's talking about staying with Thomas. Remember him?"

"Kind of, I was all caught up in my blunders with you. I don't like making you angry. Some of the men talk about how their girls are beautiful when they're angry. It hurts me to make you angry."

"Do you talk about me to your men?"

"No! You're my private *Little Flower*. Some of them tell everything. It's embarrassing. I need to go. Watch for my signal. We all look alike. That's how you'll know me." He started singing his lullaby.

There was banging. He hung up. This run just took him to the edge of town and back.

Jocelyn maintained her 4.0 average. There was only one semester to go. How did Mark put it? Graduation, master's, doctorate, work, and him. He was already planning their wedding and honeymoon.

Robert planned to leave right after his class work finished. Jocelyn challenged him on it, but he was listening to no one. She did get him to promise to tell Rose and Grandfather hi for her. She wrote to them often and enjoyed their letters in return.

Her final semester didn't sound too bad. She was already accepted to the master's program, which would start in the summer. Life was going well.

Then disturbing news came from Robert. He was talking about Christianity, the Bible, and some Gospel of John nonsense. What had Robert gotten himself into now, she wondered?

Then Dad took it up. He was talking church. Funerals and weddings—these were all church was good for. Then Dad wanted the family to go with him to church. She decided to go to keep him company. She found she could think there—just tune out what was going on. The rest, though, started giving Dad excuses. She felt sorry for him, so she kept going. Then Winnie started going too. She had Winnie sit next to Dad. That way he wouldn't notice her non-participation as much.

She started thinking about her wedding. Mark was planning it, so would she. She liked the pastor's voice. She liked the looks of the church. It didn't have a center isle, so she wondered what the wedding march would be like on the right then on the left.

Winnie had to shake her arm to get her attention when it was time to go. Then it was embarrassing when Dad introduced Winnie as their housekeeper.

Jocelyn did well in her classes. She was ahead in most. She made arrangements to be gone to meet Mark's boat when it came in. Father had an invitation to meet it with all his family and Winnie. Mark had specified that she be there too.

Jocelyn looked at each of the men as the boat sedately rode the Thames to the pier. There were men at the top of the upper part and men all over the top of the tube of the submarine as it came up the river. She saved the men on the top of the tower to the last. The man with the field glasses at the command of everyone else, shouting orders, which were repeated by those in command of the groups of men on the tube, looked familiar. He made the hand signal. She did it. He did it then had to look elsewhere. Mark was in charge. Mark was directing his submarine into its berth!

"Hey, Mark's the one with the field glasses on top!"

They all cheered as he expertly maneuvered the submarine gently in. The boat slowed and pulled around to rest against one of the piers. Someone shot a knot in the end of a line onto the shore, and something was shouted to the man with the field glasses. The men on the top of the tube were holding onto the line, which had been shot to shore. The ones on shore grabbed it and seemed to be pulling the submarine snug to its berth. The action became frantic as the groups of men handled the lines of thick rope used to tie the submarine to the pier.

There were several thousand people watching for particular men. Just before he disappeared back into the boat, he looked at her and again gave her the signal.

"Hey, Dad, Mom, that was Mark that brought the boat in."

"I thought he looked familiar. He did a great job. You'd think he was raised on a boat as neatly as he handled it." Jocelyn also heard positive comments from James and her sisters. She was very proud of this man to whom she became more committed as time went by.

Jocelyn eagerly watched as men came and went out of a hatch. Other hatches opened. A man appeared with a gun belt strapped on and a clipboard. The gangplank was stretched from the pier. Slowly, men toting heavy sea bags of their belongings checked in with the man with the gun, and it seemed that he had to clear them to leave. The Meyers family waited and watched as more family groups took their man home.

Jocelyn noticed the odd odor that came from the men. She mentioned it. Her family decided that it came from being enclosed for months with a hundred people.

One of the men brought them refreshments and suggested they go to the café at the base exchange because Lieutenant Commander Denton's watch was not over for almost an hour. The Meyers family discussed it and asked if they could stay there on the pier. That was not possible, as equipment needed to be removed and supplies brought on board. Their navy van driver made some suggestions, and a plan was formulated.

A familiar form came out of the forward hatch. They exchanged the hand signal. He set things up for his men then he went to the gangplank to talk with that man and pointed out to him Jocelyn and her family. He did his saluting and ran toward them. The rest of her family was leaving. He stopped a couple of yards away and looked in her eyes. Then he called out to Father, and Mark greeted the family. They congratulated him on his maneuvering of the boat. He thanked them for coming but asked them to go on home. He would be there as soon as he could finish his watch and drop his things off at his apartment. He hugged Winnie and shook hands with everyone else except Jocelyn.

"I'll see you later, *Little Flower*," he said more into her eyes. His crew whistled and urged him to kiss her. He never heard it and just turned and went back to work. He got his crew busy again and flashed his hand signal to her in the van; she did it back as it pulled off.

She planned to study, but images of her man kept covering the page. She saw his car pull up and saw him get out with a bouquet. She went downstairs to meet him. He watched her descend the stairs and handed her the bouquet.

Everyone was congratulating him on handling his boat. Jocelyn took the flowers in to the kitchen and got a vase to put them in.

"That's some man you got yourself there, honey," Winnie commented.

"Yes. How am I going to wait?" Jocelyn almost whined.

"You gotta save the world first."

"Okay," Jocelyn sighed.

"Take those to the table. I gotta get your dinner ready to feed that man."

"Thanks."

Jocelyn was leaving the dining room when Winnie went into the entryway to announce dinner. Mark hugged Winnie and slipped a small box into her hand.

After dinner, Jocelyn teased him for bringing Winnie a present and nothing for her.

"I brought you a whole bouquet of presents," He sounded hurt.

She laughed, and he joined her. Then he excused himself to talk with Winnie.

Later, he found Jocelyn, and they talked.

"Should I call you later and sing you to sleep?"

"No, I wouldn't rest. I have to make up the classes I missed today."

"Okay. I'm going to Hartford with your father tomorrow to learn about becoming a politician. I'll see you in the evening. Have a good night."

"You too."

The next evening, Jocelyn greeted Mark and Father as they entered the back parlor.

"Hello, Jocelyn. Will you allow me to postpone our date tonight due to the weather? It's a blizzard out there."

"You could stay here."

"Thank you for your generous invitation, but I had better not. I'll see you tomorrow if the roads are safe."

"Mark, let me pick you up in the morning. I'll call you if the Senate session's canceled," Phillip offered.

"All right. I have to go. It's snowing harder. I definitely don't want to be caught in a whiteout."

Jocelyn went to exercise and after dinner went to her rooms to study. The next morning was a whiteout. Jocelyn studied until mid-morning. She called Mark.

"Hello, *Little Flower*."

"Hello, Mark. I wish you had stayed last night. We could have spent the day together."

"Too tempting."

"Oh, I didn't think of that."

"You never do. That's my job. What if we were exploring the house and found ourselves off in one of those far bedrooms away from everyone. Looking at you is all the temptation I can handle. Being alone with you like that, I couldn't bear it. I would break every promise I have made to you, your father, and your brothers. Now to change the subject completely," he said firmly, "Has your Father talked with you about reading the Bible, going to church, or Robert?"

"Yes. I really don't get it. I go to church because he asked. I read the Bible because he asked. It's good literature and has some interesting stories, but he believes it really happened like it says."

They discussed various parts of the Book of John, the miracles she considered too incredible to be true.

"He asked me to go to church with him. Will you go with me?"

"Sure, to be with you, but how am I going to concentrate on the sermon when this incredibly marvelous, talented, handsome, Navajo Lieutenant Commander is sitting next to me?"

"You have a point, but I'll have it harder with the beautiful, intelligent, talented, graceful Senator's daughter next to me. Maybe we'll have to have your father sit between us."

They laughed and hung up. She stared out at the snow storm, seeing Mark.

The next morning, she wondered what Mark was doing, so she called him. The conversation was confusing. He seemed to be running while he was talking. He told her to hold on then just used Navajo. Finally, he gave her a confusing explanation. She decided to change the subject by asking him about a Navajo word he used a lot. They worked on the pronunciation.

"What does it mean?"

"Little Flower. That's my name for you. You were like a rose bud with great promise of enormous beauty when I first met you. As your life unfolds, you're greatly exceeding that promise. You're a flower of breathtaking beauty unfolding before my eyes."

"Oh, Mark." Jocelyn sat there stunned.

He spoke to her more, but her mind really couldn't register it.

Finally, she asked, "Mark, what's your Navajo name?"

She practiced saying it.

"What does it mean?"

"Fish."

"Fish?"

"I'm a submariner. Fish is the closest my language can come without being two miles long."

"What?"

He tried to explain how his language worked. It was all very confusing. He tried to explain using the different types of snow from this storm. He had her practice the words. She really didn't understand the distinctions in meaning he was making, but she wanted to know more about him.

"Mark, teach me Navajo."

They worked on the words she knew. Then he begged off citing a desire to talk with a real estate agent.

"Mom's a real estate agent."

"I wasn't thinking here."

She didn't hear him. She ran to her mother's study, told her that Mark was looking for a house, and handed her phone to her mother. They talked then Mother returned the phone to her and told her to end the conversation soon.

"Sure, Mom. Hey, Mark."

"Yes, Jocelyn."

"I have to go. Talk with you later."

"Yes. Later, *Little Flower.*" They laughed.

Jocelyn went to her room. She saw the bouquet he had given her. Each flower took on significance. She remembered his hurt when she did not consider the flowers a gift. He had said, "A whole bouquet of gifts." He had been honoring her with something he felt very precious. She remembered his country. There weren't many flowers there. He had compared her to a rarity in his experience. She savored the explanation he had given for her name.

She picked up a fallen petal. She studied it, and then she started crying. The enormity of his love for her was overwhelming, yet comforting. He worked hard at keeping them apart, at keeping his promise to wait until she was ready. He was putting her before himself, before his needs as a man as Mother had told her. She lay down, still studying the petal, now overwhelmed with her selfish, self-centered existence. He was working hard to care for her, and she didn't really comprehend the enormity of his sacrifice. She cried for a long time, determined to look for ways to help him.

The snow storm continued. She studied and went on to the terrace. She played the piano and played games with her family. They got into a Monopoly marathon.

She realized that as much as she enjoyed these activities, she enjoyed just sitting with Mark more. She began walking through the house and remembering Mark—all he had said and done with her. Slowly, she began to understand that his love had been there for a very long time.

She remembered her trip to Hawaii and how protective he was of her. She never thought about where he had stayed; she realized she had been too caught up in herself. She remembered how he had looked at her, and she wondered if he had seen anything else as they went on all of the tours of the islands, because each time she had looked at him, he had been looking at her.

She sat down in one of the far bedrooms and realized Mark was right. If he were there right then, they would be kissing and hugging and who knows what else. She really didn't want to think that far. Some of the girls at college told about things they did with their boyfriends that she didn't like to hear about. Right now, she wondered what it would be like with Mark.

She awoke from her reverie and went to study. He wouldn't do those things with her until she got her doctorate, so she'd better work on that, not daydreaming about her honeymoon as she knew he would never even kiss her before then.

The snowstorm ended. She dressed in many layers and went outside. Her siblings had done the same. They teamed up and were having a big snowball fight across the terrace.

"Jocelyn?"

"Yes, Winnie."

"Mark's on the phone for you."

"Okay, I'll be right in after I get some of this snow off me."

Her team pitched in and started beating the snow off very vigorously.

"Hey, you guys, you're beating me up. Let me go. Mark's waiting."

They all laughed and decided to clear off the driveway so they could get out the next day. They had a snowman-building contest with the snow on the driveway.

She used the phone in the kitchen because she still had snow on her, and it wouldn't be a problem if it got on the floor there. Mark told her he would be gone. She tried to support him, telling him to be safe and to tell his family hi for her. She asked how to say another word and practiced all of her Navajo with him. When he said he loved her, she told him she loved him too and that she thought of him every day. When the call ended, she removed her outer layer of clothes, wet from playing in the snow with her family. She went to her room and again contemplated this man, his love, and how she could support him more.

She got busy with school. Between her day off to see Mark's return and the blizzard she expected to be behind. She turned in her makeup work from her day off. Her study during the blizzard had her again ahead. She was doing well, ready for midterms.

Some days later, Robert called and spoke with Father. As soon as everyone was home, Father had them all gather in the back parlor, even Winnie.

"Dear ones, I have some bad news: Mark's grandfather passed away yesterday."

The reaction was a mixture of disbelief and grief. The sisters hugged each other and cried. Someone would tell an incident about him then they would cry. Everyone had Grandfather stories. Jocelyn told some too. She told how much he knew people by just looking at their faces. They wanted to know what to send.

"They don't have a funeral like we do. Did he die in the hogan?"

"Robert didn't say anything about that," Father said.

"If he died in the hogan, they would cave it in to bury him. Then Rose wouldn't have a place to live," Jocelyn declared.

"Neither would Jessica, Abraham, and Roger. I wonder if they would know at the Police Station," James added.

James called the Police Station. Abraham wouldn't be back for many days. The Lieutenant said that they had not caved in the house. Abraham's truck was still at the house, but the rest of the family was with Mary Rose. He assured James that there was nothing they could send, and he would contact him if he learned of anything. Next James tried Robert and left a voice mail.

Jocelyn thought about how much Mark had liked to talk with Grandfather and had revered him. As much as she missed Grandfather, she knew Mark missed him more.

She went to her room and cried for Mark and thought how much he had relied on Grandfather's wisdom. She cried for Rose, who had lost her father. Then she thought about little Roger and how much he loved his great-grandfather. She removed her clothes and crawled into bed, crying, remembering, crying, and sometimes even sleeping. By the next morning, she had resolved to make some changes.

"Dad, may we talk?"

"Come in, Jocelyn. Let's sit here on the couch."

"Dad, how can I support Mark more? I've been so selfish and self-centered. He has been so good and loving. Do you know that he won't even be alone with me? He's putting my life dreams ahead of his desire for marriage. I want to learn how to be better to him."

"My little girl is growing up."

"When I realized the enormity of his care for me, all I could do was cry. Part of my tears were over my shame at the way I've treated him. I don't want to be like that anymore. Will you help me to be better to him?"

"I'll try. Maybe it will help if you consider him as more than just a good buddy. Did you know he thinks of you as a precious flower of great worth?"

"Yes, he told me. That's when I really started thinking about this."

"When did he tell you?"

"In one of our calls during the blizzard."

"Your Mother thinks of me as her knight in shining armor, her protector, and her provider. When things come up, she talks with me about them. Maybe you could start treating him that way too, as a valued resource like you do Mother and me."

"Thanks, Dad."

"Jocelyn, Mark is a very good man. He's trying hard to please you."

"But, Dad, I don't want a clone of you, or Matthew, or James, or Robert. I want my Navajo Mark. He's so strong and courageous. His life dream is to be Captain of a submarine. The first Navajo Captain of a submarine, and he is working very hard at it."

"So ask him how you can help him, especially now that his grandfather is gone. He was Mark's father after his father died. Try to support him there too."

"Okay. Thanks, Dad."

"How are you doing with your grief?"

"I don't know. Sometimes talking about him helps the most. I cried most of the night."

"Talking about her helped me when Mother died."

"Thanks, Dad."

They had a good father-daughter hug. Phillip thought about the comment Mark had made about hugging her: it was still future, but he was sure that Mark and his daughter would fit well together.

The family remained numb, but they had to go to classes. During the next few days, Robert called several times. Everything Robert told Father, he relayed to the rest, either at dinner or family meetings.

When Mark got back, Jocelyn tried to support him by talking about Grandfather. Mark told her stories about him from when he and Grandfather were together.

"I won't talk with you this week. I have my exam for Commander."

"I know you'll do well. You have studied hard."

"For our next date, what about seafood and ice flowers?"

"Oh, yes. Dress very warmly. We'll be by the Sound."

They spent the week studying and taking exams, and on Friday night, he called. They talked about their exams, as she had taken her midterms. Both felt they had done well.

"I'm ready for our date tomorrow, so is Matthew as our chaperone."

"I am also. I guess I really didn't believe you when you told me about ice flowers."

"I'm not sure what anyone else calls them, but that's what we call them. See you tomorrow."

"Yes, see you." Mark was surprised that she kept the call short. Most of the time, he had to tell her bye more than once. She wasn't angry and was looking forward to their date. He did his exercises and turned in.

The next day, Jocelyn and Matthew were ready and talking in the entry way when Mark drove up. They went out and got in the car. They greeted and talked studies on the way to the restaurant.

Mark and Jocelyn both asked Matthew to sit with them, but he refused. He had a book he was studying.

They practiced her Navajo. They enjoyed the fish. She commented, as his Navajo name meant 'fish,' that he was nothing like what they were eating. They talked about Grandfather. They lingered over a last cup of coffee and finally left. Mark paid Matthew's bill as well. She told him to drive back to her house. Matthew put his book inside then they walked to the Sound.

"You know the tide rises and falls?"

"Yes."

"During dead high tides when the water is still before falling toward low tide, it freezes in this cold."

"Even the saltwater of the Sound?"

"Yes. So as the tide goes out, the frozen sheet of ice comes down on a rock. See there?"

"Yes."

"Then the ice breaks around the rock, and it freezes that way. The tide rises, and where the rock was fills in with water and freezes. See?"

"Yes."

"When the tide goes out again, the ice falls on the rock and forms new breaks in the ice, which freeze that way. I call those petals, like on a flower. It keeps growing as the tide rises and falls, so they become ice flowers, which grow until thaw."

"They're beautiful. Thank you for sharing your world with me."

They were looking into each others eyes when her foot slipped on the icy rock. She turned her ankle.

"Mark!"

She was falling. He caught her. The last thing she remembered as he also slipped was him catching her and her head hitting his eye.

When she awoke, she hurt. Her whole head hurt, and only one eye worked. The light hurt her eye. She tried to move.

"Jocelyn. Be still. I'm right here," Mother assured her.

She relaxed some and drifted back to sleep. The next time she woke, she hurt just as much. She tried to move. One arm was attached to a board. That hand hurt, and the other hand was caught in the covers. She tried to free it.

"Jocelyn, calm down. I'm right here," Mother tried to assure her.

Her mouth didn't seem to work right. She tried to talk, but her mouth didn't move. She tried to free her hand again.

"Jocelyn, calm down. I'll free your hand, but just relax. I'm right here."

"Mmm."

Mother pulled her hand out from under the covers and patted it. A nurse came in to check the machines and IV and then left. Mother started talking but not telling her what she wanted to know: Why did she hurt? Why did her mouth and eyes not work? Why did her hand hurt? Why was her arm strapped down? Her agitation increased the pain, which in turn increased her agitation.

"Jocelyn, please calm down. Hello, Doctor, she's awake but upset."

"Hello, Jocelyn. I'm Dr. Norris. You fell. You twisted your ankle. I have that foot in a boot. I'm going to look at it first." He raised the blanket at the foot of the bed and removed the boot.

"Your ankle is doing well. I'm going to wrap it this time. Let us know if it gets to hurting worse. Mrs. Meyers, keep this boot handy, she'll need it again later."

Then he showed her how to put it on. Mother put it into the closet.

"Mmm," Jocelyn groaned.

"Yes, your mouth. I'll check that too. You broke some bones in your face. I had to wire your mouth closed so they can heal. I'm going to check your IV next. Does this hurt?"

"Sss."

"Good. Now for the beautiful part—you have a technicolor face. That was some rock you hit. I'm going to check your right eye. Can you open the lid by yourself?"

Jocelyn tried. It was too swollen.

"Okay. I'm going to move your eyelid."

"Sss!"

"I know it hurts, but I have to check that eye. I'll try to be gentle, but your whole face is swollen. Here, lift your left hand. Show me with your left hand how many fingers you see."

She held up one finger.

"Now make a fist. Nod it this way for yes and shake it this way for no. Okay?"

She nodded her fist.

"Does the light make your eyes hurt?"

She nodded her fist.

"Does your stomach feel queasy?"

Again, she nodded her fist.

"I'm going to give you some water. Just take a sip. Put your hand in a stop sign, like this"—he demonstrated with his hand—"if you feel like throwing up, Okay?"

She nodded her fist.

He put the straw to her lips. They were so swollen they didn't work right.

"Okay, Plan B. I'm going to just put some water in your mouth. Here."

He used the straw to pick up some of the water and put it between her lips. Some dribbled down her chin. He wiped it with a tissue.

"Did you get any?"

She nodded her fist.

Then he started talking with her. The X-ray in the emergency room showed broken bones on the right side of her face. They needed more information from an MRI. He told her they would do it soon. He told Mrs. Meyers to be sure the boot was on any time they transported her.

"Jocelyn, is your stomach more queasy?"

She shook her hand no.

"Which hand do you use to write?"

She pointed to her right.

"Well, Mrs. Meyers, use the fist nod and ask only yes or no questions. Do you have any questions?"

They discussed Jocelyn's injuries and her studies. Dr. Norris wrote an excuse note on his prescription pad for the college. Soon he left.

Jocelyn felt she had let Mark down. She would have a hard time finishing these classes so she could graduate in May and start her master's in June. She started crying and fell asleep.

The next time she awoke, Mother was putting the boot on her foot. She could hear others in the room. They lowered the side rails on her bed, picked her up by the sheet, and moved her to a very hard bed. She cried out when her head touched the hard bed. Mother put a pillow under her head, took her left hand, and then walked with her to the MRI. People kept shouting at her. She tried to tell Mother, but she didn't understand. She pulled her hand from Mother's and covered her ear.

"People, she's not deaf and has a bad headache. Please be quiet," her mother said.

That helped, but when they started the MRI, they had some rock music on. Again, she covered her ear. Mother leaned near to talk with her and heard the music.

"Excuse me, don't you have anything better?"

"Kids like this kind of music."

"Not my daughter. Don't you see it's making her upset? Let me see what else you have."

"Sure, Mrs. Meyers."

Everyone knew this was Senator Meyers' wife and daughter. The technician showed her the music. At the bottom of the pile was a CD of waltzes. She looked at it carefully.

"Here, this is much better."

They put it in and turned it on in the control booth.

"Much better."

The technicians exchanged looks then the one monitoring Jocelyn said, "It's working. She's relaxing. Let's get this done."

Mrs. Meyers watched the pictures they were getting and noted their comments. They seemed very positive.

At the end, Mrs. Meyers asked how Jocelyn was. They deferred her questions to the doctor. She took on her no-nonsense steely pose, and they told her.

"There doesn't appear to be any brain swelling or damage. The facial bones are all in place. The cheekbone right here is pushed in some. There may need to be surgery to pull it out. The jawbone is better than what the X-ray showed. The doctor may be able to remove the wires soon. All in all, she doesn't look too bad. What happened?"

"She slipped on the ice and landed on her fiancé's face. He has it worse. He landed on a rock. He's still unconscious."

"Was that Lieutenant Commander Denton?"

"Yes. How do you know?"

"We heard..." An elbow stopped the flow of words.

"Mrs. Meyers, we need to get Jocelyn back to her room."

"Of course, and thank you for listening to me."

"Yes, ma'am."

They exchanged looks, but they left the waltz CD in.

They started cold compresses on her face, and the swelling went down. As Jocelyn got better, she worried about her classes. One of her professors visited and assured her that her midterm grades were all A's, and there would be accommodations made because of her accident.

Several days later, the doctor requested the name of her dentist. Doctor and dentist discussed the case and decided to remove the wires immobilizing her jaw. They had to put her to sleep to do it. With the swelling improving, Jocelyn was finally able to talk.

"Jocelyn, how is that?" Mother asked.

"How's Mark?"

"He's in the Naval Hospital. Matthew is taking care of him."

"That doesn't tell me how he is, Mother."

"He has a concussion. He hit the back of his head on a rock. His face looks like yours."

"Is he going to be okay?" Jocelyn asked.

"Matthew is working on it."

"What do I look like?"

"Quite technicolor, sister." James and her sisters walked in.

"How's Mark?"

"Matthew's taking good care of him."

"What's the matter? Why won't you answer me?"

"Mark's concussion is much worse than yours. The neurologist hasn't been there yet. He has to come from elsewhere."

"He isn't throwing up anymore," James stated.

"Commander Bright is learning to respect his Navajo taboos."

"He got upset because he was undressed. You know how he is about clothes."

"They're going to do an MRI," Brianna added.

"Can I talk with him?"

"Not yet, he's mostly using Navajo."

"Mother, when can I go home?" Jocelyn asked.

"When you're ready, dear. The doctor has to okay it."

When Dr. Norris came in, he examined her ankle and face closely. He kept feeling her face, especially the area around her eye. He pulled Mrs. Meyers into the hallway.

"Her facial bone here under her eye is caved in some from the impact. I'd like to pull it out even with the other side."

Mrs. Meyers wanted to know how it would affect her sinus cavity if left. Then what would be involved if the surgery was done.

"Let's talk with Jocelyn. She wants to graduate in May and won't be able to if you do all of that."

"As her mother, don't you want her looks restored?" the doctor asked.

"As her mother, I want what's best for her. What would not doing the surgery do for her appearance?"

"I can show you in my office. I have some software that can do that."

"Let me talk with Jocelyn."

They went back into the room.

"Doctor, how's Mark?" Jocelyn asked.

"I'm not his doctor."

"When can I go home?"

"I was just talking with your mother about that."

"I'm an adult. Tell me." She took on her mother's steely look.

"Tell her." Mary Meyers' steely look was harder to ignore.

"Well, Jocelyn, when you landed on the man—"

"Mark, when I landed on Mark's face it broke the bones around my eye."

"Yes. It pushed in these bones," the doctor explained.

"Mom, where's that mirror you had?"

"Here, dear."

"Show me."

It was the area Dr. Norris had been feeling before. "See this side doesn't come out as far as this side."

"How does that affect inside, the sinus cavity and eye?"

"It doesn't seem to have affected your eye. It has reduced that sinus cavity. It's your appearance that is most affected. See that side of your face doesn't come out as far as this side."

She felt both sides and compared them in the mirror.

"I don't see that much difference. It would take time to recuperate. How long?"

"About three or four weeks. It really won't lengthen your complete recovery time by much."

"I won't be able to graduate in May. No."

"Miss Meyers, let me return you to your pre-injury beauty."

"Why? So you can make more money? I need to get back to class so I can graduate."

"But, Miss Meyers, your appearance. You don't want to lessen your chances with the good-looking boys.

"I already have a *man*. I don't need a *man*. He looks like me right now. I did this to us when I slipped. It's more important to me to graduate so my *man* and I can get married."

"You don't mean that wild Indian that tore up the Naval Hospital Emergency room? You don't..."

"Mother?"

"Matthew says that he was trying to get to you. Mark was upset that he had not caught you and protected you. Matthew is taking good care of him," Mary said.

"Doctor, I need out of here so I can see my *man*!" Jocelyn demanded.

"Well…"

"Doctor!"

"Doctor?" Mary asked.

"Well…"

"We're checking out. Jocelyn can recover just as well at home as here, can't she?" Mary decided.

"Well, yes, but…"

"But what?" Phillip said as he walked in.

"Hello, Phillip."

"Hello, Dad."

"So what's the problem here?" Phillip asked.

Dr. Norris tried to convince Senator Meyers that his daughter needed plastic surgery to restore her face. Phillip listened to all of the arguments.

He looked at Jocelyn's face and asked her, "What do you want?"

"To see Mark, get caught up in my classes, and graduate."

"Mary, what do you think?"

"It would take a lot longer to recuperate and wouldn't change her looks that much. I want to take her home."

"So, Doctor, you heard them. Prepare the papers. We're going home."

"Dad, have you seen Mark?"

"No, only Matthew has. You can talk with him when we get home."

"Phillip, please go out so I can get her dressed."

Jocelyn got dressed. She found she could not bend over to tie her shoes without her head pounding, so Mother did it for her. They gathered all her things. Mary opened the door.

"Phillip." She got his attention.

"Are you ready to go? What may I carry?"

After she got home, Jocelyn tried to call Matthew, but got a message that he had no signal. She wandered in to see Winnie.

"How you doing, Jocelyn?"

"Tired. I wish I knew how Mark is."

"What I heard is he's okay. The MRI didn't show any brain damage. Matthew and John gave him a bath. He fought 'em over it, but John's as strong as Mark is now. He had trouble keeping water down, but they gave him something for that. He is starting to drink water. If he can keep food down, he may be able to go home in a few days."

"How do you know all of this?"

"I keep my ears open, especially when it comes to my boy."

"Who's John?"

"John Howell, that took care of Uncle Hector. Remember him?"

"Oh, yes. I liked him."

"I did too."

"Thanks, Winnie. I think I'll go to bed, I'm tired."

"Want some soup or something?"

"Soup would be nice."

"Need help?"

"Just the soup and a nap. Thanks."

"Hold on. I'll take it up with you. Want the elevator?"

"Yes. Hey, can I ride on the cart?"

"No. Remember when I'd catch you and Robert playing on it?"

"Yes." But Jocelyn really didn't like to remember playing with Robert. Some of those memories were bad.

Winnie changed the room so Jocelyn could reach the intercom system from the bed, got the boot off, helped her into bed, made her drink all of the soup, covered her, and left.

Jocelyn awoke with her ankle bent and on her right side. She was more in discomfort than pain. She called her academic adviser about catching up, who promised to bring the makeup work over the next morning and assured Jocelyn that she could graduate in May.

That afternoon, Matthew came home to clean up. She cornered him to learn exactly how Mark was. He was encouraging and assured her that Mark would go home in a few days.

"Don't worry, sis, you only put a dent in his pride and his face. He'll be fine. Say, did you know he took the exam for Commander?"

"Yes. How did he do?"

"He made a perfect score. A review board came to check it out. They thought he cheated. One of them even removed his covers. I think he thought Mark had the test answers with him. You know how he is about being uncovered. If he was up to it, I think he would have knocked him out."

"No. That's when Mark exercises. He takes it out on a punching bag instead of their face. He really doesn't like violence. Thanks, Matthew, for taking care of Mark and for telling me."

"I gotta get back, sis. I'm using Mark's car to get on base. They salute me like I was him!" He laughed.

Jocelyn relaxed. Her fears for both Mark and her graduation were unfounded.

Almost a week later, Mark was released from the hospital. John and Mark brought Matthew home. They stayed for dinner. She talked with Mark for a short time. He looked tired and in pain. He still had headaches and loud noises hurt his head, but Matthew and John both said he was doing better. John would drive and care for him.

"Call when you feel up to it."

"Does it hurt your head to study?"

"No. I'm getting caught up. My adviser is sure I'll graduate in May."

"One more milestone, *Little Flower*."

"Yes, *Fish*. I wish you had a better name." He laughed, reached toward her, turned, and left. Even in his condition, he didn't dare touch her.

She went to her classes in a cab when no one was free to drive her. Her chemistry labs were the hardest to catch up on. When that professor realized that it was hard for her to stand on her crutches and boot, she got her a stool and sometimes let her do the lab orally.

Mark was doing well until he seemed to have a relapse. He visited her with his right arm tied to his chest and his sleeve pinned up. When she asked what happened, he said he forgot it was injured.

Robert called, asking for her.

"Well, hello, stranger. You still liking Mark's country?" Jocelyn said.

"More than ever, Jocelyn. Remember I said I was still looking for Miss Right?"

"Yes?"

"I think I've found her." Robert rhapsodized on the charms of Miss Miriam Camack. "I may be in love. Thomas calls me a lovesick puppy and says I need to come back to earth. He misses the old me. I don't think I've changed. Anyway, I was telling Miriam about ice flowers. She's always lived here and can't understand. Do you think you could send me a series of pictures to show how they grow? I thought you had some."

"Sure, Robert. I think Mark would enjoy helping me find them. By the way, we're discussing the four Gospels and going to church with Dad. I still don't get it, but Mark thinks he does. He and Dad talk a lot about it too. I thought it was funny that he's named after a book in the Bible. Say, did you know Dad is named after one of Jesus' disciples? That's funny too."

"Yeah. Keep discussing it and going to church. It'll all make sense one day. I'll keep praying that it does. What about the others? I heard even Mom thinks we've gone off the deep end."

"You have to admit it's strange."

"It's not strange to me. There are some more of your pictures I'd like. You know in the fall going on I-95 toward Boston the colors change at Westerly?"

"Yes. From salmon, gold, and red to magenta, rose, and rust. I have some pictures that show that. It's the different trees, but it's amazing."

"Miriam thinks all those colors are from an artist's overactive imagination."

"Oh, remember that gorgeous maple in that dairy farm field across from the ice cream parlor on that road east from Norwich? I have some pictures of that too. We went there the other day. Mark agrees it's the best ice cream in the world."

"Could you send me some? The ice cream they have here is really flat in comparison."

"Sorry, you'll have to come get it yourself. It doesn't ship well. Gets too messy."

WANDA E. PALMER

"Killjoy." They both laughed.

"Mark wants to talk with you. Love ya, bye."

"Love ya too, bye." Jocelyn then handed the phone to Mark.

"Hello, Robert. Are you taking care of my world?" Mark said.

"Trying to. You holding that end?"

"Until Jocelyn knocked me out. Say, about this Gospel thing. You really think this Jesus did all those miracles?"

"Yes. He is the Son of God. The best miracle He has done is to change my life. I'm not searching anymore. I've found the Creator of the Universe. Did you know the Hubble telescope is finding that a lot of the stars we see at night are actually galaxies? God created it all. That's how big He is, yet He loves you and me. He's concerned about our lives. He wants to help us through our days and over the rough parts. I remember seeing that water tanker lumbering up to Grandfather's house: over rocks, into holes, one quarter up, and another down. That's the way my life was. My purpose in life was to be a teacher. When I was doing my student teaching, the kids controlled the classroom. It was a fiasco. If teaching was so bad, I had no purpose in my life. I began to search for meaning and a better purpose. I found it all in Him, Mark. He can be a better Father to you than your own would have been had he lived, or more than mine is to you now. He has answers, people only have suggestions. He goes with you on your submarine and to go get ice cream with Jocelyn. By the way, enjoy some of the ice cream for me next time you go."

"I will. Back to Jesus. If He is so good, why am I just hearing of Him now? And what about all of this prejudice from so-called Christians?"

"Maybe you're just now ready to hear of Him. I think you've hit the nail on the head by labeling them so-called. They're not following Christ in their prejudice. Read John chapter four. Jesus is talking with a woman in Samaria. First, men didn't just talk with women like that. It was a cultural thing. Then Jews didn't talk with a Samaritan. The Jews thought they were better because they were full-blood, and the Samaritans were half-blood dogs. When she came up to the well, and He asked her for water, she responded by asking how He as a Jewish man was asking a Samaritan woman for a drink. It was major, big-time prejudice. He treated her with respect. Also, she was a whore. A respectable Jewish man wouldn't talk with a Samaritan whore."

"Robert, let me get a Bible. Hold on."

"Sure." Robert prayed for Mark and got his own Bible.

"You said John chapter four?"

"Yes."

"Okay."

"See, the first six verses set the scene. Verse seven is Jesus' question. Verse nine is her question, see?"

Mark began reading aloud at verse seven. They discussed it passage by passage as he read through verse twenty-six.

"Do you believe Jesus is the Messiah, which means Savior as does Christ?"

"Yes. It says so over and over in this Book."

"Do you believe you have sinned?"

"Oh, yeah. If you knew all about me you wouldn't let me near your sister."

"I know what you mean, man. But Jesus can cleanse you from that sin. Do you believe that?"

"Yes. You say it happened to you, and so does your father."

"Then all that's left is to tell Him."

"Tell your father?"

"Yes, you can, but I meant Jesus. You need to tell Jesus that you're a sinner and want to accept His payment for your sin. Let me pray for you, and then you can pray." Robert prayed for Mark's understanding and salvation.

Mark started speaking in Navajo. Robert hoped he was praying and hence didn't want to interrupt, but kept praying silently for Mark. He heard his name. He heard Grandfather Meyers and wondered if that was his dad.

When there was silence for a while, Robert asked, "Mark?"

He responded in Navajo.

"Mark, I don't know Navajo."

"Sorry. I didn't realize I was speaking Navajo. I…I'm not alone anymore."

"Alone?"

"Yes. I've been alone all of my life since Mother moved us back to live with Grandfather. Now Jesus is here. This is more peaceful than a cleansing ceremony."

"It's a more powerful and thorough cleansing than your Navajo ceremony."

"Now what?"

"Tell Jocelyn and Dad. Go to church with Dad. Start studying the Gospels and then work your way on through the New Testament to the back of the Bible. Pray. Talk with Jesus about everything. Be thankful for your day as Grandfather taught you, but use your own words, not the rote prayer to his Navajo gods. Greet the day without the corn pollen and using your own words, talking with Jesus."

"Okay. In English?"

"He understood your Navajo, didn't He?"

"Oh. I guess so. Jocelyn is here all worried. I guess I need to talk with her."

"Okay. Bye."

"Mark, what's going on? Robert doesn't know Navajo."

"Remember how I told you that I was always alone?"

"Yes. I heard you tell Robert you were no longer alone. I don't understand."

"Jesus is here, inside me. I feel full, at peace. Clean. More clean than after a cleansing ceremony. I had always distrusted Jesus Way freaks. After Grandfather died, I took My Mother to the church that Robert goes to. I didn't like it…um…for many reasons. But your father has been discussing the Bible with me. I know the miracles are hard for you to accept, but they seem to validate the claims of Jesus that He really is God. Also, Robert showed me that the people in the Bible had prejudice, but Jesus didn't."

"Mark, what's going on?"

"Jocelyn, He saved me!"

"Who? What do you mean?"

"Jesus." He explained how alone he had been since he was young and that now he wasn't alone anymore. Jesus was there with him. He told her about the peace and contentment he felt inside. He told her that this was so much better than a Navajo cleansing ceremony. He kept talking. All of these years, she had done most of the talking; now he couldn't seem to be quiet. There was a fountain bubbling out of him. It could not be stopped. It wasn't her fluttery excitement, just a quiet, peaceful flow, and she didn't know whether to be angry or sad.

Phillip came in to ask them to go to church with him the next day.

"Phillip, I did it. I asked Jesus to cleanse me. I talked with Robert. He showed me John chapter four. See? Here?" Mark said.

They discussed the chapter and what it meant to Mark. Jocelyn listened, her emotions fluctuating between anger and incredulity. Sometimes, she actually heard what they were saying. Father and Mark seemed so tuned into this Bible-Jesus thing. Sometimes, she wanted to stomp out. Mark's flow of words kept coming. She had never heard him talk so much, but he seemed peaceful. He seemed so calm. He wasn't hiding his emotions; they seemed to be pouring out of him in this flow of words.

John came in to see if it was time to go. Phillip promised to pick them up for church tomorrow. All the way home, Mark talked, joy spilling out over John. John had to be forceful to get

Mark bathed and ready for bed. The next morning, John was awakened by Navajo singing and dancing on the balcony. He had to work at getting Mark fed and dressed for church. Then he asked Mark to sit in his chair and read his Bible while he got cleaned up and dressed. They had hours to wait for Phillip to come, so John got out his Bible, and they had a Bible study together.

John had been saved as a child but had drifted away until the incident with Mark's Uncle Hector. He had been studying his Bible but not attending church. Mark asked a lot of questions for which John had no answers. He said they could talk with the preacher about it. Mark got a new notebook and started writing his questions. He had trouble writing with his left hand, so John started writing the questions. Mark's questions aroused questions in John. The questions mounted.

On the ride to church, the discussion had a lot of, "I don't know, write that one down too."

Jocelyn wondered where her Navajo Mark had gone, and Matthew was totally bewildered but was glad that Mark's injuries were improving.

While shaking hands with the pastor in the end of the service, Phillip mentioned that they would like to get together and ask some questions. Pastor Smythe invited them to lunch with his family.

"There are five of us. Are you sure?" Phillip asked.

Mrs. Smythe concurred with her husband.

Seated in the living room, Pastor Smythe asked, "Are all of these your children?"

"No. Only two, there are three others at home and one in New Mexico."

"What is that one doing in New Mexico?"

"Robert's teaching at a Navajo college near Albuquerque. This is Matthew, my eldest. This is Jocelyn, my eldest daughter. This is Mark, Jocelyn's friend, and John, Mark's friend. John is staying with Mark at present. They started writing down questions for you as they were studying the Bible this morning."

"Where were you studying?"

"The Gospel of John. May I just go through our questions one at a time?" Mark requested.

"Sure."

The questions and answers lasted all afternoon, the discussion of one question leading to others, and had to be suspended to go to church that night. At times, Matthew joined in the questioning. Before leaving for church, Pastor Smythe made a date with them the next Sunday morning in his study before church. They made a copy of the questions in the church office.

Jocelyn really didn't like these new developments in Mark's life, especially these meetings with Pastor Smythe. It was much harder to ignore what was being said when it was just the six of them. Occasionally, what was said piqued her interest. Matthew didn't believe either, so at times they commiserated. Matthew had to go to his next training, while Mark and John had to go to New Mexico for some mysterious reason. That left just her and Dad. It was a very uncomfortable two hours at church that morning.

~ *8* ~

Jocelyn's graduation was coming up. There was no doubt Mark could attend. He was looking forward to it, as he figured her bachelor's degree as the halfway point to their wedding. She was graduating with honors, even though she had missed classes during her recovery from their fall. Mark and John argued about what he should wear to best honor her in this achievement. He thought of wearing his Navajo dress and jewelry. John said he should wear a plain suit or his tuxedo. He asked Phillip, who thought it should be his Commander's uniform. He asked Jocelyn.

"I don't care. You can go naked and kiss me."

"Jocelyn, I'm being serious."

"Okay." She took four cards and wrote Commander on one, Navajo on another, Suit on the third, and Tuxedo on the fourth. She turned them over and shuffled them. He added some blank cards and shuffled them again. She closed her eyes. He spread them out. She dropped her hand on one and turned it over: Commander.

"I hereby declare that you shall attend as Commander Denton. You shall sit with my family in my place in the family order and dance with me at the party afterward."

"You know I can't do that."

"I know, but soon we shall. Mark, when we get married, I want to go somewhere private where we can do all these things like dancing and swimming."

"And hugging and kissing."

"I'm glad you're my friend."

"So am I. I'm dreaming."

"Not a pipe dream but a future dream."

He got up and left, and she followed. They looked for someone, anyone to keep them apart. They found Winnie and discussed her graduation party.

The graduation ceremony was a lot of music and talking. Mark watched Jocelyn or looked in her direction the whole time. The rest washed over him. When she received her diploma, he stood and yelled her Navajo name. People behind him were amazed at this dignified Commander in dress white uniform, including gloves and sword, yelling like that.

Afterward, when everyone was congratulating and hugging her, Mark looked into her eyes and said, "Four years."

"Yes." A sigh escaped her. At the party, he just sat there, watching all she did. When she came near, they either said, "Four" or held up four fingers. He left feeling contented. She had been accepted in the master's program in chemistry and would start in the summer semester.

One evening, they were sitting in the porch swing, talking. "Mark, you don't seem as…well…you don't seem to have to leave so suddenly. You seem more at peace. More like your old self."

"Yes. With Jesus in control of my life, the lust does not overtake me so much. I still have to pray it away sometimes, but I am more at peace. Having Jesus is very peaceful. Have you thought about having Him in your life?"

"Well. Subject change."

He prayed that she would accept Jesus as her Savior soon.

"Why do you sit at my feet when you propose and times like that?"

"To honor you as my woman. I'm putting myself in subjection to you, to your wishes. When I propose to you, I'm putting my self, my heart, my life in your hands. I am at your mercy. You are the woman. You have the power. I'm offering myself as servant to your power."

"Mark!" She stared at him. "Is that a Navajo belief?"

"Yes. We're a matriarchal society. I'm here to serve you. You're in charge."

"I like to think that you're in charge. Would the woman make the plans for the date?"

"At least have veto power."

"Would you accept me if I bossed you around?"

"You're not like that. Subject change. John has found a lady he wants to know better. He wants to double-date. Is that okay?"

"Sure. It might be easier because I can have someone to talk with when I need to."

"Good. What about lunch after church tomorrow? We can meet her. Maybe come here to talk."

"Sure."

Jocelyn liked Amy. She was like Winnie in some ways, they were both black and had a similar outlook on life. After lunch, they spent the afternoon talking on opposite benches in the shade of an old tree in the garden, the men on one bench and the women on the other. They had supper with Jocelyn's family then went to church.

After he got home, Mark called Jocelyn to see what she thought about the date.

"I enjoyed John much more than when he was just a shadow in the background as our chaperone. I like Amy too. I think it will work well. Mark, how's your arm? It's still in a sling. Does it hurt you?"

"I still have to be careful, but it will be fine. Do you still have headaches?"

"Only when it's damp. I wonder what this winter will be like. What about you?"

"I can't read for long periods yet. Good thing I'm a fast reader. See you next week. Take care. I love you."

"I love you too. Have a good week. Bye."

"Bye, *Little Flower*."

In May, Phillip was not feeling well, so he went to the doctor, who did some tests. He had had a mild heart attack. They made changes in his diet and routine, and he started walking more.

A couple of weeks later, he was heading to Hartford to close his office for the summer when he had some pain. He pulled to the side of the road. With difficulty, he dialed 911. The operator kept talking to him until the state trooper located his car, took his phone, and talked with her. The ambulance arrived shortly. The trooper stayed with the car, located Mary's number in Phillip's phone, and told her to go to the hospital and that a tow truck would take the car to her house. Mary called her office and arranged for someone else to meet her two clients and show the houses she had lined up for them. Someone took her to the hospital and sat with her. The children came and went during the day, trying to care for her between classes.

The doctor told her that it was a heart attack. They inspected his blood vessels and found some blockage, which they cleared with the balloon procedure. Phillip improved, and they sent him home. One of the children was with them most of the time. At night, the boys took turns with him, and the girls took Mary to bed; she slept from exhaustion.

Mark came to see Phillip and Jocelyn as much as he could. John offered to spend the nights with him. Everyone agreed that it was not necessary.

Phillip improved. The surgeon scheduled open heart surgery for June fourteenth. June first he had a good day. On the second,

James helped him to the rose garden terrace to enjoy the glorious spring with the roses. He had a good day.

In the middle of the night, Mary awoke to find Phillip struggling. She called 911 and called on the intercom for James, the only son home. She threw on a robe and tried to help Phillip. James and the girls tried to help. Mary told them to get dressed so they could let the EMTs in and take her to the hospital.

After the ambulance left, Mary got dressed, and the family drove to the hospital. The doctor greeted them and took them to a conference room.

"I'm sorry, Mary. Phillip is gone."

"No! No! He was better. James, you took him outside."

"Yes, Mother. You sure doctor? Can't you resuscitate him?"

"We tried."

"Mother?"

"James?"

"Doctor?"

The family huddled around Mary in pain, confusion, and tears. Finally, they started to leave.

"Doctor, what do we do now?" Mary asked.

"Go home and rest. Let me know which funeral home you want me to send him to."

"Funeral home?"

"What's going on?" Matthew rushed in.

"Dad had a heart attack," James lamented.

Matthew looked at the doctor, who shook his head no. He looked at his sisters clinging to each other in tears and his Mother who was being held up by James.

"You mean…?"

"Yes, Matthew. Take your mother home. Let me know which funeral home to send your father to," the doctor said.

"Funeral home?"

His sisters let out a wail. Jocelyn hugged Matthew.

"May we see Phillip?" Mary asked.

"Mary, I don't think that's a good idea."

"Mother, he won't look natural," Matthew objected.

"I want to say good-bye."

"Mary, you really don't." The doctor tried to dissuade her.

"Yes, Doctor, we really do need to see him and say good-bye now."

"He's over here," the doctor relented.

Mary and the children gathered around the bed. They straightened his body and his pajamas. They each kissed him and told him they loved him. They replaced the sheet over him and went home.

Mark wanted to take Jocelyn in his arms to comfort her but knew he dare not. They were both vulnerable. He had to be strong for them. They sat in chairs near to each other and talked. He sang Navajo lullabies to her.

The family was discussing the funeral.

"When's Robert coming?"

"Who's picking them up?"

"Them?" Brianna asked.

"He's bringing Thomas."

"Oh, yeah. I forgot."

"Mark said he and John would pick them up," James stated.

John helped Winnie when they were there. Since John and Mark were not family, they could not get bereavement time off so they came to see the family when they could.

"Mark, let's go on a date."

"John? You're my friend but…"

"You and Jocelyn, Amy and me. How about a picnic at that park with the great view of Long Island Sound?"

"Whew. For a minute there I was worried about you, Black Man."

"Really, I'm serious. All you and Jocelyn have been doing is moping around here. You can cry just as well out there as in here. Maybe the good salt air will help you some."

"Well…"

"It's settled then. Show me again how you put on her jacket and escort her to the car." John urged them out.

"We need the picnic."

"In the trunk with your lantern. That's a fancy lantern. Here, Mark, we have to put the bad arm in first."

"Oh, yeah."

"Now let's go." John held the door for them. "We have to pick up Amy."

At her door, John helped Amy into her coat, and he held out his arm as he had seen Mark do for Jocelyn. He was awkward at helping her into the car. He appealed to Mark for help.

"Amy, would you mind?" Mark asked.

"Mind what?"

"I want to show John how to escort you to the car and seat you."

"I want to learn how to treat you like a lady," John said.

"Oh pshaw. I'm no lady."

"I would like you to be my lady."

"John!" Amy blushed.

"I want to learn how to be a gentleman like Mark."

A crowd started to gather.

"Gentlemen," Jocelyn said, "What if we go on to the park and practice there?"

Mark and John looked at the crowd growing about them and got into the car.

They practiced. They talked. They saw a submarine coming in. They laughed over the lantern. Amy learned why John wanted to learn about being a gentleman. They laughed over some of

Mark's fumbles over learning to escort Jocelyn. John felt his idea was a success.

A cold wind came up. They reloaded and picked up the picnic basket. John escorted Amy to the car, following Mark's lead. On the way back to their apartments, John and Mark discussed future double dates.

Jocelyn, her brothers, Mark, and Suzanne were selected as pallbearers at the funeral. Jocelyn was in a fog of grief during the funeral. Life seemed to stand still. At home, she played the piano—sometimes something sad, sometimes something violent like Wagner, and sometimes something frantic like Chopin.

They became worried about Mother.

"Hey, guys, we need to do something about Mother." Matthew worried.

"She won't leave her room."

"She won't come down to eat."

"She's not touching the trays we take in to her," Jocelyn added.

"She's the most depressed of us all."

"They were married a long time," Suzanne stated.

"They had been talking about taking a special trip."

"Yeah, for their anniversary."

"Hawaii or Cancun," Brianna explained.

"Her whole world has caved in."

"I can understand wanting to cave in the house," Robert proclaimed.

"That has to do with their Navajo belief in ghosts and ghost sickness."

"I know. I said I could understand that desire," Robert offered.

"Okay, guys, we don't need to argue," Brianna suggested.

"Back to Mother, if she doesn't start eating soon, I'll have to give her an IV. Is she drinking anything?" Matthew asked.

"Only sips. I have to keep reminding her to drink."

"Let's keep getting her to drink, add fresh apple juice, and clear soup in a cup, or I'll have to start an IV. I've got to go. Keep close track for me. I'll see you after work."

They all hugged him and promised to keep track of how much Mother drank.

Jocelyn wandered into the music room and started playing the piano.

"Hi, Jocelyn, how are you?"

"Hey, Mark. Have a chair. I don't know whether I'm glad to see you or not. This is a very depressing place."

"That's what Winnie said. How's your mother?"

"She's the most depressed one of all."

"Do you think she would see me?"

"We could try. Don't get your hopes up, okay?"

"Okay. Would you go to church with me Sunday?"

"That stuff again? How can you believe that when *He* took Dad away?"

"*He* helped me get through my grief. I was growling at John before I left for New Mexico. I prayed and read the Bible the whole time I was gone. Now I'm ready to face this cruel, mean world again. It was Satan who took your father away, but he's in heaven with God and Jesus. He's doing fine. It's us that have to live without him."

"How are we going to do that?"

"With the Holy Spirit's help. He's been through it with everyone else who has lost a loved one. He'll do it for us too."

"You'd better not talk like that with Mom. She'll throw you out her window."

"She likes challenges. I have one for her," Mark declared.

"What? Read the Bible? Been there, done that," Jocelyn sneered.

"No. Let's go see if she'll see me first. I'd like to see her alone if she will. Please?"

"Sure. Come on," Jocelyn answered.

Jocelyn knocked on her mother's bedroom door. "Mom?"

"What, Jocelyn?"

"Mark wants to see you."

"Okay. Tell him to wait. I'll let him in my study when I'm ready."

"Okay. I'll let him know," Jocelyn agreed.

Mark had gone to the window seat at the end of the hall and sat down, praying for Mary.

"Mark, she'll open that door when she's ready for you."

"Thank you. Maybe we can go for a little drive later?"

"Maybe." Jocelyn was noncommittal, she went downstairs.

Mark and Mary took a drive. When they returned, they were early for supper, so they went to the back parlor to join her children. Jocelyn and her siblings were grateful for the improvement in Mary. Matthew drew Mark into the library.

"How did you get Mother out, let alone to eat?"

"She's a businesswoman. I've seen her change from a sentimental mother to a sharp businesswoman in seconds. I gave the businesswoman something to do. She took over the grieving wife."

Several days later Matthew, James, Robert, and Mark had spent the entire night talking in the library. The next morning, Thomas and the ladies were in the back parlor talking.

Robert and Mark came into the back parlor.

"Robert, may I?"

"Sure."

Robert watched this very Navajo man in awe.

"Ladies and Gentleman, would you do Robert and I the honor of accompanying us to Phillip Meyers' church in his honor?"

He bowed with a flourish before them.

Jocelyn rose and curtsied with flourishes. "I would be honored to, Sir Pinto."

Brianna and Suzanne mimicked her. Not to be outdone, Mary joined her daughters, trying to out-flourish them all. They all laughed. Winnie checked on them as laughter was a big change from the crying she had been hearing from the family. Mark repeated his performance for her.

Then he added to all, "Ladies, this gentleman needs to retire to adorn himself properly. I suggest—only a mere suggestion as you ladies need no adornment—but should you so desire, go and add what little adornment you require and meet in the library at…What time, Robert?"

Robert joined in with his own flourishes and comments.

"Hey, Mark, I didn't know you were a Shakespearean actor."

"Many things you don't know about me, White Man. See you there."

During the service, the tissue box was passed, but the family seemed to drink in the message. Afterward, many people offered their condolences with sidelong glances at this strange man with all the jewelry, standing proudly with the oldest daughter.

At lunch, Robert said, "Mark, you have a name for Jocelyn, but you call us guys all White Man. Is that all you call me?"

"No. Your Navajo name is *Dream Teacher*, which means Dream Teacher."

The rest, including Winnie, asked him to name them. He gave each the name he used in his Navajo for them.

"Winnie, you have been like a second mother to me. I call you Little Mother."

"Mary, you are wife of my good friend Senator Meyers. You're also mother to my Little Flower. When I think of you, I call you Mother-in-law. In my culture, it would be my job as husband of the oldest daughter to care for you. I have promised myself to do all in my power to care for you."

The family was stunned.

Matthew said, "In my culture, it would be my job to care for my mother. Mother, I also promise to do all in my power to care for you. This will always be your home. To Mother," He raised a toast to her with the water as they no longer had wine at every meal.

"To Mother," The rest, even Thomas who had felt at a loss to help this grieving family, stood and toasted her. Then everyone was seated.

Mary rose. "Since we are in the toasting mode, I would like to toast my son-in-law. Jocelyn, it's out of your hands. He's my son-in-law, and I'm his mother-in-law. You have changed this family for the better in so many ways. I will only name two: you have taught us the value of other cultures, and you love my daughter beyond comprehension."

Mark blushed, looking only at Mary.

The rest shouted, "Hear. Hear."

"Who else would be willing to wait almost a decade for a lady to fulfill her dreams? But at the same time, you are fulfilling your own dreams. To Commander Mark Pinto Denton!"

The rest again stood and raised a toast to the blushing man dressed in his best Navajo clothes and all his jewelry.

When the table settled, Brianna asked, "What's my Navajo name?"

"You too are a flower—a delicate lily that grows in the dessert. You are Mariposa Lily."

"And me, Mark?" Suzanne asked.

"You are the rose that blooms on the cactus—much different from your mother's roses but still with the thorns. You are Cactus Rose."

"What about me?" James asked.

"Grandfather named you. You're interested in water usage, food production, life in an arid land. He called you *Life*, which means 'life.'"

"I remember him calling me that, but I didn't know what he meant. He would say '*Life*James' like it was all one word."

"What did he call me?" Matthew asked.

"*Physician*, which means 'doctor.'" Mark stood. "I've never made a toast, but I need to honor this *Physician*. He saved my life. When I was in the emergency room, all I could think of was my Little Flower. I hadn't caught her. I hadn't protected her. I had failed her. I needed to go to her, care for her. Those *stupid white men* wouldn't leave me alone. I fought my way to Little Flower. In doing so, I tore the IV needle out of my arm. *Physician* calmed me and told me that Little Flower was okay. He strapped me to the bed so I could not get away. If I had gotten away, I would have bled to death. *Little Flower*, thank *Physician* for saving me for you."

Jocelyn rose and thanked her brother.

"To *Physician*!"

"To Matthew!" The rest seated.

"Mary Meyers, my mother-in-law, I want to emphasize the agreement I had with Phillip Meyers. I love your daughter Jocelyn Jeanette Meyers very much. She's my Little Flower. I will honor her and care for her every day of my life. I promise to not touch her until the day you give her to me to be *My Wife*, my wife. At that time, I promise to gently love her and make many grand-babies for you. To Little Flower!" Then he sat.

"To Jocelyn!"

Jocelyn stood. "Mark, you are my enigma. You're so strong and yet so gentle, so commanding and yet so yielding, so precise and yet so full of abandon. From the moment I first met you, you've greatly enriched my life. You've taught me your culture by taking me to live with your family. You've been willing to learn my culture by letting my father and brothers teach you. You're so flamboyant and yet so scared. When you asked Father to marry me, you were so scared I thought you were going to faint."

"Hear. Hear." There was much laughter as the men remembered.

"But you just told us how much you wanted to care for me when I knocked you out." She saw Robert and Thomas, realized they had not been there when it happened and explained, "I was showing him ice flowers at the estuary. I slipped. Mark tried to catch me, and he slipped. My face here landed on his face there. Show them, Mark. His head landed on a rock. He was knocked out and brought in to the emergency room, crazy with a concussion because he was trying to care for me as he promised you, Mother. And yet he rebuked me for interrupting by only a look and a very slight turn of his body. I believe you, Mark, that you will always honor and care for me. You won't spend the night here in a blizzard for fear of dishonoring me and not caring for me. Commander Mark Pinto Denton, I love you and promise to marry you. I will wear your necklace."

Mark stood. "Jocelyn Jeanette Meyers, I give you my necklace as a promise to marry you after you have earned your doctorate and are working for Baker. I won't take you until then and you and your mother say you're ready." He walked around the table to her, removing one of his necklaces as he did so.

"But that's Grandfather's necklace. You bought the other one for me."

"It's the necklace he gave my grandmother when he…when they got engaged. He wanted me to give it to you while we were there. When he died, he told me it was for you."

He put it on Jocelyn. It was the closest he had been to her since they had been together in New Mexico. He blushed and stepped back. He sat on the floor at her feet as he withdrew something from his pocket. He made a long speech in Navajo. He held up a box and then opened it. There was a velvet box inside. He held up that box and opened it. She gasped! There was an elegant diamond ring. She looked at Mark and then back at the ring. He just sat there, holding the velvet box out to her. They locked eyes.

Mary stood and went to them. "Mark, are you giving this to Jocelyn as an engagement ring?"

"*Yes.*"

"I don't speak Navajo. Please tell me in English."

While still seated, he turned toward Mary, held out the ring box, and said, "My Mother-in-law, will you accept this token of my love for your daughter and my promise to marry her when you're ready to give her to me to be My Wife by placing it on the third finger of her left hand?"

"Mark, aren't you carrying this 'no touching' idea too far?"

"No!" He looked in Mary's eyes. "If I were to touch her right now, I would take her right now, right here in front of you."

Mary took the ring and placed it on Jocelyn's finger. Then she guided her to her chair and sat down in her own seat. The people were stunned. They sat there, and then they heard singing. Matthew went to look. Mark was singing and dancing with glorious abandon in the ballroom.

He ran up to Matthew and yelled at him. "Did you hear? She said yes! She loves me." He danced away yelling at the top of his voice. "She took my necklace. She took my ring. She loves me." He lapsed into Navajo.

Matthew steered him out the door and onto the terrace. They went for a very long walk. When he was no longer yelling and only occasionally beating the air with his fist and jumping around, Matthew asked, "Did you mean it when you told Mother you were ready to take Jocelyn right there?"

"Oh, yes. Oh, yes. I was so happy. When I put the necklace on her, a shock of electricity went through me. It didn't matter that you were right there. I had to get away. But I also had to give her my ring so everybody will know she's mine. My Little Flower will be taken by me one day." He bounded away.

Matthew remembered he had blushed and stepped back. This man's strength was greater than his desire. Mark was babbling and bouncing all the way to his car. Matthew watched—sure, the car was bouncing. He went to find Jocelyn. She was vigorously attacking the piano.

"Jocelyn, are you okay?"

"No. Yes. Did you see the ring?" She held up her hand. "Matthew, what do you do when you want someone very much? Mark was right. If he…we…I would have torn my own clothes off and attacked him right there. Do you know he never says 'I love you' unless we're *not* going to be together? Like if he's going to have duty or go to New Mexico. Do you think Mother understands?"

"She has six kids. I think so. Do you realize none of us are married? We're all in the same boat, and only Mark says what he's really thinking. He actually told on himself. We think we're so sophisticated. Did you hear him tell Mother he would make many grand-babies for her?"

"But did you notice how he promised to do it? Gently. When I tell him I don't want to wait, he tells me I have to. We have to honor our promises. Oh, Matthew, we have to make Mark's commissioning ceremony better than last time."

"And we don't have long to do it. Let's talk to Commander Bright and Admiral Sullivan."

They talked with Mark as well. He already had most of the arrangements made. He told them when his family was coming.

The commissioning ceremony for Commander Mark Pinto Denton went well. There was not the media circus there had been last time, but the pageantry was greater, including a sword arch from the ballroom to the terrace. There were more people present, and the refreshment table was outside. There was a butler and maids, a chef and cook's helper. The Meyers men and Thomas were in tuxedos, and the ladies, including Winnie, were in formals. Mark was pleased, so Jocelyn was as well.

The uncles were surprised he used his full name at this commissioning.

"Will you use your Navajo name next time?" Uncle Raymond asked.

"I'm considering it. *Little Flower* wants to change it though," he said, looking at her on his arm.

"How do you want to change it?"

"Something that reflects this man's character better. He's not just a fish. He's strong and noble. He's gentle and kind."

Soon, the Meyers family and the Pinto family as well as their friends began to discuss the characteristics of appropriate animals, fish, and fowl, and compare them with Mark's character. They told stories about him to make their point. The choices narrowed down to Eagle.

Then they had a naming ceremony, the non-Navajo following the Navajo lead. They had their naming dance in the ballroom, the Navajo singing, the rest doing as told.

Jocelyn wanted him to drop Mark Denton, but he refused to deny his father.

"Remember, he made me just as I am going to make our babies."

He went to the legal office and had his name changed to Mark Eagle Pinto Denton.

Something else changed. Mark and Jocelyn were no longer fighting lust. They still stayed with their chaperone or double-dated. They still did not kiss, but they were able to be near each other without lust tearing them apart. Every time it surfaced, he prayed it away.

A couple of days later, Mark, John, Thomas, Robert, and James were sitting on the terrace laughing when Matthew, Jocelyn, Suzanne, Brianna, and their mother joined them. The men stood until the ladies were seated, except for Brianna who leaned on the back of Mark's chair.

"Whatcha laughing about, Mark Eagle?" Brianna asked.

"What it takes to get a man to accept Jesus as his Savior, Brianna Lily. Come sit by me."

"What does it take?" Matthew challenged.

"Coming face-to-face with myself," Robert asserted.

"Stripping the mask off."

"Acknowledging me for what I am," James added.

"Being hit with the truth."

"Finding the one who really cares," Mark emphasized.

"Jesus did that to you?" Matthew asked.

"Yeah."

"For me," Thomas declared.

"Sure did."

"Yep," James expressed.

"And more."

"All of you?" Mother asked.

"Yes, Ma'am," John continued.

"Yeah," Thomas replied.

"Yes."

"Yes, Mother."

"Yes, Mother."

"He's taking over my family," Mother complained.

"Best takeover that ever happened to me."

"Yes. I was searching for something better than the mess I was making of my life," Robert agreed.

"Robert, your life was not a mess."

"Mother, you really don't want to know."

"Robert, you were a good boy."

"I was a filthy, rotten, no-good scoundrel. I could have gone to jail for the things I did. James, how many times a week did you have to lie for me?"

"Oh, fifty on a normal week," James answered.

"You're lying to me now," Mother charged.

The brothers looked at each other, "Naugh."

"James?"

"Yes, Mother, me too. I'm probably worse than Robert because I gave a better show, but it was all hypocrisy. Since I accepted Jesus, I don't feel I have to use a woman anymore. I'm looking at church for a real angel like Robert and Thomas and John have found. I'm praying hard for God to clean me up so I can deserve her."

"James, what about me?" Jocelyn asked.

"You're no angel, Jocelyn. Oh, you didn't like guys, but you were an alcoholic like us and, boy, did you tell tall tales. You made up some whoppers. It's a good thing you didn't know what we were really doing."

"Remember me playing with you?" Robert asked.

In a small voice, Jocelyn said, "Yes, and you, too, James."

"Yes. I'm sorry Jocelyn. Will you forgive me? I have been freed from those demons. I'd like to help you get freed from yours as well," James proposed.

"Me, too, Jocelyn. I'm so sorry I ruined our lives. Would you forgive me and let us pray for you?" Robert asked.

Mary Meyers got angry. "What are you saying?"

"Remember that nurse we pushed off the roof?" James asked.

"You didn't push her"—Matthew cut in—"She was chasing me. I was going to tell on her when I learned what she was doing to you. I ran on to the roof and sidestepped, so she couldn't catch me. She kept going off the roof. That rotten girl went with her too."

"You mean we didn't kill her?"

Robert and James looked at each other.

"But I remember pushing them."

"So do I."

"No. That's one thing you're not guilty of. But I feel guilty for letting it happen to you," Matthew lamented.

Suzanne asked, "Did you do things to me? I remember Robert playing with me."

"You were so little. I threw up when I remembered. That's why you keep everyone out and can't stand anyone close. Mark calls you Cactus Rose because you are so thorny."

"I want to be freed from my demons," Suzanne requested.

"So do I," Jocelyn agreed. "I drank to try to forget those memories and the nightmares they caused."

"Like we did," Robert agreed.

"Wait a minute," Mother demanded, "What are you saying?"

James explained, "That nurse fondled us, and made us do it to each other and her girl."

"That's why we didn't like her," added Robert, "That's why the gardeners found them in the bushes."

"All of you?"

Matthew said, "Not me. Just James, Robert, Jocelyn, and Suzanne. I learned about it from James. I was headed to tell you when the nurse and her girl went after me. I ran to the roof, sidestepped their grasp, and they slid off."

"That's how they got in those bushes? Phillip, the police, and I thought it was someone else who came and killed them, or suicide, or something."

The group sat in silence. Those who didn't know about this past horror in their lives were stunned. Those who remembered were saddened by those nightmare days.

James lamented, "I should have gone to the mental hospital then. I was searching for relief and didn't find it until the other day when Thomas helped me accept Jesus."

Robert added, "I did all those terrible things because of that nightmare. I went to New Mexico searching for peace. I thought I would find it in Mark's Navajo beliefs. Mark, I envied you and your family their serenity, but what I have found in Jesus is so much greater. This is not just a band-aid over the cancer—it is radical surgery. My whole way of thinking, my whole life, even who I am has changed."

"I want that change," Suzanne requested. "I really don't like who I am."

"Me too," requested Jocelyn and Brianna.

Thomas led them in prayer. The others accepted Jesus as their Savior after further discussion, including Rose's brothers.

Jocelyn sat there in silence. She was at peace for the first time in her life. She looked at Mark and Brianna talking. She understood! What he had said after it happened to him made sense. Her reticent Navajo had bubbled over with joy. She was experiencing joy as well, but hers was quiet. Not her usual fluttery excitement over things, but a calm quiet peace like a pond on a still day. She really didn't hear the commotion around her. She kept looking at Mark.

He looked over at her, "How are you?"

"Peaceful. You were like a bubbling brook. I feel more like a quiet pond." They drank in each others eyes.

His mother and uncles came to the group. Everyone started dancing in the joy of their salvation. The Navajo taught the rest the simple steps of a round dance in celebration. They made an open space on the terrace, by moving the chairs and the group danced.

Brianna asked, "You two going to join us?"

Mark looked at Jocelyn, "No. We'll stay here. You go on."

Mark and Jocelyn sat and looked in each others eyes. Occasionally they talked, but Jocelyn didn't really want to talk, she wanted to think.

Because of a cold wind that came up, everyone else started to go in. Brianna came back to them. "Hey."

Mark smiled at her, "Hi."

"Aren't you two getting cold?"

Mark looked at Jocelyn, "Want to go in? We could sit in the music room."

"Mark, I think I want to go to my room. I think I want to read the Bible. Where did you start reading, at the beginning?"

"No, the beginning starts with creation. The Book of John is a better place. Do you have a Bible in your study?"

"No. Maybe Robert will let me use his."

"Let's go talk to Robert. I will bring you one later."

They talked with Robert, who had some booklets which only had the Gospel of John.

Jocelyn and Mark followed Robert to his room. He gave her one, but Mark already had a full study Bible like Robert had, so didn't take one. Robert and Thomas got their supply to hand out to everyone who did not have a Bible, and went back downstairs to give out their Booklets. Mark took Jocelyn to the door to her study.

"I'll return soon with a Bible for you like Robert has. Jocelyn, you don't know how happy I am for you."

"Yes I do. I could see it in your eyes. Mark, what will this mean for us?"

"A better marriage when you are ready."

"You still want to wait?"

"You are even more worth the wait than ever. I have been praying for this day since I got saved." His eyes portrayed his love for her as he turned and left.

She went into her study and sat on the couch, holding the Booklet. She thought and prayed.

Soon Mark returned with a Bible for her in a nice leather cover with her full name printed in gold. When she answered his knock, he handed it to her and left. He joined his family downstairs.

Jocelyn thanked him, closed the door, and put both Books on her desk. She took a hot, soaking bath, thought about her life, and prayed. Things she had heard at church and in the Bible study in the pastor's office with Mark and her father came back to her. If asked at the time, she would have said she hadn't heard a word, but some things had lodged in her mind. Sometimes she could hear the pastor's voice as he had said it. She ended up in bed, thinking, sleeping, waking, and thinking some more.

In her reverie, she thought of Marcie. Her deterioration had been hard for Jocelyn to accept, so she had stayed away from her. It went against all that Jocelyn had been taught. According to conventional wisdom, Marcie should be fine. The conviction of the rapist should have removed the problems caused by his actions. The abortion should have removed the problem of the pregnancy. The result should have outweighed the bad, but that wasn't what happened for Marcie. The bad so overwhelmed her that she was helpless.

"Like James! What had he said? He didn't get relief until he believed in Jesus. Robert! Robert said the same thing. Maybe Marcie needs Jesus!"

Jocelyn got a robe and slippers on and padded across the hall to James' bedroom. She knocked on his door as she went in, "James? James?"

"Umhm?"

"James, did going to the mental hospital help you as much as finding Jesus?"

"What?" He turned on his bedside lamp. "Joss? What's the matter?"

"I need to talk to you."

He looked at his clock on the nightstand. "Jocelyn, it's 2:30 in the morning. Can't this wait a few hours?"

"No. Oh. Yes. But..."

"Give me a minute. Go in my study. I'll join you."

Jocelyn went through his bathroom.

"Hey, shut the door."

She closed the bathroom door to the study and the hall door. She got comfortable on his couch. Their suites were mirror images of each other, exactly alike except for personal belongings.

Generations of the family had lived in these suites, leaving their mark on the furniture, but very little had changed since the house had been built over 300 years before.

She could hear James as he used the toilet, and washed his hands and face. When he entered the room, she was looking out the window. "I like your view."

"You didn't get me up at 2:30 to admire my view. What's up?"

Jocelyn discussed her thoughts about Marcie with James. His knowledge was limited since he had gotten saved less than a week before. Jocelyn wanted answers, so James got Robert. They talked for a time, but ended up getting Thomas. The four talked for hours.

"Anything else, Joss?" James asked.

"I don't think so. At least not right now."

"Anyone else hungry?" Robert asked.

"You're always hungry," Jocelyn teased.

"Yeah. I'm gonna change and fix breakfast, you're welcome to join me," Robert said as he left.

They met in the kitchen, and Thomas and Robert made them breakfast. Before they finished, Winnie came in to prepare breakfast for everyone.

Robert told her she had four less to fix for. Jocelyn said that it was six because Robert and James ate enough for four. They laughed and joked, but Jocelyn said she wasn't going sightseeing, she was going to contact Marcie instead.

When it was a reasonable hour to call, Jocelyn called Marcie's house. The phone was disconnected. She went to the house. They had moved. It took almost a year to find Marcie and get to see her. Jocelyn talked with Mrs. Rogers many times before Marcie was willing to see her. Even then it took several months to reconnect, but over that time, Marcie noted differences in Jocelyn. Over the following year, Jocelyn was able to lead Marcie to Jesus and start a weekly Bible study in the Gospel of John with her.

Mark started noticing changes in Jocelyn right away. She wasn't as caustic and sarcastic in her remarks.

The Sunday after her salvation, Jocelyn was sitting beside Mark in church waiting for the service to start. She looked at the Bible Mark had given her. "Mark, how did you get the Bible engraved so quickly? It usually takes days to get it done."

"I got it for you and had it engraved when I got mine. I wanted to give it to you then, but something made me wait. I have kept it in the center of my dresser all this time. Every time I would see it, I would pray for you to be saved. Jesus has answered my prayers. May we have a Bible study together?"

"I'd like that. Maybe this time I'll pay attention."

They laughed, remembering the Bible studies in the pastor's office after Mark got saved and her boredom. He watched her during the service and realized she was paying attention for the first time. On the way to lunch, she wanted to discuss the meaning of the sermon. This became a habit for them. She seemed like a thirsty sponge to Mark—eager to soak up the truths of God.

Her siblings and Mother joined them in their Bible study. Everyone was surprised that Mother invited Winnie to join them because she had always been adamant about keeping servants in their place.

One of the nicest changes Mark saw in Jocelyn was her lying seemed to disappear. Most of her lies were so far-fetched that they were readily noticeable. Many made him laugh, but some caused trouble between them. He confronted her on it.

"Why did you tell me that you had an agreement with your parents to not kiss before the wedding?"

"It kept you at bay, didn't it?"

"Yes, but you telling me that you didn't want to kiss until our wedding would have done the same thing. Any more lies?"

"None I can think of."

"How did you accept me?"

"Because I could trust you."

"So I'll need to be sure you're not lying to me so I can learn to trust you."

"I'm sorry," Jocelyn apologized.

"Tell me when you realize that you've lied. It hurt me when I realized you had lied to me and you lied often, why?"

"It kept the guys away. Most guys would leave me alone when they realized I lied to them, but you wouldn't leave. I'm sorry. I promise to try not lying any more."

Jocelyn was still grieving over her father when she was due to start her master's degree program. She went to her academic adviser and asked if she could wait until the fall semester to start. Because of her record, they readily agreed. She again excelled. She took a very heavy load and accelerated her program. She graduated in eighteen months.

For this graduation, Mark again wore his full dress uniform with his sword. He yelled, "*Little Flower!*" when she received her diploma. When Mark was congratulating her after the graduation ceremony, he said, "I think you were very anxious to finish."

"No. To kiss you, Captain Pinto."

"I don't have the results of that test yet."

"You took the exam, didn't you?"

They both laughed, remembering his treatment when he made Commander, the review board certain he had cheated. He did very well on the test and was made Captain.

When they had the commissioning ceremony for Captain Mark Eagle Pinto Denton, his uncles and mother again came. Robert had brought his fiancée Miriam Camack to meet his family. Somehow Jocelyn thought it was more a family gathering, including all of the pageantry accompanying this commissioning. Mark had achieved his goal to be a young Navajo Captain of a submarine. He seemed to enjoy being Captain of his submarine.

One day, they were sitting on the porch swing.

"Jocelyn, why do you call this a porch swing? It's on the terrace, and you don't have a porch."

"I don't know. That's what they call it at the store. Mark, it almost seems like your men are children with petty grievances and squabbles."

"Maybe some men haven't grown up. They're getting better though."

"Do you want a large family?"

"As many as you'll give me. What about you?"

"Yes. But I don't want them cared for by a nurse. I don't want anything to happen to them, like what happened to me."

"I've been thinking about home schooling them and taking them with me when I go…places." He almost slipped and talked about his ranch.

"Sorry, I shouldn't think about making babies."

"It's not long now." He wanted very much to kiss her. "Good-bye, love." He went home and dreamed of her that night.

Jocelyn was accepted readily in the doctorate program. She had not worked on it long before Baker contacted her about working for them. She started working with the proviso on both sides that she complete her doctorate.

She asked only one question: "What will happen when I get married and get pregnant?'

"We have less hazardous work if that happens. Do you foresee that in the near future?"

"I'm engaged." She showed her ring.

"Do you have a date set?"

"A year or two."

"Keep us informed if you might be pregnant."

"I will."

Mark and Jocelyn were talking one day. "Oh, Jocelyn, one more step accomplished."

"Yes, dear. What do you think about Robert's children's home? Have you ever thought about adopting? In many ways, you have adopted all of your men you have commanded."

"I've never thought about that. Do you want to adopt some of our children?"

"What I'm thinking about are all those children that the police keep bringing Robert to care for in the children's home. He says that some of them are going to need homes. He can't adopt them all. Those children are already here. They need homes through no fault of their own. You could teach them to be Navajo—"

"Only the boys. I don't know how to be a girl."

"Mark, you interrupted! You are becoming too Meyers. I want you to keep your Pinto."

"Sorry."

"Do you think your mother would help me with the girls?"

"She's helping Robert, living at his house."

"I know, but I could call her, and when we visit she could teach me. Let's call and ask her."

"But, Jocelyn, I want to make our babies."

"I want to also. These would be in addition to every baby we make."

"I'll think about it."

Mark's boat went on sea trials just after he took the Rear Admiral exam. His Rear Admiral commissioning was held at the Submarine Base. His mother and uncles again came.

"Rose, may we talk?"

"Of course, My Daughter-in-law."

"I want to hear about all of the children Robert has."

"How long do you want to talk? What is your question, My Child?"

"If Mark and I adopt a girl from you, would you help me to teach her to be a Navajo lady? Mark knows how to teach the boys, but I would need to learn how to teach the girls."

"What about your own children? Will you teach them Navajo Way?"

"Oh! You're right. I'll need to learn anyway. So will you teach me?"

"It will be hard to teach them to make bread and mutton stew with you living here. If you bring them to visit me, I can teach them those things I cannot teach you on the phone."

"Okay, that will work. We'll need to talk with Mark to schedule their visits."

"We have already talked. Mark asked me years ago when you came to visit."

"Did he know then we would get married?"

"It was before he asked you. He was still assuming. He has matured greatly."

"I hope I have too."

"Yes, My Child."

"Thank you."

"We will not come any more for his navy. Next time, it will be for your wedding."

"I'm looking forward to it."

"Let me tell you about ram and ewe, red and white."

Rose's instruction was very thorough.

"Now, My Child, you are ready to be taken by My Son. I will instruct you more then. I will instruct him more as well."

She held Jocelyn's face in both hands, kissed her on both cheeks then left the room. For a while, Jocelyn thought about what she had learned before she too left.

Mark made Rear Admiral a year before she graduated as Dr. Meyers. At her graduation, Jocelyn, James, and Matthew laughed about the fact that they now had three doctors in the family.

"Jocelyn, when do you want to get married?"

"Oh, Mark, I don't know. Is it really time?"

"Yes, Jocelyn. It's now my time to take you. When will it be?"

"May we talk with Mother?"

"Yes, but don't make it too long. I've been very patient for years. My patience is at an end. My expectation is here."

"Let's go talk with Mother."

"Now." He got up and headed to her mother's office and knocked on the door.

"Yes."

He waited.

"What do you want?"

"To take your daughter."

The door flew open.

"Mark, what do you mean?"

"I want to take *Little Flower*. She has finished her dream. Now it's my turn to have her."

"Mark, will you wait for a wedding?"

"Yes. When?"

They had never seen him so demanding. The three discussed dates. Mary called a family conference to discuss dates.

Mark was adamant that it be soon. "I have waited nine years. You knew I was waiting. Why do you want to wait more?"

"We need a dress."

"I have it made. What else?"

"Invitations."

"What else? I'll hire the people to make your wedding, but I want it soon."

They agreed on a date two months away. Mark refused them any more time. He took Jocelyn and her mother to a dressmaker with whom he had already talked about what he wanted. Jocelyn tried on the dress he had had made. She requested lace on it. After they left, she made him stop the car.

"Mark, how did you get the dress to fit so well?"

"Remember that blue dress I like so much?"

"Yes."

"Winnie gave it to me, and I gave it to the dressmaker. You may have it back. It's there beside your mother."

Mary said, "Mark, I've never seen you so impatient."

"Impatient! Nine years isn't impatient!"

"Mark."

"Yes, Jocelyn!"

"Why are you angry?"

"You want me to wait more. I have fulfilled my part of the bargain. I want my reward. You knew. Why is this so hard?"

Jocelyn and Mother looked at each other.

"Mark, I'm afraid. I don't want you to do to me what my brothers did."

"*Little Flower*, I'll kiss you once at the wedding. On the honeymoon, you'll tell me what pleases you. I promise to be very careful and gentle with you."

"Mark, you're right. We're acting like a fact is a surprise. Like when I went to your home in New Mexico, you told me what to expect, but I didn't accept it. Mother, how soon can we get the invitations printed? Mark, let me see your calendar."

He got his phone and opened his calendar. She saw notations on it.

"Mark, what are these?"

"Your red and white."

"You're already keeping track?"

"Yes."

"When do you want to get married, Mark?"

"Here. It's just after your white, so we will not make our first baby the first time I love you. It gives us a month to learn how to please each other with a few days off for your red, before your next white."

Mary stared at him. "What are you talking about, Mark?"

"You've had babies and don't know this?"

"No, tell me."

"When she gives the white flow is when we will make our babies."

"White flow?"

"Between your red flows."

He was embarrassed.

"What date is that?"

He told her, and they agreed, so it was settled. They went to the printer. He showed Jocelyn and her mother his three top choices for invitations. They decided on one. He gave the date and time, and Mary gave the number of invitations wanted. The invitations were ready in a week. Mark's Yeoman made the address labels on Mark's home computer. Several of Mark's men helped put the labels on the invitations.

"Mark, you shouldn't make your men do this."

"They volunteered when they learned I was getting married."

"You told them?"

"No, John did."

They were ready for the wedding in three weeks.

~ 9 ~

Mark retired as Rear Admiral Mark Eagle Pinto Denton the day before their wedding. That noon, Mark took Jocelyn and her family, the members of his family present, and some close friends to Martha's Vineyard for lunch on his Admiral's yacht. Upon returning, the yacht was tied up at the Meyers' dock. After the civilian party left the boat, there was a brief ceremony, which ended Mark's command of the vessel.

The wedding party changed clothes and then had the rehearsal and the rehearsal dinner. Before he left, Mark and Jocelyn were talking in the swing.

"Dr. Jocelyn Jeanette Meyers, are you ready?"

"Why don't I just kiss you and get it over with?"

"In the morning, you will. What will we say then?"

"We'll think of something. I hope I don't mess up my speech."

"You won't, Brianna has helped you with it every day."

"Where are we going on our honeymoon?"

"Away from everyone."

"New Mexico?"

Mark just smiled.

That night, Jocelyn lay there thinking of the last nine years. Some had been very good. Some had been very bad. It was almost over. She missed her father and Mark's grandfather. It would have been nice to have them here, but tomorrow she would finally marry Mark. She laughed that now she would know what his arms and legs looked like. She wondered what lovemaking with him would be like. She knew he would be tender and gentle with her, but she had heard horror stories. She was still afraid of him touching her.

Suddenly, her radio came on. It was morning—the morning of her wedding to Mark. She got up and bathed in the special bubble bath she had been given at her bridal shower. She put on the special underclothes for her dress. The dress was beautiful: white satin with lace at the throat and sleeves. She was wearing her necklace and earrings from Grandfather. Her sisters, dressed in their bridesmaids' dresses, came in and fixed her hair. Mother came in and inspected all three daughters. They were ready. It was time to go downstairs to Matthew who was going to give her to Mark, along with Mother. Mother and Jocelyn walked arm in arm down the stairs; her sisters preceded them.

Matthew hugged her, "You look beautiful. Ready?"

"Yes."

Jocelyn took Matthew's arm and Mother's arm, and they escorted her to the ballroom, up the aisle, past the guests, to the place where she was to stand in front of Mark, who was seated on the floor. They hugged and kissed her. Matthew escorted his mother to their seats. Jocelyn looked at Mark, awaiting his speech.

He looked into her eyes. "Dr. Jocelyn Jeanette Meyers, would you do me the honor of joining my life, entering my home, bearing my children, being my wife for the rest of my life?"

"Yes."

"Then I pledge myself to you for the rest of your life."

She reached out to his hands as he raised them and stood, still looking into her eyes. They held hands as she said her speech.

"Rear Admiral Mark Eagle Pinto Denton, retired, would you do me the honor of joining my life, sharing my home, fathering my children, being my husband for the rest of my life?"

"Yes."

"Then I pledge myself to you for the rest of your life."

He stood there quietly, awaiting their first kiss. She gently took his face in her hands and slowly bent forward to kiss him for a long time. As she released him, he took her right hand and brought it around his left arm. They faced Pastor Smythe, who had watched in place, along with the rest of the wedding party.

"Dearly beloved, we are gathered today to unite this man, Rear Admiral Mark Eagle Pinto Denton, retired, and this woman, Dr. Jocelyn Jeanette Meyers, in holy matrimony."

The ceremony proceeded normally, except Mark had the rings. He laid them on Pastor Smythe's Bible at the appropriate time.

When it came time for him to kiss the bride, Mark took her face in his hands, slowly bent and met her lips with their second slow, satisfying kiss. As he moved his head away, she squeezed his hands. "We did it!" she whispered. They turned to face the guests and were introduced as Mr. and Mrs. Mark Denton.

He escorted her to their place near the refreshment table. His family followed, standing next to Jocelyn. Her family followed, her mother standing next to his uncle. Pictures were taken then Pastor Smythe led the way to the receiving line and out on to the terrace. The honor guard came last, forming an arch of swords for them to walk under from the door to the terrace. After they emerged from the sword arch, Mark turned, thanked everyone for coming, and told them to enjoy themselves, but he and his bride had a long trip ahead. Everyone called good-bye and waved as the white limousine carried them away to Trumbull Airport. It stopped at a small plane. Their luggage was transferred to the plane, and they took off.

"Mark, can you tell me now where we are going?"

"I can, but I won't. It's very private. There will be just you and me for a month."

"Who's going to cook and clean?"

"I will."

"Oh, Mark, you can be too reserved sometimes."

"Wait until we get there."

He put his arm around her and drew her close.

When the plane landed, Mark helped the pilot remove their things from the plane and turn it around. He unlocked the door to a house in a meadow with nothing else around then he picked her up and carried her in. They went down a hallway to a beautiful garden, which had a fountain, and set her down near it. He put their things inside the door and locked it.

He took her into a very large bedroom with a king-size bed. He took her in his arms and kissed her.

"Mark, I'm scared."

He gave her some tea.

"Do you want me to sleep in another room?"

"No. This is like the tea from the engagement ceremony."

"Yes. What do you want?"

"I don't know. I'm scared."

"Have some more tea. Want me to leave while you get ready for bed?"

"No. I want you to undress me, and I want to undress you."

He kissed her as he unzipped her dress. He carefully removed it and hung it up in the closet. When he turned back around, she was next to him.

"How do I get your shirt off?"

"Like a T-shirt. Over my head and then pull the sleeves."

"Mark, this is beautiful."

"My mother made it."

"It's…It's not cloth."

"It's bleached antelope skin. Mother has saved every antelope skin I have killed for food to make my white wedding suit."

"This fancy stitching?"

"Yes, she did that also."

"How do I get it off?"

He raised his arms and told her to pull it over his head then pull on the sleeves. He took it when he was out of it and hung it up. When he turned around, she was across the room.

"Jocelyn, I'll get out your nightgown."

He opened her suitcase and got out her gown and then got his pajamas out of his bag. He put on his pajama top then took her gown to her.

"Drink more tea."

He put her gown on her. He noticed the effects of the tea as she relaxed and removed his shoes.

"Are these antelope too?"

"Yes. My mother made these also."

He gave her another long kiss.

"Mark, how do I get your pants off?"

"Untie the bows just like my shoes."

She froze when she realized he had nothing on under the pants. He removed them, hung them up, and put on his pajama bottoms. He pulled the covers down, picked her up, laid her on the bed then covered her. He went around to the other side of the bed and got in.

"Mark, kiss me."

He did so as he caressed her.

"Are you okay?"

"Yes. Love me."

He smiled as she removed his pajamas and he removed her gown. He kissed her as he made love to her.

She was disappointed.

"Jocelyn, what's the matter?"

"I was expecting something more. I'm not sure what."

"Jocelyn, I'm being gentle with you. You're a virgin. I could hurt you if I'm not careful. It will get better as you get used to me."

In a small voice, she said, "I hope so. I'm getting hungry. I haven't eaten since this morning."

"I haven't eaten since the rehearsal dinner. Let's go eat."

"Where?"

"The kitchen. There's lots of food. Come on."

"But, Mark, I'm not dressed."

"There's no one to see us. You sit here and watch me make you an omelet. Oh, I need to get the food out of the entryway."

He didn't know how long the effects of the tea would last, but he was hoping she would get used to seeing him by then as he had no more. He went to get the food. It took two trips. She liked what she saw of his body in motion, the muscles strong and firm. He put the groceries away and made the omelet. Then he put it on only one plate. He filled one cup with coffee. He fixed the coffee as she liked it. He took them to the patio, sat down, and sat her on his lap. He started feeding her. Then she took the fork and fed him. They alternated feeding each other from the same plate, looking deeply in each others eyes, and giving each other sips of the coffee.

"Mark, do you like your coffee with cream and sugar now?"

"If you do."

"You're enduring my coffee?"

"Jocelyn, I endured nine long years without you. I can endure a small thing like cream and sugar in my coffee."

He kissed her, "Jocelyn, why were you dragging your feet over getting married?"

"I was afraid."

"Are you still afraid?"

"No."

They kissed. Loving did get better with each time they tried.

"Mark, will you hug me?"

"Sure."

"Ah. We do fit nicely. My head right here on your shoulder."

"Mmmm." He kissed her deeply.

She took his hand and studied his ring.

"When did you get our rings?"

"I went back to Samuel Nakai and got them the next day after you got the gifts for your family."

"Are these the ones you showed me?"

He held her hand and looked at her ring.

"Yes. This is the one I had you try on. I asked him to set this pair aside for me."

Then she compared his hand and his arm.

"I've been wondering what your arms and legs looked like under your clothes."

"Do you approve?"

"Oh, it wasn't that. I was wondering what color they were, the same or lighter than your hands."

"So what's the verdict?"

"Other than handsome, they're only a little lighter. Do you tan?"

"I don't know. I've never tried."

"Let's lie here on the grass and try."

"But it won't be fair."

"Why?"

"I'll be getting my back tanned, while you won't be getting any tan at all."

"Let me get on top."

"You want to try?"

"Yes."

It was very satisfying. Then they laughed that he still wasn't getting tanned.

They were snuggled together. Jocelyn asked him if he was going into politics now that he was retired. He had told her before that he couldn't while he was on active duty with the Navy.

"I don't know. I am so used to being in charge as an Admiral and ranch owner, I'm not sure I could cooperate like a politician has to in order to get votes on my bills. Your father talked with me about that when he was teaching me. I haven't thought about it since he died."

"Let's pray about it."

They did and received no clear direction. Many years later, after they moved to the ranch, the Farmington Republican Committee asked him to run for the New Mexico State Senate. He did, won, and soon gained a reputation for being honest, hard working, and plain spoken. His children were being home schooled, so the family moved to Santa Fé for the senate session and back to the ranch the rest of the year. He bought an old hacienda to live in while in Santa Fé.

Later he requested, "Teach me to swim."

She started looking for her swimsuit. He stopped her.

"Do we need it?"

"Well."

"Come on."

He led her to the pool. She led him to the deep end.

"Take a deep breath. Then we'll jump in."

They held hands and jumped in. He expected to touch the bottom, but she pulled him up.

"Move your feet back and forth. Move your hands in figure eights. I'll be right here, but you really won't go down."

He laughed, "Now what?" He quit moving his hands and legs and went under.

She pulled him up by his arms, "You gotta keep moving, silly."

"Okay."

"Now as you're *moving*, lay back."

He did. He laughed, and she joined him. He was moving across the pool on the water. She swam beside him.

"We're in the shallow end. Bring your feet under you and stand up."

He hugged and kissed her after he stood, his hand caressing her.

"Which do you want to do?"

"Both."

"I don't think we can in the water."

"Let's try."

They ended up in bed.

"I think swimming will take many lessons," he whispered into her ear.

Another day, she asked, "Now what do you want to do?"

"Dance. Teach me your slow sexy dance."

This was harder because she had to lead him in leading her. He kissed her and danced her to bed. At one point, she showed him what to do while he held her from behind. That was less successful. Then suddenly it all fell into place. She relaxed into him. They still ended in bed, but he was making the right dance moves to get them there.

"Jocelyn, I want to love you under the stars."

"Where?"

"On the grass in the patio."

She kissed him. He danced her out. Afterward, they lay there looking at the stars, talking.

One morning, he awoke to her inspecting him, her fingers feeling each muscle. He could hear her naming each one as she fingered it.

"Mark, remember when you said you like me soft and curvy, not with hard muscles?"

"Yes."

"Were you referring to your hard muscles?"

"Yes. I want you to look like you, not like me."

"So what's your verdict?"

He kissed her as he ran his hand down her. "I like the way you are."

"I like the way you are too."

He kissed her and rolled her over to make love to her.

"No, Mark. I'm not ready."

"You've been playing with me for a long time. Why aren't you ready?"

"You have to get me ready. I don't work like you do. You can just look at me and want me. I have to feel you petting me, understand?"

"Yes."

She combed her fingers through his hair. "Mark, do you want to grow your hair long like Grandfather now that you're not in the navy?"

"I never thought about it. What do you want?"

"How do you fix it?"

"I could show you with yours and some yarn, or rubber bands, or something to hold it."

"Isn't there some string in the pantry?"

"That will work."

They got the string and a chair. He sat her at an angle to the mirror. He talked with her about what he was doing as he did it. When he finished her hair looked like his mother's, except the binding was plain white twine instead of her colorful yarn.

"What do you think, Dr. Denton?"

"Mark, I never thought what my new name would sound like. It's nice. Say it again."

"Dr. Denton, would you wear your hair like this to work?"

"Oh, yes. It would work well. I have to have a net over it there anyway. Did you know I fix it in a bun for work?"

"No. This is a Navajo bun."

"Would you have to do this every day?"

"Not unless you really got wild and messed it up so bad I couldn't just comb it back into place."

"Would you keep my hair like this except the weekends?"

"Yes, Dr. Denton, I'll do this for you so you can save the world."

"How long would it take for your hair to be long enough for me to fix?"

"Hair grows about a half inch per month. You do the math."

"Turn around."

Measuring with her fingers, she figured.

"More than a year. You'll look shaggy till then. Does that bother you?"

"Does it bother you? You'll have to look at it."

"Then you'll look like the wild Indian they all think you are. I'll be able to run my fingers through your hair."

"Like this?"

He removed the twine and ran his fingers through her hair as he kissed her. She sighed into his arms.

They danced. They kissed. They swam. They hugged. They loved each other.

One day, his phone beeped at him. "*Little Flower*, we need to clean up the house and pack."

"Oh! It seems too soon."

"We will return often. Definitely, for all of our anniversaries."

"Thank you, *Eagle*."

They kissed, and she learned something about cleaning the house as she helped him. He did laundry. He did something to the pool and fountain. He cleaned the bathroom in their bedroom and the one in the pool room. He cleaned the bedroom and the kitchen and swept the rest of the house. She wondered what his Admiral would say about him doing all of this.

"Mark, does it bother you that I don't know how to clean and cook?"

"No. Does it bother you?"

"Well. If you're sure it's okay with you. It is woman's work. I guess you'll have to teach me, or do you have a housekeeper?"

"At the ranch house, I do."

They packed their suitcases, and they both heard the plane coming. She hugged and kissed him then took his arm, ready to leave.

He told her about everything she saw as they flew to the ranch house.

"Jocelyn, this is all my ranch. I told you we would see it. Here we are at the main house. I have some work to do in addition to showing you around. What do you want to do while I'm working?"

"I want to follow you. There are no secrets here like on your submarine, are there?"

He laughed, hugged, and kissed her. "No secrets. A lot of people for you to meet though."

He had introduced the pilot as Martin and told her of his other duties. Then they met the head foreman, Jonathan. There was a secretary, a bookkeeper, a housekeeper, gardeners, foreman of the stable hands, foreman of the cattle hands, foreman of the crop hands, and so many more that she was totally lost. They all called him Boss and her Mrs. Boss, even though he gave her name.

He had a meeting with all of the foremen. There was not a chair for Jocelyn, so he pulled her to his lap, his arms around her as he looked at the various reports. Each man discussed his area of responsibility. The stable foreman talked about mares with fancy names ready to drop foals. They all talked about sales and profits, soil and moisture.

Jocelyn really didn't try to follow what they said. She tried to read the reports, but Mark turned the pages too fast. Then she heard him say something about her. They were talking about showing her the ranch.

The meeting adjourned, and a meal was brought in. Someone brought her a chair. He teased the man that he liked holding her better.

"Shore, but the Misses may want to feed herself."

Jocelyn looked at Mark. Mark looked at her. They laughed; they had fed each other for a month. They all laughed, the rest not knowing what the boss thought was so funny.

After they ate, they started their tour. They saw orchards and fields of grain. They saw meadows with horses and large pastures with cattle. He kept saying, "And over that way is…" She realized the foremen were also giving him details on their reports.

When they got back to the house, he took her into a large room with a large desk, computer, bookshelves, sofa, chairs, and a wall of windows. He took her face in his hands and kissed her.

Someone walked in. "Oh. Sorry, Boss, I didn't know you were in here. I'll just put the mail down, supper's almost ready."

He looked at the housekeeper. "Thank you, Mrs. Pete."

He drew Jocelyn into a close hug and kissed her again. "Welcome to my ranch. *Little Flower*, I love you so much."

He picked her up and swung her around and then kissed her again.

At supper, they were talking about a certain mare probably dropping that night.

"Get me when it's about time. We want to watch," Mark requested.

"Yes, Boss."

They talked about other things.

After supper, he took her on a tour of the house, ending at a door, which he unlocked. He picked her up and carried her in.

"Welcome to my ranch."

He kissed her, let her stand, and showed her a suite of rooms with a living room, study, bedroom, and bath. She saw their suitcases.

"Maybe we should unpack."

"Mrs. Pete has taken care of it."

He opened a closet door, and she saw her clothes hanging on one side. He opened some drawers, and there were her things.

"I have servants like you."

"Mark, I never had anyone but Winnie."

"They will take care of us so when we come we don't have to worry about those details. I have you to care for now." He caressed her face.

"Mark, what were the men talking about when they said 'dropping a foal'?"

"Yes. Your mare's going to have her foal while we're here. Isn't that great? I've only seen one other born. *Little Flower*, may I watch when you have our babies and give them their first bath? I did it for Roger. I want to do it for our babies too."

He held her tightly, looking into her eyes.

"I guess so. I never thought about it."

He turned on a fancy stereo set and started dancing with her. He kissed and caressed her.

She stopped him. "Mark, you asked them to come get us. What if they walked in on us like Mrs. Pete did?"

"I locked the door. They have to ring the doorbell like at my apartment in Groton. This is my apartment. That was my office, but she puts the mail in there. Jonathan works some in there when I'm not here. But here they have to ring the bell, and I let them in. If I'm loving you, I will finish then we will get dressed and go watch. We'll have to stay out of the way. We'll get in a corner where we can see and watch your foal being born."

"But Mrs. Pete has a key."

"She only comes in when she knows I'm not in. No one will walk in on us."

He started dancing, kissing, and petting her again. She laughed and just enjoyed the moment with him.

They were sound asleep when the bell rang. He reached over, pressed a button, and said, "Thank you. We'll be there soon."

He urged her to dress warmly then led her to the fancy stables. It was obvious where the mare was: there were people standing around. There was soft indirect lighting in the walls near the ceiling. There was a thick layer of straw on the stall floor, and he led her to a corner at the tail end of a horse lying down on her side. She was a dark red. Jocelyn would have called it auburn on a woman.

Mark sat down and pulled Jocelyn down on his lap, both of them facing the tail of the horse. His chin rested on her shoulder, and his arms wrapped around her. He whispered into her ear about what they were seeing. She turned and whispered into his ear when she had a question.

The mare's sides started heaving.

"She's having a contraction."

Another came soon. Someone was timing them. The people in the stall were whispering.

"She's dilating. See that hole getting larger?"

Jocelyn nodded her head.

"A hoof is poking out. Another contraction. The other hoof. The muzzle should come soon. Another contraction. Uh. The muzzle. Now it should go pretty fast. They're pulling on the hooves. I don't know what's happening."

They sat there watching as one of the men removed his shirt and covered his arm with an ointment. Then he pushed everything back in.

A man came over and sat next to Mark. "They's twins. Vet's trying to sort 'em out."

Mark had been excited, but now he was worried. He put his forehead on Jocelyn's shoulder and started praying in Navajo.

"I think he's got it. He's pulling on a pair of hoofs."

Mark raised his head, and Jocelyn could hear him say, "Thank you, Jesus. Thank you, Jesus."

"Mark, you're too tight. Mark, let me go. Mark, turn me loose."

"Boss."

"Yes?"

"Turn Mrs. Boss loose, you're squeezing her too tight."

"What? Oh! Jocelyn! Are you okay? Did I hurt you?"

"Mark, you hurt me. Turn me loose."

"Okay. I'm so sorry. I'm so sorry."

She turned her head to his ear. "Talk with me later."

"Sure. Oh, look, hooves, muzzle, eyes, ears, neck. Oh, *Little Flower*, look. You have a filly. Another one is coming."

He kissed her on the cheek.

"Aren't they beautiful?"

"Boss! Turn her loose! Here, Miss, sit beside him. He gets a little lost sometimes, but he's the best boss I ever had. You okay?"

"No. I think he bruised my ribs."

"He weren't trying to hurt yo. He just got excited. Hol on his arm. He can't get yo then."

"Thanks. I'm sorry, what's your name?"

"Pete, Miss. I'm gonna train yor fillies if yo keep 'em."

"Maybe you can help me train him." They smiled.

Mark kept talking about the foals being born, the men cleaning them, the mare getting on her feet and cleaning her foals, and the men guiding them to drink from her.

"Boss, that's all for tonight. We'll call yo when the next one's coming. Go on in and take Mrs. Boss. She's done in."

Pete helped her stand.

Mark finally looked at her. "Jocelyn, what's wrong?"

"Boss, I think you better carry her."

Mark picked her up and easily carried her to their suite. He put her down in their bedroom.

"Oh, wasn't that great?"

"Mark!" She held his face and put her forehead on his. "Mark, listen to me!" She didn't raise her voice, but there was an edge he had learned to attend to.

"Yes, dear."

"I think you bruised my ribs. You kept squeezing too hard."

"What?"

She had his attention finally. She removed her shirt. There were arm and hand imprint bruises across her rib cage.

"Oh! No! Oh, Jocelyn!"

"You have some medicine. Get it."

He put the medicine on her, put an old T-shirt of his on her, and they lay down. He kept apologizing. She covered his mouth.

"I love you. Now go to sleep."

She got comfortable and slept. It was late the next morning when she awoke. He had put more medicine on her and covered her bruises with the T-shirt. She got up and slowly got dressed. She wore the largest shirt she could find over his T-shirt. She went toward the kitchen. Many people greeted her. She smiled and slowly moved on.

She heard Mark talking in the conference room. She went in. There was now a chair next to his. She eased herself into it. He froze when he saw her.

"Oh, J—"

"Sshh." She put her hand over his mouth, looked him in the eyes, and said, "*Eagle,* you have a job to do. Do it."

He blushed, looked down, told the man to continue, and looked at him. The meeting was about over, but there seemed to be two more items.

"About Jose Mendez, he's a good worker, but his wife's sick."

"How long has he worked here?" Mark asked.

"At least thirty years."

"We'll retire him at full pay," Mark decided.

Jocelyn joined in the conversation. "Mark, what if he wants to return soon? How about adding a proviso that he's welcome to come back any time, since he's such a good worker? Don't say anything about his wife in relation to the retirement. Let him know what a valued employee he has been."

They agreed it was a good idea.

"Now, Jocelyn, what are you going to name your fillies?"

"I have no idea of good names. What are good suggestions?" She looked at Pete.

Several men supplied names. Pete cleared his throat. "What about the roan as Storm Cloud and the dun as Star?" He then gave their full registry names.

"Do those sound like good names to everyone?" Jocelyn asked. Everyone agreed.

"Fine, that's what we'll call them, Mark."

"Then you need to sign the registry papers, Miss."

"Why me? Mark's the owner." She was confused.

"No, Jocelyn. When I bought this ranch, I chose that mare for you. She's in your name. She has paid your master and doctorate degree bills. She's yours."

"You didn't do this today?"

"No."

"Oh, what do I do?"

They told her. She followed their instructions. Then they cleared the table, and lunch was served.

As they were leaving, Jocelyn followed Pete. "Pete. Pete!"

"Yes, Miss."

"Thank you."

"You're welcome, Miss."

"I'd like to see the next one too. But why do you say 'drop'?"

"'Cuz in the wild the mares usually don't lie down."

"They literally do drop?"

"Yep."

"You said something about training the fillies. What's that?"

"Well, I mostly train 'em for racing."

"How do you know if they would be good at racing?"

"You don't until you race 'em, but they have good blood and good lines. They might be good. Boss really don't like to race 'em. He's been sellin'. The older colts from the mare are winnin' races."

"Then how are you training them?"

"Mostly, I just help out in the stable, exercising and such, and gentlin'."

"Thank you, Pete."

"Yes, Miss." He glanced at Mark. "Boss," then turned and went to the stables.

"I think we have some talking to do." She took Mark's hand.

"Yes, dear." He followed her into their suite.

She sat on the couch and looked at him, waiting. He told her the history of the mare. The previous owners had raced many of their horses. That was one source of their income. The winners were considered good stock animals for producing future winners. Mark didn't like racing, but breeding and selling possible winners had produced a lot of income. This mare had been a winner, and her offspring usually became winners, so her colts brought high prices.

"You kept saying she was mine, but it didn't make sense to me, so I ignored it. How did you register her colts when I wasn't here to sign the papers?"

"You gave me Power of Attorney. Remember all of those papers I had you sign at the legal office?"

"What else did I sign that day?"

"You gave me control of the stud fees from the best stallion, which also belongs to you. He usually produces winners as well, so people pay a high price to let him take their mares."

"What kind of price?"

"Ten thousand dollars."

"May I see him?"

"You have. Remember the breeding field?"

"That's what you meant?"

"Yes. The men put the mares in there when we want him to take them then remove them when they're close to dropping."

"How do you know?"

"I have two women to watch them and keep track. They tell their foreman, who schedules the mares to be brought in."

"You said the horses were profitable. No wonder you need a secretary and bookkeeper."

"But the breeding stock is getting old. We need to change to show animals from racing animals."

"Do they bring the same prices?"

"No, but there's the same competition."

"May I see a show?"

"I'll schedule us to see one."

"Why did you say the foals paid for my schooling?"

"They did. When Phillip died, James and Robert asked me to help your family financially. Robert was the only one working then. Matthew and James each had another year of training to go. Suzanne had finished her second year. Brianna would start in the fall. My Mother-in-law didn't have that kind of income. Winnie gets the mail, so she has been giving me the school bills. I've also been putting some into her account regularly. When Matthew started working, I started cutting back on what I gave her. Please don't tell My Mother-in-law or Matthew."

"How did you do this?"

"My navy income was large. My retirement will have us living very well. This place has been very profitable for me. I consider it an investment to educate your family and a help to My Mother-in-law."

"Any other secrets?"

"My Groton house. If you don't like it, I'll sell it and buy what you like. It was paid for by the profits from the ranch. This place is almost paid off as well. I bought this as a retreat, especially the hideaway. That's where I would go when I got out of harmony. The Groton house I got for my privacy. I have lived next door to you for years but would not let your mother tell you so we wouldn't be tempted."

"Privacy? Next door? The nudist camp?"

"Yes. You'll check it out when we go back next week."

"Tell me about it."

"Well, there are about ten acres. There's an orchard, a garden plot, rose bushes—not a formal garden like you have—tennis courts, indoor pool, nine bedrooms. There's a gatekeeper's house, a pier, and a boathouse. I'm not sure what else right now."

"If I like it, may we keep it?"

"Of course."

"Mark, I want to see the foal born, but I'll sit beside you this time."

"Yes, dear. I'm so sorry."

"I know. You didn't mean to hurt me. You got excited over the fillies being born. That's one thing I like about you—your excitement over life."

"Is that all you like?"

"No. I like everything about you—your bearing, your gentleness, your strength, your peace, your love. Right now I don't know how I'll be able to love you for a while though."

"Yes, dear. Let's take a nap."

"That sounds good."

They watched the next colt come that night. Jocelyn sat next to Mark. She wouldn't let him touch her as he gave his excited commentary on the birth, but she held his arm, her head on his shoulder.

One morning after breakfast, Mark said, "Jocelyn, I have buyers coming today. What do you want to do?"

"I'd like to see the horses. I'm going to the stables."

"Okay. See you."

They kissed. He went to the house living room. She wandered toward the stables, looking at everything on the way. She looked at each of the horses.

Pete came to her. "Stay away from her."

"Why?"

"She bites."

"Are you busy?"

"Not right now. Whatcha need?"

"I'd like to see the horses."

"Wait a minute." He came back with a bag of apples and took her to a meadow. "I'm gentlin' these colts. Hold your hand out flat."

She did. He put a quarter of apple on it and told her to hold it out to the mare. The horse took the apple. He told her to pet her face.

"She's soft."

"Here, feed the colt and pet 'em."

"Oh, he's so soft."

She ran her hand along his neck. Pete kept putting apple pieces in her hand. She kept feeding and petting the foals and their dams.

"This is fun. They're so soft. Now don't let me keep you from your job."

"You're doing it."

"Me? Explain."

"This is gentlin'."

"I like your job. Oh, Mark's coming."

Several foals pushed against her to get some apple. She lost her balance. The foals shied away. Pete offered her his hand, but she didn't see it as she got up. Mark walked up.

"Boss."

"Pete. Jocelyn, are you okay?"

"Yes, Mark. Oh, you should pet the foals. They're so beautiful and soft."

"Jocelyn, don't get attached. I just sold most of them."

"Oh, but can't I enjoy the feel of them? Pete, I like your job. May I help you again when I'm free?"

"Shore, Miss."

"Jocelyn, we need to go."

"Okay. Thanks, Pete."

"Boss. Missus."

They talked as they walked back to the house. He promised to bring her to the ranch as often as she was free. The next morning, they left with Martin, Mark's pilot, for Groton.

When they got to Groton's Trumbull Airport, Mark carried the suitcase they brought back with them and took her to the taxi stand. He gave the address, but the cab driver did not know where it was.

"Do you know where the Meyers Mansion is?"

"No."

Mark directed him to his gate, paid him, and got Jocelyn and the suitcase out. Then he waved the cab on. He went to a keypad and passed a card by the reader. The gate opened. They went through. He pressed a button on the other side, and the gate closed. He escorted her along a winding driveway. Lights on motion sensors came on as they passed the sensors. He told her about the property as they walked along. When they got to the front door, she thought it beautiful, as the glass in it was worked in a butterfly pattern.

"Oh, Mark, did you buy this?"

"It came with the house. I have added or gotten rid of very little."

He passed his card by the reader twice. The door opened. He picked her up.

"Welcome home, *Little Flower*."

He kissed her as he stepped into the entry way.

"Thank you, *Eagle*."

He set the suitcase down and closed the door, but continued to carry her as he went from room to room throughout the downstairs. Then he carried her upstairs to each room. He ended the tour at the pool.

"Now, Dr. Denton, which bedroom do you want?"

"Your bedroom, Admiral Denton."

He laughed and kissed her. "I will share whichever room you choose."

"May we see the choices again, as I wasn't thinking of choosing as I looked before."

He slowly took her room to room, showing her all of the amenities of each one. They entered one she didn't remember from the first time through. It had a large walk-in closet with built-in storage, a large bed with a canopy top, a couch and chairs, a desk, a marble tiled bathroom, and a wall of windows overlooking the rose bushes.

"Mark, can anyone see us in here?"

"Not that I know of. Long Island Sound is that way. Your house is that way."

"Did you show me this room before?"

"No."

"Tease." She kissed him. "What about this room for tonight. Have you slept here before?"

"Every night. I wanted to see if you liked it as much as I do."

"Do you run around naked here?"

"Most of the time, unless someone is here working."

"Do you have servants here?"

"Only a gardener once a week and a housekeeper once a month. How do you like my Groton house?"

"Well, I'll have to see more of it to give you an answer."

"Fair enough. What do you want to do now?"

"A bath and bed. I'm tired."

"Are you too tired to love me?"

"Check my calendar. We're getting close to my white."

"That was over while we were at the ranch, and you were too sore to let me love you."

They bathed each other and enjoyed their first night in his home. She called it "Mark's Nudist Camp" in private.

The next morning, she got dressed. He teased her that he knew every inch of her anyway. She asked if he was going to show her around like that. He relented and dressed.

"Mark, you call me an exhibitionist for letting my arms show. I don't understand you wanting to run around here without clothes."

"Oh, I don't know. Rebellion, I guess. Remember that bad blizzard and my neighbor kept after me?"

"Yes."

"I wanted some place where I could go without clothes, and no one would bother me. In the apartment, I slept in my underwear. I've never had pajamas until now. I got tired of sitting around studying, so I went out on my balcony. The snow felt good on my skin, so I took my shirt off and started throwing snowballs, reveling in the snow. She saw me. I never thought about anyone seeing me. I decided then I wanted a place where I could run around naked, and no one would see. That day when I got your grieving mother to eat and drink, my challenge to her was to help me find that kind of privacy. She found me this. I don't dress because I don't have to. Maybe I was getting prepared for our honeymoon. Did you like it?"

"Yes, Mark, I liked it very much. But when you asked me if I wanted you to sleep in another room, would you have?"

"Yes, Jocelyn. That's what I was expecting to do. Then you told me to remove your dress. I got excited that maybe I'd get you that night. Then you got scared, and I had to remind myself to be glad I could spend the night in your bed. When you asked me to love you, I was so excited I had to keep reminding myself to be gentle. What would you have done if I hadn't been gentle?"

"You might not have gotten a second chance. But you were so gentle it made me want you more after loving you started getting better."

"My question for you: why did I have to force you to set a date for the wedding? I was planning it for years. I don't understand."

"Mark, you know what that nurse had Robert and James do to me. It made them want to do it more. It made me despise men. You got past my defenses to get me to love you. But when it came time to get married and to let you do those things to me, I got scared."

"Did I hurt you?"

"No, Mark. You were almost too gentle. At first, I was wondering what's so great about this."

"And now?"

"What do you think?"

"You have attacked me."

"Mmm." She caressed him.

"Love, how did I get past your defenses?"

"I could trust you. Remember when I got to Hawaii and was sick?"

"Yes." He remembered that he caused her sickness.

"You held me as I threw up. You cared for me. My brothers said you wanted sex. You easily could have taken me then."

"No, Jocelyn, not while you were sick. I would never do that."

"Exactly! I could trust you to care for me. That opened the door for me to be able to love you. See, Mark, I love you because your Navajo honor cared for me. That's what I love most about you. So keep your Navajo to please me. Is that more clear?"

"Jocelyn, you really like me for me?"

"I really like My Navajo Mark being Navajo Mark."

He showed her his Groton house and property.

"Mark, let's keep this place. I like it very much."

"I'm glad. I like it too. See, God made us for each other."

That week, he took her to the Sub Base to get her a dependent's ID card. They walked over to visit her family often.

~ *10* ~

"Love, I need to fix your hair."

"Why tonight?"

"So it will take less time to get you ready in the morning."

"Okay."

She sat on the chair he had for her with his supplies on the vanity top.

"How do you do those curly things?"

"What?"

"I want to make those curly things by your face here and here. How do you do it?"

"You mean this?"

She looked in the mirror and made a long curl beside her face, showing him how to do it. He tried on the other side but thought hers looked better. She showed him how each side had to curl toward her face.

"Why do you want these curls?"

"I like showing off my beautiful bride, and I like you curly and curvy and *womany*."

He kissed her.

"Mark, is feminine the word you're looking for?"

"Yes. I like my feminine wife. Now where is that spray stuff you put on it to make it stay?"

"It's called hair spray. Here."

She covered her face as he coated her hair with the hair spray. She started coughing, choked by the heavy cloud with which he covered her.

"Jocelyn, are you okay?"

"I think you overdid the hair spray."

"Oh, I'm sorry. Will you be okay?"

"Yes. Maybe don't use quite so much next time."

"Okay. Jocelyn, I'm nervous."

"Why?"

"We are going to be apart."

"No more than when you were working at the ranch. Sweetheart, it's the same thing. I'll be fine, and so will you."

They kissed.

"Come on, I have to bathe you."

"Mark, if you do that I'll need another bath in the morning."

"Okay, I'll never get tired of bathing you."

"But we won't have time for the loving and another bath and the loving and another bath and the—"

He kissed her quiet. The next morning, he fixed breakfast as she got dressed. They ate, and he drove her to her building.

"Park over here. See my sign?"

"They will need to change your parking sign, Dr. Denton."

"Yes, Admiral Denton. Park here and wait for me."

"When?"

"I should come out about 5:30."

She started to get out.

"Wait, I will escort you."

"Only to the door."

"Yes, dear."

He kissed her at the door and caressed her face.

"Have a good day saving the world."

"Thank you."

She went in, and he went home, did the laundry, cleaned house, worked on the garden, took care of the vegetables, made chicken stew, did the ironing, ate lunch, and lay in the hammock to read the Bible. He awoke two hours later, afraid he had not picked her up on time. He set his phone to alert him to go get her. He had a couple hours, so he walked over to visit Winnie and whichever in-laws were home.

"Mark, how was your honeymoon?"

"Great, Winnie."

"And Jocelyn?"

"She's at work. I had some time before I go pick her up, so I thought I'd visit. Any school bills for me?"

"Yes. You still want them?"

"Yes. I will put all of the Meyers through college in honor of my good friend Phillip Meyers and to care for My Mother-in-law. What is it, Winnie?"

"My boy is married. You's all grown up."

Tears flowed down her face. He hugged her.

"Winnie, do you realize I was already twenty-two when I met you?"

"Oh, I know, but you was still a scart little boy. Now you's been a Captain of your submarine and an Admiral and now married. One of these days, you'll have your own scart little boy."

She hugged him.

"Was I that scared?"

"Yes, Mark, you was. Remember that first time you come to help Marcie? Now that was one scart youngin. But after that was over an you just come to see Jocelyn, you was white as that platter, scart stiff. Then they all welcomed you, and you calmed down. Then you come to ast Mr. Phillip for Jocelyn, and you was scart again. We wondered if you'd get her safely to the resrant. Now here you are all married. Let me see your ring."

He held his hand up to take his wedding ring off.

"No. No, you don't take it off. Let me see it on. Don't you never take it off, you hear?"

"Yes, ma'am."

He held his hand out to her.

"An hers is jus like it?"

"Yes."

"Nice."

She smothered him in another hug. He saw the clock.

"I need to go, Winnie, I have to pick up Jocelyn. Thanks for being My Little Mother in Groton."

"I'll always be here, Mark."

They hugged again, and he left. He parked in Dr. Meyers' parking place about 5:00 and walked back and forth in front of the building, anxious to see her. Every time the door opened, he looked at the person coming through. He saw her coming out with two men. He ran up the stairs and smothered her in a bear hug with a long kiss.

"Oh, I missed you so much."

"I missed you too, *Eagle*. I'd like you to meet my lab partner, Dr. Anders, and my supervisor, Dr. Williams. This is my husband, Admiral Pinto."

Mark shook hands with the men, but his other arm stayed around Jocelyn.

Dr. Anders asked, "Will you be coming to the Fourth of July picnic?"

"If Jocelyn wants to."

"I hope that you do come to the picnic," Dr Williams invited. "We'd all like to have more time to get acquainted."

"We'll discuss it and get back to you. Nice meeting you, gentlemen. Oh, how do we get a sticker for my car and change the name on her parking place? She's Dr. Denton now."

"Oh, I have your sticker, and I already asked to have my sign changed to Dr. Pinto."

"You want my Navajo name?"

"Yes, I put your name as Eagle Pinto."

"Jocelyn!"

"Yes, *Eagle*."

She moved them to the car. He helped her in, went around, and got in.

"Take us home, *Eagle*."

"Okay. Then will you tell me what's going on?"

"Yes, dear. Dr. Anders is following us, let him."

"Okay."

"Don't let him come in though. Open the gate, turn in, and close it. Aha."

Pleasure covered her face as she saw Dr. Anders stopped by the gate. Mark parked in the garage, and Jocelyn led him into the living room with the beautiful view of the Sound.

"Mark, I want to change the furniture around so we can see the water from here."

"Not now, after you explain Dr. Pinto."

"Dr. Anders had the mistaken idea that I belonged to him since we're lab partners. Then when he learned that you were that wild Indian that tore up the Naval Hospital Emergency Room, he has been after me even more. So I was egging him on. I was bragging about your estate."

"You didn't call it the nudist camp, did you?"

"No, just told how big the house and grounds were and the ranch in New Mexico. I couldn't remember how big it was, so I said a thousand acres."

"That's true."

"And I said your name is Eagle Pinto. I was wishing your hair was longer."

"This is a side of you I have never seen."

"You have never seen me around other men."

"I saw you around Pete and the foremen."

"They treat me with respect as Mrs. Boss. He treats me as his personal slave. *Eagle*, will you go to the picnic, and when he challenges you to a feat of strength, accept and quietly, Navajo, beat the socks off him?"

"Have you talked with Dr. Williams?"

"Yes. They're waiting for him to blunder so they can fire him. They have me on separate projects."

"Okay, Jocelyn, but if he ever hurts you, I will hurt him."

"Oh, and call me *Little Flower*. I'll call you *Eagle*."

"Did you really have them put your name as Dr. Pinto?"

"Yes."

"Aren't you carrying this too far?"

"No."

"Did you give them the Navajo spelling for Pinto?"

"I don't know it. Write it down."

He wrote *Pinto* and then *Eagle Pinto* on a card and gave it to her.

"*Eagle*, let's go swimming."

"Aren't you hungry?"

"For you. I missed you so much. What did you do all day?"

He told her as they swam.

"How do you like your hair?"

"I love it. I got many compliments. To those who asked me to teach them how, I said they had to get their own Navajo husband."

"So when is this Fourth of July picnic?"

"The fourth of July!"

"Oh! Sometimes! Anyway, do you want to go to the picnic?"

"Yes, dear, I'd like to introduce you to everyone."

"Am I your exhibit?"

"Mm. Yes. I like showing off my handsome Navajo husband."

"Do we need to take anything?"

"No, Baker furnishes it all. Stand up."

She kissed him as she snuggled up to him. He whispered Navajo terms of endearment as he carried her up the stairs to their bed. The next morning, he smoothed her hair, sprayed her lightly with the hair spray, and then fixed them breakfast. He pulled into her parking place. The sign said Dr. Pinto. She laid the car sticker on the dashboard of his car. He escorted her toward the door. Dr. Anders was there.

"So what's this lie about a ranch? There's no Eagle Pinto ranch in New Mexico."

"Look under Little Flower Ranch near Farmington."

"And that place you went to last night is registered to Mark Denton."

"Yes, that's my English name. Excuse me, I have to wish *My Little Flower a good day*."

He kissed her and called her the Navajo terms of endearment she knew. He caressed her face and turned her loose. She went inside. A crowd had gathered around them.

"There's no registry for your marriage either. You're a fake."

Mark reached over, picked him up, and brought his face to Mark's face.

"Leave My Wife alone, understand?"

Dr. Anders hung there limply.

"Go clean up. You smell bad."

Mark stood him back in the corner of the building. He crumpled. He did not land hard, but his pants were wet. Dr. Williams came out.

"Admiral, what's the problem?"

"He has been harassing My Wife."

"What did you do?"

"Picked him up and told him to leave her alone."

A lady who had watched agreed. "Dr. Williams, that's exactly what happened. Please make Dr. Anders go home to take a bath."

"Why?"

"He messed his pants."

"You picked him up?"

"Want me to show you?"

"On me."

"Okay. I picked him up like this and held him like this and told him to leave My Wife alone. Then I set him down like this. His legs couldn't hold him. He messed his pants on his own," Mark said as he showed Dr. Williams exactly what he did to Dr. Anders.

"Admiral, where do you work?"

"I talk with my foreman and take care of my house and grounds. Why?"

"One of our studies is on muscles. Would you help us?"

"I would need to know more about it."

"Come in, I'll show you. Excuse me. Dr. Anders, go home and clean up."

Dr. Williams asked Mark to show him his house and ranch on the internet.

"Why?"

"To verify Jocelyn's claims."

"Look, she doesn't have to work. I can take her home right now, and we will live very well. Working here has been a dream of hers for almost twenty years. If I show you, will that be the end of it?"

"Yes."

Mark showed him the Little Flower Ranch website, which listed Mark Denton as owner. Dr. Williams asked questions, which Mark answered by showing him the information on the website.

"How much is this colt?"

"Five hundred thousand dollars."

"A half million?"

"Yes."

"Now show me your house."

At Google Maps, he typed in his address and requested satellite view. He brought the picture close so they could see the fence, house, outbuildings, orchard, and pier.

"Where did Mrs. Pinto grow up?"

Mark pulled the view back, and the Meyers Mansion was there with its grounds, next door.

"Did you know Senator Meyers?"

"Yes. He was my friend. I miss him very much. I'm especially sorry he wasn't at my wedding."

"Where did you have the wedding?"

"In his ballroom."

"Why did you sit on the floor?"

"You were there?"

"Yes."

"Then why are you asking this?"

"To see if I can get you angry."

Mark laughed, "Why?"

"Part of the study. Were you angry with Dr. Anders?"

"No, just warning him to leave My Wife alone."

"I'll need to have you measured. Please take off your clothes and put on this gown."

"No."

"What?"

"I will not have my body measured by some stranger. My body belongs to My Wife. She is the only one who has access."

Mark walked out to his car and drove home. His phone rang. He looked at it.

"Jocelyn, is something the matter?"

"You have Dr. Williams' shorts in a knot."

"What?"

"He's all bugged because you're not a docile, civilized Indian who'll jump through his hoops. Thanks for letting him see your ranch and your house, but now I wish you hadn't."

"Why?"

"Because he thought you would comply. What did you do to Dr. Anders? He treats me like I have the plague."

"Warned him to leave you alone. Are you sure you want to work with those crazy people?"

"At times, no. But the work I'm doing is important."

"Okay. So what do you want, love?"

"To hear your voice. I'll go on. Thanks for being you. Bye."

"Bye, *Little Flower*."

When he picked her up that afternoon, they had an audience. He still ran to her, hugged, kissed, and escorted her to his car.

"Mark, I like your car."

"Why? It is the same one I've had for years."

"It made Dr. Anders think you really didn't have the ranch and all because it's just an old compact."

"Maybe I should get a bumper sticker that says my other car is a Cessna."

"Or a stallion."

"Or a John Deer."

"Or a race horse."

They laughed. He took her to work every morning and picked her up every evening except when he went to New Mexico.

A few weeks later, he was grouchy.

"What's the matter?"

"Love, I know you want my hair long, but it's bugging me."

"Oh, Mark, you can wear your hair any way you like. I was just wondering if you would like to have it long. Sweetheart, do whatever pleases you."

"Jocelyn, I want to please you."

"Mark Eagle Pinto Denton, you please me. You don't have to do anything special, just be your own special Navajo self."

"Really?"

"Come on." She took his hand and led him to the garage. She made him get in the passenger seat and got in the driver's seat. She pressed the button to open the garage door, drove out, pressed the close button, drove to the gate, pressed the open button, drove out, and pressed the close button. She drove to the base exchange, let him out, and told him she would be at the commissary. After his haircut, he joined her and pushed the cart around. He paid for the groceries, and she got the car while he tipped the bagger. He waited for her, loaded the groceries into the car, and drove them home. After they put the groceries away, he hugged her.

"Jocelyn, do I really please you?"

"Yes, Admiral Denton, very much. Do I please you?"

"Yes, *Little Flower*. It is as though God changed your self into silver."

"You're so romantic."

Their first anniversary was coming soon. She again took six weeks off because she wanted to spend time at the ranch. Pete had said he would teach her to ride. Work was going well. Her life with Mark was a dream come true: being married was more than she had hoped for.

Lightning Source UK Ltd.
Milton Keynes UK
UKOW07f2120141214

243121UK00014B/178/P

9 781630 638962